The
BEAUTY
of
BROKEN
THINGS

ALSO BY VICTORIA CONNELLY

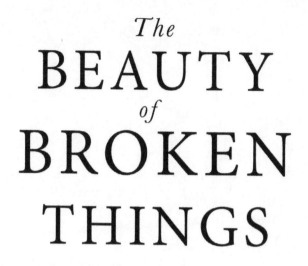

The
BEAUTY
of
BROKEN
THINGS

VICTORIA
CONNELLY

LAKE UNION
PUBLISHING

Text copyright © 2020 Victoria Connelly .
All rights reserved.

No part of this book may be reproduced, or stored in a retrieval system, or transmitted in any form or by any means, electronic, mechanical, photocopying, recording, or otherwise, without express written permission of the publisher.

Published by Lake Union Publishing, Seattle

www.apub.com

Amazon, the Amazon logo, and Lake Union Publishing are trademarks of Amazon.com, Inc., or its affiliates.

33614082056275

ISBN-13: 9781542008167
ISBN-10: 1542008166

Cover design by The Brewster Project

Printed in the United States of America

To Fiona and Richard with love

In the beginning . . .

'Of course, it needs a bit of work,' the estate agent said.

The woman looked around the room, noticing the crumbling plaster, the damp stone and the rotting timbers.

'Yes,' she said. 'It does.'

'And that has been reflected in the price.'

She nodded, knowing that she was lucky to be even considering buying a place like this.

'Would you mind if I walked around on my own for a while?' she asked.

'Of course not. I'll wait for you outside.'

She watched as he left her, listening to the sound his neat shoes made on the old flagstone floor. It was a good floor, she noticed. Perhaps it was one of the few things in the place that didn't need fixing. She looked up at the ceiling high above her and gasped. There was so much space here. Not that she needed a lot of space, being on her own, but she appreciated having it around her because it meant that other people wouldn't occupy it. It would be all hers and that was important.

So there was a bit of work to do, but there wasn't anything insurmountable, was there? Not after what she'd been through. A little painting here, a little carpeting there. Okay, maybe some new timbers, plastering and stonework. She'd look into that at some point. And some window shutters to block out that appalling draught coming straight off the North Sea. But – oh – how lovely the building was. She adored the way the honeyed light streamed in through the arched windows, and how the old stone walls were pitted and mellowed by the centuries, and the steps worn away by generations of feet. It would be a privilege to own something so old and beautiful, so ancient and age worn.

Maybe it was a little extravagant to buy something so big and so ridiculously fairy tale but, she thought as she walked down a corridor lined with arrow-slit windows, what better place was there to hide from the world than in a castle?

Chapter 1

Helen Hansard was a dreamer, but the nine-to-five usually got in the way. Not that it stopped her completely. She always made sure that there were little pockets of time to daydream, no matter how busy she was. She'd never make management – she knew that – mostly because a good portion of the time she sat in meetings was spent staring out of the window, watching the way the wind moved through the one beautiful tree that grew in the central London street, or the way sunlight flirted with the office windows opposite. It had been the same at school. Helen's teachers had been constantly shouting at her for staring out of windows. But it couldn't be helped. Helen had that rare quality of being able to see beauty wherever she went and, luckily for her, it made her rather mundane job bearable.

She'd spent the last ten years working for a small advertising company, Fiennes and Fairchild, taking a graduate placement straight out of university. She hadn't meant it to last so long, only life seemed to have settled in this particular rut and the dreams she'd had of doing something better, more interesting, more *creative*, were always on hold while matters like paying bills took precedence.

But, oh, how she lived for the little moments in-between her job. It was as if she became a different person as soon as she left the office, shaking off the shackles of her administrative role and entering her other self – the truer version of the person she knew she was: the version she put out onto her favourite social media site, Galleria.

Helen had discovered Galleria during an aimless ramble around the internet and had soon been swept up by its magic and the photographs of beautiful gardens, of footpaths through woods, and smallholdings where people were growing their own food and delighting in every minute of it. Here, she'd thought, was a little corner of the web that wasn't concerned with politics, that never discussed the horrors of war and that didn't encourage debates you couldn't win with strangers who didn't really care anyway. Galleria felt like a safe haven where people shared their happiest pictures, beautifully framed, with gentle words to accompany them.

Helen adored those little square boxes of joy and would happily scroll through them several times a day to keep up to date with the people she was following. Some of them, she knew, were making a living from their art. They'd gathered thousands of followers and were now being courted and paid by companies for product placement. Helen wasn't sure how she felt about that. On the one hand, it was always an admirable thing to be able to make a living from doing what you loved most, but she had to admit that the product placement thing did rather detract from the whole ethos of being oneself.

Mind you, that was another issue with social media sites such as Galleria. How much of what you saw was true, or rather the whole picture? Helen had often asked that question and had become very aware of it when she posted her own photographs. The Helen she was presenting to her followers was the fun, free version, whose world was full of beauty and charm. Gone were the spreadsheets, databases, endless emails and conference calls. She

4

had happily banished the photocopier, the filing cabinets, the board room meetings and the many other dull bits of her life. Galleria was most definitely a highlights reel of her and everybody else's life, for who really wanted to take a photo of a sink full of dirty dishes or share that mouldy patch on the north-facing bedroom wall or the mountain of ironing waiting to be done? Oh, no. Galleria was a blissful escape from all of that. It presented the very best pieces of people – the beautiful bits, neatly edited into one perfect square, accompanied by a poetic sentence or two – and Helen had bought into it big time. Only, her photography was slowly becoming more than that. She didn't always want to squeeze it into one perfect box per day. She wanted to experiment and explore. She wanted to flex her creative wings and see if she could fly.

She was thinking about all this as she got off the Tube and headed across the concourse of the train station to catch the 17:54 train home to her village in Kent after a particularly dull day at the office. It was early April and there was still a full hour of light left, which meant Helen could gaze dreamily out of the train window and enjoy the changing landscape. As much as she was addicted to Galleria, she never forgot the primitive pleasure of being able to just sit and stare. So many of her fellow commuters had forgotten the simple delight of doing that. Now, gazes were locked onto screens as work was no longer left at the office, but followed one home. Helen refused to allow her work to accompany her home. She switched off her phone. Or rather, she switched off her work phone. She had a personal one too, and she got that out now, quickly texting her husband, Luke, to tell him she was on the train. As was her habit, she took a quick accompanying photo out of the window as they sped through a crowded station.

It was on her personal phone that she connected to Galleria and with which she took the majority of her photographs. She had several very good cameras at home too, but she liked the portability of the phone and the camera on it was good quality. Now, she scrolled through her most recent images. There was their recent weekend walk through the woods when she'd caught the purest of spring light and the fresh foliage of the beech trees. There were a few shots of the grey and fuming sea from their visit to the coast, when they'd had to bend their heads into the buffeting wind in order to remain upright. And there were several shots of their garden, full of the colours of spring, with her beloved tulips in terracotta pots and the crocuses crowding around the foot of the apple tree.

There was always something magical about taking a photograph, Helen thought, of preserving that single moment, capturing the light, the feelings, the emotion behind a scene. She was addicted to that and had often wondered if, perhaps, she'd be able to make a living from her photography. But maybe it wouldn't be so much of a joy if it became a job. There was always that concern, and yet Helen didn't believe her photography could bring her anything but happiness.

She took a deep breath and then wished she hadn't. Somebody was eating a meat and egg sandwich behind her. How wonderful it would be to live without the daily commute, she thought. How exciting to make a living from creating beautiful photographs. But could it be done?

She looked out of the window at the same view she had been looking at for ten years. Ten long years of travelling in and out of London. How many more did she have to go before she could retire? The thought paralysed her. Unless . . .

She scrolled through some of her photos and messages on Galleria, reading the comments as she went.

You're such a gifted photographer!
Do you do this for a living? If not – you should!
Love your pics. They always brighten my day.

6

Helen smiled, buoyed up by the support she had, but was it enough to build a new career from? Luke's business as a self-employed builder was doing well, but could they afford to take a drop in their combined income while she got a new business off the ground? And could she really run her own business? She had no idea how to be self-employed and solely reliant on herself for an income. The prospect was terrifying and yet exhilarating at the same time. If she didn't do it now, then when? Nobody was going to come up to her and offer her a more fulfilling life, were they? She had to go out and find it for herself.

Without waiting a single second, because she'd waited and wasted far too many of those already, she quickly sent Luke a text.

Got a proposal for you. H x

A moment later, his reply came.

I love a proposal. L x

She smiled.

You might not like this one. H x

Tell me! L x

When I get home. Not long now. H x

Looking out of the window as the suburbs slid into the countryside, a glowing feeling of hope filled her. She might just be able to do this. She was ready – *more* than ready. With a little bit of luck and a lot of determination, she could change her life and do a job she was passionate about. And, if she was working from home, maybe she could finally have that much-longed-for Labrador.

The train began to slow for the next station and Helen held her phone up to take her daily photo of the oak tree that she thought of as hers. Today it was silhouetted in front of the setting sun, strong and solid in the landscape around it. Helen smiled as she captured its beauty, looking at the screen, happy with the image.

It would be the last photograph she'd ever take.

The April evening air cooled quickly once the sun had set and it was long after dark when the police car pulled up outside the house. The occupants waited a moment, seeing the light on and the figure of a man walking around inside. The husband. He was at home.

They got out of the car and walked towards the house.

Chapter 2

Bill Wilson collected up his tools and went to the old shed in the corner of the walled garden. He'd been working at Lorford Castle since he was a little boy, helping his father keep the modest grounds under control. Now aged seventy-three, he couldn't imagine any other life for himself but gardening. It had been a quiet life, but he hadn't wanted it any other way. A wife, two daughters and a bit of gardening in Suffolk. He was a happy man. Which was more than could be said of his employer, the mysterious Miss Kendrick.

Bill glanced up at the castle, wondering if she was watching from behind one of the windows. He still hadn't met her. Two years he'd been working for her and she hadn't even bothered to say hello. Well, some people liked to keep to themselves, didn't they? He could understand that. He wasn't the most sociable man himself. Why, only last week he'd turned down an invitation to dinner at a neighbour's house for no reason other than he preferred to spend the evening in his own home. But Miss Kendrick wasn't just anti-social. She was on a whole other spectrum.

There were rumours, of course – so many rumours. Some had heard she was a widow, some that she'd recently been released from prison. One person believed she was a deaf mute and others thought she was just some kind of artist. After all, didn't those airy-fairy sorts always lock themselves up in towers in pursuit of their muse? Bill didn't really know what to make of it all and didn't spend much time thinking about what the truth might be. But he would have liked to have met her at least. Call him old-fashioned, but he couldn't help feeling odd about working for a person he hadn't even met. The one who paid the wages got to make the rules, however, and his wages were paid electronically once a month. All neat and impersonal.

Returning his tools to the shed, he tidied up for the day. It might be a very odd arrangement, but he wasn't going to complain. He needed the work and the job was relatively easy and within walking distance of his home.

Once everything had been put away, he left the shed, locking it behind him. He kept the key. That had been arranged ahead of his employment. He was in charge of all gardening equipment and, if anything ever needed mending or replacing, he was to post a note through the back door letter box informing Miss Kendrick.

He straightened his faithful woollen cap, the one he'd been wearing for the past two decades and the one his Jack Russell favoured sleeping with when he could get away with it. Then he turned to look at the castle, as he always did, hoping – just once – that today she might be there at a window, ready with that long overdue nod of recognition.

Standing in the shadows by one of the second-floor windows, Orla Kendrick watched as Bill Wilson left and breathed a sigh of relief. The place was hers again. Oh, how she hated intruders, even those whose help she needed. She just couldn't feel at ease with somebody else around.

When Orla had been looking for a home, she had chosen Lorford very carefully. The small Suffolk village on the peninsula, which stuck out into the great grey North Sea like a dainty little finger, appealed to both her sense of the aesthetic and also her practicality, because Lorford was a dead end rather than a thoroughfare. People didn't just happen upon it or pass through it on the way to somewhere else. One really had to want to go there because it was miles from anywhere else and, while it was quaint, it wasn't overly pretty. It wasn't the sort of place which attracted coachloads of tourists.

Then there was the beach. Like the village itself, the beach wasn't particularly attractive to holidaymakers. Part sand, part shingle, there was no parking nearby and, with sandier, more attractive beaches further up the coast, it was only of real interest to those who lived on its doorstep. But how it had spoken to Orla when she'd first seen it – that tang of salt spray and the freedom to be found in all that wild ozone. She loved that she was frequently the only one walking there with her dog or that the other few dog walkers allowed her the space and privacy that she so craved.

Winters in Lorford were especially quiet. The little village seemed to lock itself away from the rest of the world and hunker down. Orla liked that, appreciating the special peace which winter brought with it. It was a dark gift at the end of each year when one could shut oneself away at home.

Of course, when Orla had first arrived, she'd had a stream of visitors to the castle. Naturally, after sitting empty for five years, people were curious to see the new resident. Orla had quickly told them through the closed door that she didn't receive visitors. People meant well, but she didn't want them to mean anything at all. She just wanted to be left alone. There were a couple of particularly persistent callers. The vicar and a woman with a big bank of a bosom who was always carrying a wicker basket full of Tupperware. Orla dreaded to think what would happen if she let *her* into her home. She'd never be rid of her. She'd be back at some indeterminate time in the future to collect her Tupperware and use it as an excuse to drop something else off. No, Orla thought, neighbours meaning well and her leading a quiet life simply didn't go hand in hand.

Life hadn't always been so quiet, though. When she'd lived in London, she'd enjoyed socialising and had always had a full diary and a small circle of friends she enjoyed being with. Looking out of the castle window into the garden now, she couldn't help comparing the view in her mind's eye to the one she'd had in her London flat. The busy street lined with bus stops had been noisy with twenty-four-hour traffic and yet it had never really bothered her. It had just been a part of the city she'd loved.

And she *had* loved it. In the not-too-distant past. But all that had changed after the incident.

She closed her eyes. How long ago that old life of hers seemed, yet it was only a memory away. Although she didn't think of it very often, she found herself smiling as she thought about it now – of the evenings spent drinking cocktails with her friends and long lunches with work colleagues in swish restaurants. And her work. How she'd loved her work in the photography studio. Why had she ever let that go?

Orla took a deep, stilling breath as she let the memories of the past fade. She liked her new life, didn't she? She appreciated the quietness of being alone and the safety that the thick castle walls provided. Sometimes it did get a little too quiet, she had to admit that, but it was safe. Quiet meant safe, she told herself, and there were other ways to reach out to people. She'd slowly learned that over the last few years, dipping into the virtual world via the internet. It felt far more comfortable than the real one, and the people who joined her there lived at a safe distance and wouldn't be likely to turn up on her doorstep. She might never meet these online friends, or even know their real names or where they lived, but she felt all the happier for that.

Sitting down on the old sofa in the great hall of the castle, Orla picked up her phone, logging on to Galleria. She'd been using the site for two years now and had tens of thousands of followers while following just a couple of hundred accounts herself. One of her favourites was *Trees and Dreams*. She couldn't remember how she'd first discovered the account, but she'd been immediately captivated by the beautiful images there, spending many happy hours looking at the world through the eyes of the photographer, taking in the scenes of cool country lanes and the gentle folds of the Kent Weald landscape and the quirky photographs often taken from train windows. There was a softness to the pictures – a delightful delicacy that resonated from the screen and completely enveloped you so that you felt as if you'd entered the picture itself. And it wasn't just the whimsical subject matter that made one feel like this – the frothing fields of cow parsley, the shimmering leaves of an oak tree – Orla felt that this photographer could take a picture of a barbed wire fence and make it seem beautiful. Actually, come to think of it, there was a photo of barbed wire, with a spider's web sparkling with dew suspended across it.

As Orla visited the account now, she noticed that there hadn't been an update from *Trees and Dreams* for a while and, now that she thought about it, there hadn't been any messages from her for a while either, which was unusual. Perhaps she'd been away. Orla checked the date on the last photograph. It was over a month ago. In social media terms, that was an eternity. One could easily commit social media suicide if no postings were made within the space of a single week. The world rushed by in a mad fury and, if you didn't make yourself heard, you could be quickly forgotten. But Orla hadn't forgotten her online friend for, unlike so many other accounts she followed, she had struck up something of a friendship with the woman behind this one. No names had been exchanged, but she knew a little bit about her, like she was happily married to a builder who specialised in old buildings and that she was forever trying to persuade him to get a dog. Messages of warmth and mutual appreciation had flown between them. From what Orla could make out, *Trees and Dreams* did something in the city – something she never wanted to talk about but which obviously wasn't making her happy. But her world outside her work was one full of joy and light. Orla had always encouraged her to pursue that.

Perhaps she should send her a message now, she thought. That wouldn't be too intrusive, would it? It was one thing to send messages about one's online account, but quite another to ask too many questions about one's personal life. So Orla hesitated, then decided it would be best not to.

That was the only downside with virtual friends. One could never be sure what was really going on with them. For one thing, there was the time difference with friends based in other countries and continents. If you messaged them, they might not receive it for hours and, by then, it could be lost in a jumble of other messages. Then there were the vagaries of the internet, with connections often being lost in Lorford. Orla gave up hope of linking up successfully on some days, which often meant she didn't talk to anyone either in real life or in the virtual one for days at a time. She also found the language of the internet very limiting. She did her best to express herself with a few brief but carefully chosen words, but it wasn't the same as being in a room with someone, where the tone of your voice or a glint in your eyes could make all the difference to the way you communicated with somebody.

But she didn't want to be in a room with people. *This* was her world now.

Orla sighed. Feeling at a loss as to how to reach out to her friend, she switched her phone off. Perhaps she'd check in again later.

Walking across to the window, she saw that a van was pulling up outside her gates. She kept them shut and the delivery men were used to taking any goods to the back door. She never answered the doorbell. Occasionally, a persistent delivery man would ring the bell a few times and hang around as if Orla was going to make an appearance and offer to sign for something, but that was never going to happen. Instead, she watched now as a young man got out of the van and opened the door at the back to retrieve a small box. Orla knew what it was – a very pretty cup and bowl she'd just bought at an online auction. She couldn't wait to see it and to run her fingers over the little hairline cracks and the sweet chips along the rim which would catch the light when she photographed them.

She watched the man approach the castle. Suddenly, he glanced up at the very window where Orla was standing, causing her to shoot back into the shadows. She closed her eyes, waiting for the moment of panic to subside. She counted slowly, as she'd been told to do in such situations. The fear was only in her own mind. The man was outside. He wasn't near her and he wasn't going to come any closer than he already was. She knew that, and yet the fear felt real all the same.

She waited a few moments, her back straight against the cold wall of the castle as she slowly breathed. It was okay. He'd leave the parcel by the back door and then he would go. She'd seen the pattern time and time again. It would be no different now.

Sure enough, a moment later, she dared to look out of the window. The van had gone. She was safe once again.

She walked through the living room and down the stone spiral staircase to the back door. It was a large, ancient wooden one with both a modern lock and iron bolts. The estate agent had seemed embarrassed by it when he'd shown her around, but it was exactly the kind of door Orla needed in her life these days.

Opening it now, she picked up the little box and took it inside, shutting and bolting herself in once again. She then took the box upstairs and placed it on a table in a special place she called the china room where she opened all her new packages. Orla took her time to remove the tape and the layers of tissue paper to reveal the delicate cup and bowl. They were a classic blue and white willow pattern that she adored and she examined them now, her gaze taking in the chips and cracks, a little smile tickling the corners of her mouth.

They were beautiful. Beautifully broken.

Chapter 3

Luke opened his eyes, blinking in the brightness of the May morning and cursing the fact that he hadn't drawn the curtains the night before. He couldn't really remember how he'd found his way to bed, but the empty glass on his bedside table and the throbbing behind his temples as soon as he tried to move quickly jogged his memory. Another evening lost in a wine-induced haze, he thought, pushing himself out of bed and going into the bathroom. He'd lost count of how many of those he'd had since the accident, but it was costing him a small fortune, he knew that much.

What on earth would Helen say, he wondered as he stared at the strange, bearded reflection in the mirror? She'd be appalled at the state he'd let himself get into.

He took a quick shower and then returned to stand in front of the mirror. He really should shave. Dishevelled wasn't a look he carried well. But the truth was, he really didn't have the energy. Or the inclination. What was the point? What was the point of anything any more? He just couldn't see it. Why bother shaving in a world without Helen? Why bother doing anything? Why bother even being? These questions rattled around his brain in an endlessly painful cycle as he did his best to get through the days, counting down the hours until he could find some comfort, some release, in a few glasses of wine in the evening.

It had been during one appalling evening just a month ago when his life had come crashing down around him. The signs had been there, of course, but he hadn't put them together. First, when he'd got home, he'd been surprised not to see Helen's car in the driveway. He'd been running later than usual at work, but she was normally home by the time he returned. Maybe she'd stopped off at the shops, he thought. He just remembered his haste to get out of his work clothes and into the shower. He'd been working on a fifteenth-century cottage in a picturesque Kent village, knocking the walls back to their original lath and plaster, and it had been a very dusty job. But, by the time he'd come back downstairs, she still wasn't home and, when he'd rung her phone, it had gone to voicemail. He hadn't left a message, sure that she'd be home soon. Only she never did come home that night.

He'd been cooking pasta when the doorbell had rung. Pasta! How on earth could he have been doing something as mundane when his wife . . .

He closed his eyes as he thought of the dreadful sight of the two police officers standing in his doorway. A man and a woman with pale, serious faces.

At first, Luke thought they must be lost, because why else would they be knocking at his door? He didn't imagine for a moment that their arrival and Helen's lateness were connected.

He remembered the strange expression on the woman's face, one that he hadn't been able to read. She'd been talking about the trains from London – the train that his wife was on. It never made it to its destination. Some kind of signal failure, they thought. Not confirmed. Nothing had been confirmed at that stage except that there were two trains involved. And Helen. Helen was dead. That, at least, had been confirmed.

Helen. Was. Dead.

Luke couldn't remember what had happened after that. Phone calls. Paperwork. Death made a lot of admin. That was a lesson Luke had quickly learned. Luckily, his business partner, Chippy, had been a stalwart, stepping in and stepping up at work, allowing Luke the time and space he needed.

In fact, he was due round any minute now, Luke remembered, glancing out of the living-room window just as Chippy's van pulled up.

Luke smiled. He liked Chippy. They'd been working together now for four years and Luke believed he couldn't find a better colleague.

'Hey,' Luke said as he greeted him at the door.

'All right?' Chippy asked, removing his steel-capped work boots before coming in.

Luke nodded. That was about as deep as it got between them and Luke was glad of it. He instinctively knew that Chippy was there for him, but he felt relieved that his friend and work colleague didn't expect anything of him.

'Cup of tea?'

'Great.'

Luke did the honours in the kitchen.

'You cut your hair?' he asked.

'Girlfriend told me it was time,' Chippy said, self-consciously running a hand through the short fair hair that, up until recently, had hit his shoulders.

'It suits you,' Luke told him.

Chippy grinned as he took his mug of tea from Luke and they both sat down together in the dining room.

'I've taken some photos,' Chippy said, reaching for his phone from his pocket and finding them before handing the phone to Luke.

'You working okay with Mark?' Luke asked him.

'Marcus.'

'Right.'

'He's doing okay, but he's not up to your standard.'

Luke looked through the photos of the sixteenth-century house. 'Ah, you found that fireplace!'

'Yes, and it was just as big as you said it would be. We've opened it right up.'

'Looks great.'

'The owner's delighted.'

'Well, it looks like you're making good progress,' Luke said, handing the phone back.

Chippy popped it in his pocket and finished his tea before heading towards the door, where he stopped and turned around.

'You coming back soon?'

Luke was about to reply when Chippy glanced at the mantelpiece and his expression changed. Luke knew what he'd seen: the wedding photo of him and Helen. It was his favourite one, where they were both laughing as confetti floated down around them.

Chippy quickly averted his gaze, his face flushing red, and Luke instantly felt bad that his friend might be feeling uncomfortable. Death had a way of doing that, he'd learned.

'Yeah,' Luke said. 'I'll be back soon.'

Chippy nodded and gave an awkward smile and Luke watched as he got into his van and left for a day's work.

Luke sighed as he closed the door. He missed his work, but he couldn't face it yet. He couldn't face *normality* just yet. He walked towards the mantelpiece, picking up the photo and looking into Helen's laughing face.

'Why did you go?' he whispered, feeling, once again, total disbelief that he wasn't ever going to see that sweet freckled face of hers again.

It had been several weeks since the accident, but it still all felt so raw. May had arrived along with the first swifts, the apple tree had burst into blossom and the woods had turned hazy with bluebells. Luke cursed it all because Helen wasn't there to see it. He felt bitter with anger. How could something as simple as a signal failure take a life? He wanted to lash out and punish somebody, but there was nobody to blame. At least, nobody they'd actually named. But somebody must have been in control of that damned signal, and their lapse in judgement or concentration or whatever on earth it was had cost eleven people their lives. It was the worst accident that line had seen in decades and there'd been an outpouring of grief not just locally, but nationally too, with people arriving from all over the country to lay flowers at the scene where the two trains had collided.

Luke hadn't laid flowers. Helen wasn't there. It was a strange feeling, but he honestly thought that she was somehow still at home. Every now and then, he'd just *feel* her, and he'd spin around, sure he'd find her standing behind him. It was the craziest thing, and he genuinely thought he was losing his mind. He felt like that a lot since that dreadful night when the police had knocked on his door.

A few of Helen's things had been recovered from the accident. Her handbag with the faulty zip, which had contained all the usual things a working woman carried with her throughout the day, together with a few unusual ones, like her journal. Luke hadn't yet had the courage to read it. He knew Helen liked to keep a brief record of all her thoughts and feelings about her day – and he felt it would be intrusive to look at it, although there'd been many an evening when he'd sat holding it in his hands, feeling that it was the last true piece of Helen he had left.

Looking through her handbag had been a cruel agony. There were so many little bits of Helen in there – a wrapped lemon drop;

a pencil covered in a marbled paper, an old paperback collection of poems, her favourite cherry-red lipstick, her mobile phone, and a little mirror backed with a William Morris print. But the thing that got to Luke was the keyring in the shape of a Labrador. Helen had always longed for a dog. It was one of those things they'd kept putting off and now it was too late. He had cursed himself a thousand times over that, holding the keyring tightly in his hand as he'd cried, believing that he'd been a bad husband and that he should have listened more to her. Had she been happy – *truly* happy – with her life? She'd always seemed to be and yet he knew there was more he could have done to make absolutely sure of it.

He was staring at the handbag again now. He hadn't looked inside it for a while, but something drew him to it now and he opened it up. There were all the familiar bits and pieces that he'd handled so many times, thinking of how these inanimate objects had been with her when she died, and how she'd carried them with her on her last day. He picked up the Labrador keyring again. It was like his own personal torture device and he felt a lump lodge in his throat as his anger arose again. Why hadn't they got a dog? Why hadn't he taken more notice of that dream of hers and made it come true?

Because you thought you had more time, a little voice inside himself said – the kinder Luke that he wished he could thump. He didn't deserve any kindness. He'd been a bad husband who hadn't given his wife nearly enough of what she deserved.

As he put the keyring back into the bag, he spotted a piece of loose paper folded in half in a section of the bag he hadn't noticed before. He took it out now and unfolded it, seeing the name Oak Tree Antiques. It was a handwritten receipt for something which Helen had paid thirty pounds for. But what was it? He couldn't quite make the writing out. A Victorian *something*.

'Vase!' he cried out as the letters made sense at last. A Victorian vase. Luke frowned, looking around the room as if the mystery vase might materialise, but there was no sign of it.

And he began to remember something.

'Luke?' Helen's voice was bright and excited as she entered the house. 'Wait till you see what I've got!'

Luke had been sitting in the living room. It was the weekend and he'd declined going antique shopping with Helen. She hadn't minded, laughing at how bored he got when she dared to drag him to one of her favourite shops and knowing she'd enjoy the experience far more if he wasn't there. How he wished with his whole heart that he'd gone now just so he could have spent a few more precious hours with her.

'What have you got there?' he'd asked as she came into the room carrying a paper bag.

She smiled one of her big wide smiles as she popped the bag on the sofa beside him and took out the bubble-wrapped object.

Luke watched, unable to guess what it might be and feeling slightly underwhelmed when she revealed a blue and white vase.

'Isn't it beautiful?'

'I suppose,' he said, trying to show some enthusiasm, but failing. 'It's got a chip in it – there.' He didn't want to point out the imperfections, but the craftsman in him just couldn't help it.

'I know! That's why it was so cheap,' she told him, her hazel eyes bright with excitement. 'Anyway, chips are good.'

'Really?'

'They show that it's been loved and used.'

'Or knocked.'

'But that's all part of its life. I learned that from BB.'

'Ah, BB!' Luke said, recognising the moniker of Helen's online friend. 'The chipped-china woman!'

Helen pulled a face at him.

'Look,' she said, pulling her phone out of her pocket. 'BB's posts are so beautiful.'

Luke smiled. Helen's greatest obsession was her photography and sharing her pictures to a site called Galleria. Whole hours could be gently lost in the pursuit of beauty, of sharing content and swapping comments. His wife now had thousands of followers on her page and was following hundreds of others. It was a world that Luke hadn't so much as dipped a toe in, but he was aware of some of the online friends his wife had made, including the one referred to as 'BB'. *Beautifully Broken* was her account name. He didn't actually know her real-life name and neither did Helen. She was one of the people who hid behind a handle, who created a whole world without giving away very much at all about their private lives. Even her avatar was carefully obscure, merely showing a china vase filled with flowers, not dissimilar to the one Helen had just bought, and it gave absolutely nothing away about the person behind the pictures taken.

Luke peered at the screen.

'What is it about women and old bits of china?' he asked, genuinely baffled as he looked at a few of BB's photos.

'Just look at those darling little rose buds and the hairline crack below the rim,' Helen said, tucking her chestnut hair behind her ears as she pointed to one of the pictures.

That was *Beautifully Broken*'s signature, Luke had learned – collecting the flotsam and jetsam of life, the pieces often overlooked by others, the damaged, the dirt-encrusted, the chipped and the chucked away. BB had an eye for the unlucky and the unloved.

'So you bought a chipped vase because of BB?'

'No, silly! I bought it *for* her. It's a present.'

'You're going to *post* that thing?'

'I'll make sure it's wrapped well. In fact, I think I've got some ribbon somewhere which would look just perfect with it.'

Luke thought about the conversation now. It had been just a week before the train crash and, as far as he knew, Helen hadn't posted the gift to BB.

He left the bedroom, knowing that he had to find the vase. Their home only had two small bedrooms and the second housed a single bed for guests and what they called their overflow wardrobe. There was also a tiny chest of drawers in there. It was the only place Helen could have put the vase, Luke thought.

Sure enough, as he entered the room, he saw it. He walked towards it, picking it up carefully in his large builder's hands, knowing that the last hands to have held it would have been Helen's. He hadn't really shown any interest in the piece before, but he did now. This beautiful, imperfect vase had been a gift his wife had bought for BB. He put the vase down and saw that there was a box on the bed and the large piece of bubble wrap that the vase had been placed in when she'd bought it. There was a piece of sky-blue ribbon too. It was just like Helen to make this gift as beautiful as possible, he thought.

He sat down on the bed and was just moving the box out of the way when he saw there was a card inside. Picking it up, he saw Helen's handwriting and his eyes misted with tears. She had such pretty writing and had always written their Christmas cards, and all of his family's birthday cards too, because Luke's own writing was so awful. Seeing her writing again now, he remembered how she'd once laughed as he'd attempted to write out a thank you letter to his mother.

'Let me!' she'd said, taking the notepad away from him. 'It looks as if a spider's dipped its legs in ink and crawled all over the page when you write!'

He smiled as he heard her voice again and then he read the words she'd written to BB.

I wanted to send you something to thank you for all the kindness you've shown in encouraging me in my photography. You've made such a difference to my confidence. I feel so much braver in the decisions I make now in taking pictures and in sharing them with the world. I realise that I've only been living half my life up until now.

Luke read the phrase again, feeling increasingly disconcerted. *Half my life.* Is that how Helen had really felt? How had he not known that Helen was unhappy? Had he been so wrapped up in his own little happy world, building his business and going about his day-to-day activities, that he hadn't seen her dissatisfaction?

He read on.

I only wish there was something I could do to help you as you have helped me. Helen. x

Tears blurred his vision and he felt that awful sick emptiness in his stomach. He knew what was coming and there was nothing he could do about it. So he gave into it, his body doubling over as he cried, the world shrinking around him so that nothing existed but his all-consuming grief.

He wasn't sure how long he sat there for, the sobs wracking his body, but he felt strangely calm afterwards, sitting there on the edge of the bed in the spare room. He picked up Helen's letter again, able to look at it now without breaking down. How like Helen it had been to want to try and help somebody. But how had she wanted to help BB? What help had she needed? Or what help did she still need?

Luke put the card down, feeling sad that it would never be sent and that BB would never see the beautiful gift Helen had chosen for her or receive the help that Helen wanted to give.

Later that day, Luke wandered through to the kitchen, acutely aware that another evening was about to descend. Another evening when Helen wouldn't be arriving home. He made himself some tea, which consisted of toast and a chunk of rather tough cheese. But it was good enough for him; he wouldn't taste it anyway. He put the radio on for a bit, welcoming the inane chatter of another human voice and then switching it off when it began to grate on him.

And then the phone rang.

He sighed, getting up to answer it.

'Hi, Mum,' he said, knowing it was her without even looking at the caller ID. She always rang the landline because she didn't trust mobiles. He shook his head. 'You really don't need to ring me every day.'

'Well, of course I do. I need to know you're all right.'

'I'm fine.'

'Are you eating?'

'I've just had tea.' He raked a hand through his hair. Every night, it was the same questions.

'What did you have?'

'Mum!'

'Because you've got to look after yourself.'

'I am.'

'But you're not always answering the phone, are you?'

'What do you mean?'

'I mean, I had your Aunt Petra on the phone. She called you last night. Several times, she said.'

Luke took a deep breath. 'I must have been asleep,' he lied, remembering the barrage of calls that had assaulted him all evening. He'd pulled the phone cable out of the wall after the third call, but he wasn't going to tell his mum that.

'Well, she sends her love.'

'Send her mine,' Luke said, 'and tell her she doesn't need to call again. Please.'

He heard his mother sighing. 'Shall I come and stay for a while?'

'God, no!' Luke cried. 'I mean, you don't need to, Mum. It's a long way.'

'We do have trains in Yorkshire, you know. It's an easy enough journey.'

'Really, I'm better on my own.' He closed his eyes, wondering if he could make an excuse and end the call.

'I'll leave you to it, then,' his mother said.

Luke felt a surge of relief as she said goodbye and then immediately felt bad. She was, after all, only worried about him. As was everybody. That was the problem really.

If only he could talk to Helen. She'd laugh, wouldn't she? He knew she would. Wherever she was and whatever she was doing, she'd laugh. That much he knew.

He walked through to the living room and glanced at the table where he'd placed her journal, before making a decision. He just needed to hear her voice and, if he couldn't do that audibly, he could at least read it. So he opened the journal. It began with a list of things she wanted to photograph, and he smiled as he read them. She wanted to capture her beloved oak tree every week for a complete calendar year. She wanted to visit the great gardens of Kent, photographing them in all their summer splendour. She wanted to spend the night in a wood, waking at dawn to photograph the wildlife there, and she wanted to visit the local old people's home and photograph the residents.

Luke read in wonder. How had he not known all this about Helen? Sure, she'd mentioned a little of it to him now and then. He couldn't not be caught up in her passion for photography. But this little journal proved to him that there was so much about her that he didn't know. All those hopes and dreams she'd kept locked inside. Luke felt frustrated that he hadn't known about any of this before, and a heavy sense of guilt weighed upon him as he thought of all the ways it seemed he had failed Helen.

He flipped through the pages. There were more lists, simple things like the equipment she would buy for her photography if she could afford it. There were other lists too – more mundane things like work targets and everyday shopping. But there were longer passages of writing as well, perhaps written on her train journeys in and out of London, describing the view from her window or funny little character studies of her fellow passengers. Luke smiled as he read them, hearing her voice so clearly in his mind – her brutal honesty and her naughty humour.

His fingers were almost trembling as he turned the pages, knowing that he would soon come to her final entry. It had been written just two days before the crash. There wasn't much, but the words touched Luke deeply.

BB has been so kind helping me to discover what it is I really want. I wish there was something I could do to help her. She sounds so isolated. So alone. And scared too, although she won't tell me why. That's no way to live, is it? I wish she'd confide in me. I'd love to help.

Luke turned the next page and the next in the vain hope that there might be something more, but there were only empty pages. He swallowed hard, feeling again that anger at a life cut short. A life filled with so much potential and passion and care for others.

He gently placed the journal on the table and looked at where he'd plugged Helen's mobile in to recharge. Her two phones had been recovered from the scene of the accident. Her work phone, which had been in her handbag, was in perfect condition, but her personal one had two large cracks across the screen. Luke hadn't dared to switch it on. Until today. It had been recharging for a few hours now and he unplugged it and turned it on. It was still working.

He watched anxiously as it lit up, his finger hovering over the keypad, entering her code, which he knew was his birthday. He'd warned her that it wasn't safe or original to have such a predictable code, but she'd merely laughed at him, and he was glad she hadn't changed it now for he was able to scroll through the last photographs she'd ever taken, seeing the world through her beautiful gaze once again. He smiled sadly at the final image of the oak tree he knew she loved so much. It had been her last post to Galleria too – her last public communication with the world. How could someone who saw so much beauty in the world be taken so brutally he thought for the thousandth time.

He scrolled through the other photographs. They were mostly little corners of their garden and details in the landscape like an old wooden gate covered in moss, a happy clump of wild garlic, or raindrops sparkling on a tulip. Each image was bewitching in its simple beauty. Helen really had an eye for the beautiful in the everyday. She appreciated the tiny things in life, like the serrated edge of a leaf, the patterns frost made on grass and the swirling shapes in a frozen puddle. And now that view of the world was lost for ever.

He looked at the photos one last time before visiting her Galleria page and tapping on her final post of the oak tree. There were dozens of comments, some made after the accident. Then something occurred to him. They didn't know Helen had died. They were still leaving likes and comments. Maybe they were even messaging her and waiting for a reply, he thought. Oh, God! What a mess. Nobody had told him about the ramifications of social media when a person died. What was the etiquette? Should he make some kind of public announcement on the site? The thought horrified him, and yet it seemed so heartless not to let them know what had happened and for them to go on imagining that Helen was still there.

He switched off her phone and sat in silence for a moment, not knowing what to do. He didn't have to do anything, really. He could surely choose to ignore it all. After all, it wasn't the real world, was it? Helen had spoken about a lot of the people she followed on Galleria – the gardeners, the weavers, the potters, all those creative people who added to the world's sum total of beauty – but these online friends weren't real friends, were they?

And yet that wasn't completely true. There had been that one special friend. BB: *Beautifully Broken*. Should he let her know about Helen's death? He felt that he should, and yet wouldn't it be awful just to message her via the Galleria website? What on earth would he say?

> Hi there. You were online friends with my wife.
> But I thought you should know that she's dead.

It seemed so cold and heartless and he knew right away that he couldn't do that to someone. He checked Galleria on his own phone, quickly finding *Beautifully Broken*'s page. He took a look around, hoping there'd be a link to a website or an email address or something, but there was nothing. He didn't even have a name to go on. Luke wasn't used to social media. He had a Facebook account, but he only really used it for his business page, which had a modest following. He wasn't sure how these things worked. Should he message her for contact details? He felt decidedly uncomfortable about doing that. This was the sort of thing one did in person or – at the very least – on the phone.

Then there was the issue with the unsent gift. Luke put his phone down and returned to the spare room, searching the box and the bubble wrap for BB's address, but there was nothing there. Had Helen even had it? He returned to the living room and flipped through her journal again, but there was no address written down there. Maybe she'd been about to ask BB for it and, if Luke could find it, he could send Helen's gift. The idea really appealed to him. He felt it would be something he could do to make up for not always seeing what Helen was thinking or feeling. This, he thought, might go some way towards helping him feel just a little bit better about that.

Luke picked up his phone again, looking at BB's page, but there were definitely no contact details there. He could message her, asking for her address, but it wouldn't be easy or honest without him first telling her that Helen had died, and that felt wrong somehow. If only there was a way of finding her and giving her the gift and telling her about Helen. That, he felt, would be the human thing to do – the thing that Helen would want him to do.

Luke scrolled through BB's gallery. He couldn't help feeling a little stalkerish as he looked for clues about her, but there wasn't really much on her page that gave anything away.

Ah, wait a minute.

He scrolled back.

The sea. That was definitely the sea. But was that where she lived or a day trip or holiday shot?

Slowly, an idea began to form. If he could find out where she lived, he could visit her, couldn't he? She was definitely in the UK, judging by the photos of the countryside. It didn't look hilly so it probably wasn't the north or anywhere like Devon or the South Downs. He glimpsed a few blurred images of red-bricked cottages and, crucially, flint. And there was a round-towered church. Very idiosyncratic. Drawing on his builder's knowledge and passion for vernacular architecture, Luke would hazard a guess that those clues led to East Anglia. Not terribly helpful seeing as East Anglia was comprised of several large counties, most of them with a coast, but at least he'd made a promising start.

He glanced up from the phone and rubbed his eyes. It wasn't healthy to look at these screens for so long. He never knew how his wife did it – moving from PC to laptop to phone with such ease. It would drive him crazy. But it was the modern world, he realised, and it was one his wife had embraced.

Sighing, he continued to scroll, ignoring the plethora of teacups and floral displays in chipped vases and focusing on the few interspersed images of landscape. Now that he'd got his eye attuned, he definitely thought it was East Anglia, possibly Norfolk, or Suffolk, which was famous for its brick and flint cottages. If he could find one particularly striking image that he could use to do a reverse image search, that might just help him pinpoint where she was.

Sure enough, a round-towered church seemed to be a recurrent theme with BB. Taken from different angles and in different seasons and weathers, it was never photographed as a whole, but the little sections she captured of it were very distinct and might just be enough to help Luke in his search.

Carefully, methodically, he searched Google for a little while longer, examining image after image of round-towered churches, comparing the flint work, the porches and the shapes of the windows, and he soon had a result. The church he was looking for was St George's in a village called Lorford on the Suffolk coast. He googled Lorford, recognising some of the cottages he'd seen in BB's photos and the stretch of lonely beach too.

Then he went back to her account, looking at the still-life photos, seeing what he could learn about the rooms they were taken in. One thing was certain – they were no ordinary rooms. He saw great grey flagstone floors, deep stone windowsills and – wait a minute – was that an arch flanked by a column? This was definitely not a modern home, Luke thought.

He looked at a few more images and smiled as realisation dawned.

BB lived in a castle.

Chapter 4

'Luke? Take a look at this. What do you think?'

Luke looked up from his phone, where he was trying to find a footpath on an Ordnance Survey map. Helen was holding her camera out towards him.

'I can't really see it,' he said, squinting at the screen on the back.

'Move into the shade and shield your eyes,' she told him, and he did.

'Ah, nice!' he said, looking at the fern Helen had captured, half in sun, half in shadow, its unfurled form like an ammonite fossil he'd once found on a beach in Dorset on a family holiday.

'Do you think so?' she asked with all the uncertainty of a naturally talented artist.

'It's beautiful.'

Helen smiled, obviously relieved. 'I've been learning about chiaroscuro.'

'Bless you!'

She laughed. 'It's Italian! It's the effect of light and dark working together.'

'So you didn't completely waste your time on that course, then?'

'No, I didn't learn it there. You can't learn everything in a single day and we focused mainly on composition. Basic stuff, really.'

'But it was good?'

'I enjoyed it, yes.'

He watched as she bent down, her camera poised in front of her as she took some more pictures. Luke went back to examining his phone.

'I can't tell where the footpath goes.'

'Does it matter?'

'It does if we don't want to get shot by a gamekeeper.'

'Let's just wander around here for a while,' she suggested. 'We don't have to rush off anywhere, do we?'

'Well, I'd quite like to get to this pub for lunch.'

'You and your stomach!'

'What?' he protested. 'It's only demanding its rights. One square meal a day!'

'Well, all right, then.' She got up and put her camera away. 'Let's find this pub.'

Shortly after that day, Helen had printed out the fern photograph and placed it on the dresser. She'd spend hours looking at it, her eye always critical.

'How could I have made it better?' she asked Luke.

'I'm not sure you could have,' he told her.

'Should I have moved an inch to the right perhaps?'

'No, I don't think so.'

'What if I'd knelt down lower? Would the composition have been better then?'

'Probably not,' he said. 'You might just have ended up with damp knees.'

He smiled sadly now as he remembered. She was always so harsh on herself.

Nicola, Helen's sister, had said it would be nice to get a few of her photos enlarged and framed for the funeral. Luke had agreed; he'd left Nicola to it, but he'd never forget the sight of them all lined up together at the reception afterwards. Words like 'gifted' and 'talented' had floated through the air to distress him even more than he already was.

And one of the photos had been of that unfurled fern, half in sun, half in shadow. Perfectly captured.

Nicola had brought the photographs round a couple of days later and Luke had put them in the spare room. He looked at them now, marvelling at their beauty, the words 'gifted' and 'waste' circling tauntingly in his mind again. He'd never really encouraged her, had he? Not really. Not seriously. If only he could go back to that walk in the woods and really listen to her instead of making silly jokes and going on about his stomach. What would he have done differently, he wondered, if he could go back? He'd have put his phone away for a start. What on earth was he doing staring at that when his beautiful wife was in his company? He'd watch her instead, bending and stretching, squinting and smiling as she captured the beauty around her. And he'd listen instead of talking. He'd wait for her to make suggestions and take the lead and, if that meant they got lost in the woods or chased by an angry gamekeeper, then so be it. She would have been happy to spend all day there with her camera and that, in turn, would have made Luke happy too.

Luke couldn't help feeling that he'd failed Helen in so many ways, but perhaps he could do something really special now in taking her gift to her friend, BB.

It didn't take long for Luke to make his mind up. It was as if he instinctively knew that this was the right thing to do.

The first thing was to ring Chippy.

'Listen,' Luke said, 'this is going to sound strange, but I'm going to meet a friend of Helen's.'

'That doesn't sound strange,' Chippy told him.

Luke paused before continuing, wondering how his friend would react and if he'd think he'd gone completely mad. 'They never met. Actually, they never even knew each other's names.'

'Okay,' Chippy said, 'that *does* sound a little strange.'

'It just feels right, though,' Luke tried to explain. 'I think it's what Helen would have wanted me to do.'

Luke told Chippy about the gift and how strongly he felt about delivering it in person and how he also didn't want to tell the friend the news about Helen's death via a cold and impersonal email.

'Well, don't worry about anything here,' Chippy told him.

'I was hoping you might keep an eye on this place while I'm away. I'm not sure how long I'll be gone for.'

'No worries.'

'Make sure there aren't any stacks of sympathy cards sticking out of the letter box,' Luke said. 'I'll drop a key round to yours before I go. Thanks, mate. I appreciate this.'

The next thing Luke did was to shave. It felt odd seeing the old Luke after so long a disappearance, but there he was, staring right back at him from the bathroom mirror, with his slightly too long dark hair and his brown eyes which still had that haunted look about them.

Then, after packing a few things in an overnight bag, and with only a vague idea about where he might stay, Luke went through to the spare bedroom and carefully wrapped the Victorian vase in its protective bubble wrap and box, together with the blue ribbon and Helen's card.

'I'm taking it to BB for you,' he whispered into the room, hoping, somehow, that Helen knew what he was doing.

It was almost a three-hour drive from Kent to the Suffolk coast and, with each mile, Luke became more and more nervous. To drive across the country to tell a stranger that his wife had died and to give her an unexpected gift was the craziest mission he'd ever contemplated, and he was beginning to wish he'd simply sent a message via the Galleria site.

Don't give up now, a little voice said, and he had the feeling that it wasn't his inner voice but that of Helen.

Go and see her because I never did.

'Okay,' he said as he took a road which headed east, straight to the coastal village of Lorford, driving through deep forests and passing heathery heathland.

He wasn't sure what he was expecting when he arrived, but he drove down to the small quay and parked his van, getting out and stretching his legs and inhaling the fresh, salty air of the estuary. The water was wide and calm and a silvery blue. A few boats bobbed about on their moorings and a couple of waders ran up and down the pebbled shore and then out into a vast expanse of shining mud. It was a beautiful spot and he spent a moment drinking it in before returning to his van.

The centre of the village was easy to find. He simply followed a road leading from the quay which passed rows of tiny cottages. A gentle incline towards the church followed and he immediately recognised the round tower from the photos. He was definitely in the right place, he thought, looking around for his destination. Surely a castle shouldn't be hard to find, he told himself, coming towards a small square around which sat a baker's, a village store, an antiques shop and a pub. But no castle. He drove on, leaving the square and reaching a bend in the road, and then he saw it.

Set back from the road, it soared five storeys up into the glorious blue sky like a rectangular rocket. The pale golden stone was peppered with arrow-slit windows and larger arched ones which winked at him in the sunlight. At its centre, at the top of a steep flight of steps, was a large wooden door. The castle had obviously been built for defence rather than beauty and it puzzled Luke as to why BB, who had such an eye for the beautiful in life, had chosen to live in a rather unforgiving sort of building rather than one of the pretty cottages he'd seen in the heart of the village. Mind you, he had to admit that the castle was impressive. From the little he knew about castles, this looked like the keep; its curtain wall and the protective buildings which would once have surrounded it had long gone.

A wrought-iron gate stood across the driveway and he parked outside it, staring up in wonder at the building that greeted him. He couldn't tell how many sides the building had, but it was at least five, which made it polygonal – a word that he loved. It was quite unlike any other building he'd ever seen.

'Remarkable,' he said to himself, getting out of the van and walking towards the gate. He expected to find some kind of intercom, but there wasn't one. However, the gates weren't locked so he opened them and walked up the driveway flanked by neat lawns. A hedge divided the garden and he caught a glimpse of a long greenhouse, a wooden shed and stunning flower borders. So she grew her own flowers for the arrangements she photographed, he thought. Helen would have loved to have seen this.

Reaching the steep steps at the foot of the castle, Luke paused, looking around in case somebody had spotted his arrival. It felt eerily quiet standing at the huge wooden door of the castle, and he turned back to look at the village, which suddenly seemed a long way away.

An old-fashioned bell with a rope hung outside the door and he pulled it now, wondering if it was loud enough to hear from inside. It probably wasn't for humans, but it didn't need to be because there was a dog inside who had no trouble hearing it. His loud barks made Luke realise he might be unwelcome. He really shouldn't have come.

Don't lose your courage now.

There was that voice again.

'Helen?' he whispered.

'Who is it?'

It wasn't Helen's voice this time, but a woman's on the other side of the castle door.

'Hello,' Luke called. 'My name's Luke. Luke Hansard. You're friends with my wife, Helen.'

There was a pause.

'I don't know anyone called Helen.'

Luke frowned. He couldn't have got the wrong place, could he? And then something occurred to him.

'You know her as *Trees and Dreams*. On Galleria.'

'*Trees and Dreams?*'

'That's right. She said you were good friends.'

'We are.'

'And I – I have something to tell you about her.'

'What?'

Luke took a deep breath. 'Look, I'd really rather not shout all this through a thick wooden door.'

There was another pause as he waited for the door to open. Only it didn't.

'I don't see people.'

'Pardon?' Luke said, wondering if he'd heard her correctly.

'I don't *see* people,' she repeated.

'But I've come a long way,' he told her.

'Then I'm afraid you've had a wasted trip.'

Luke blinked. She really wasn't going to open the door?

'Please, I think you'll want to hear this. I have something for you too. A gift from Helen.'

Only silence greeted him, and he couldn't even tell if she was still on the other side of the door or if she'd walked away. He thought about ringing the bell again but decided not to. He hadn't expected this, he thought, as he sat down on the cold stone doorstep of the castle. Why on earth wouldn't she let him see her for just a moment? Some friend, he thought. If Helen really knew the truth, she'd likely change her mind about BB. But that was the problem with online friends, wasn't it? It was easy enough to type a few messages to one another, quite a different thing to be civil in the real world.

He reached into his pocket and got his phone out, bringing up the messages he'd swapped with Helen on the night of the accident.

Got a proposal for you. H x

Luke looked at the message, as he had hundreds of times already. What had Helen been going to say to him? Their unfinished conversation tortured him to distraction. Perhaps it was something simple like replacing the ancient bedroom curtains or perhaps it was more life-changing, like having a baby. That was one of the other things that they hadn't had time for. Maybe she'd even talked to BB about it. It was one of the things he'd planned on asking her. But that didn't look as if it was going to happen. At least not today.

Well, Luke had nowhere to go. He didn't fancy driving all the way back to Kent tonight so he might as well hang around Lorford for a while. He had some sandwiches in the van and a flask of tea. He'd have himself a little snack and see how the evening unfolded.

A few minutes later, he sat himself on a garden bench in view of the castle, knowing full well that BB would be able to see him. Surely, he thought, she would open the door at some point and, in the meantime, he really was exceedingly comfortable.

Orla crept closer to one of the windows that looked out over the drive to the front gate. What had he said his name was? Luke something. Hansard. That was it. Anyway, his van was still there but, as far as she could make out, he wasn't in it. Had he walked into the village? If so, it was pretty cheeky of him to leave his van at hers.

Her heart was still racing at him having called. She couldn't remember the last time somebody had rung the bell and actually expected her to answer the door. All of her shopping was done online and her obsession for collecting meant a constant stream of packages arriving at the castle, but she never answered the door.

She was just withdrawing from the window when something caught her eye. It was him – Luke Hansard – and he was sitting on a bench in her garden. He hadn't left at all. And he was – what was he doing? Eating a sandwich! Orla's mouth gaped open at the cheek of it. Her garden wasn't a public park, for heaven's sake! For a moment, she thought about knocking on the window, but he might see her if she did that. She could send One Ear out to frighten him off, but the dear dog wasn't really up to the job. He might look the part with his huge, wolf-like body, but he was far more sheep than wolf in nature.

'What should I do?' Orla asked him. One Ear cocked his head to one side, but he really wasn't any use when it came to such dilemmas.

Orla looked out of the window again, watching as Luke Hansard opened his flask. He was there for the duration, it seemed. Well, there was no use in her standing there watching him. No doubt he'd grow bored once it got dark and would make a hasty retreat when he realised she wasn't going to talk to him.

She twisted her hands together. There was the tiniest part of her that wished she knew what it was he wanted to tell her about her friend. Helen. Helen Hansard. She'd never known her name. She'd always been *Trees and Dreams*. But knowing her name now

43

suddenly made her seem more real. Was she in some kind of trouble, Orla wondered? Why else would her husband be here? And why hadn't he just sent an email like a normal person? He could have contacted her via Galleria, surely.

Orla sat down on the squashy Knole sofa she'd bought via an online auction, not noticing the big rip down the right-hand side. She'd get that fixed at some point. What was troubling her more than the ripped Knole sofa was how Luke Hansard had managed to find her. She hadn't given out her address to anybody other than her mother, and Luke's wife hadn't even known her name. So, how had he found her? As much as she wanted to ask him, she wasn't sure she wanted to speak to somebody who had so clearly tracked her down. Surely he wasn't to be trusted. Maybe she should message Helen.

She got her phone out and went to send a message via Galleria.

Hello dear friend. This might sound strange, but there's a man here who says he's your husband. Is everything okay?

She hesitated before sending it.

Then she waited, putting her phone down and pacing up and down the room.

Her phone chimed a moment later. She had an answer. Helen at last.

Only the message wasn't from Helen. Orla gasped as she read it.

This is Luke on Helen's phone. I really need to talk to you.

Orla usually liked to take a walk on the beach just as the sun was going down, but that wretched man was still there. He'd been sitting in his van for a while, perhaps listening to the radio, but it looked like he was staying the night. He was practically laying siege to her castle and he probably realised that she'd have to come out at some point.

For the first time in her life, Orla cursed having a dog. If it wasn't for One Ear, she could happily manage without surfacing for at least a week. But there was no way she was going to leave the safety of the castle tonight. One Ear would have to make do with a quick run in the garden.

'Come on, boy,' she said, tapping her side. The great beast, whom nobody else had wanted to take away with them from the rescue centre, was up from his mattress like a cannon being fired.

'Not so fast. It's just the garden tonight.'

She walked down the spiral stairs to the ground floor, to the door that led into a secluded part of the garden at the back of the castle. The evening air was warm and still and full of the sound of the crows that lived in the ruined part of the keep. Like Mr Luke Hansard, they seemed to be bedding down for the night.

Orla followed One Ear into the garden, taking in deep, settling breaths. She still couldn't shake the feeling of anxiety that had taken up home inside her chest since this man – this stranger – had rung her bell. He might profess to be the husband of her online friend, but what did she really know about him? Anyone could say anything, couldn't they? She had to remain vigilant.

Watching One Ear as he happily galumphed around the garden, she began to wonder if her home was as secure as she'd thought it was. She'd naively thought that living in a castle with a large dog was enough and yet here was this man outside her gate. *Inside* her gate! She'd have to get that sorted out for a start. It had been much too easy for him to walk right up to her front door and then to sit on her bench in the garden. If he could do that, then he could find his way around the side of the castle to the garden she was in right now. It would be a scramble over the wall she'd had erected, but it was probably very easy if somebody set their mind to doing it.

'One Ear!' she called softly. The dog looked up from a clump of grass he'd been sniffing and trotted towards her. They were going inside, she determined, closing the heavy ancient door behind them and bolting it. One large key and two metal bolts made her feel a little better but, when she walked towards the window and saw that the van was still parked outside, she could feel her guts churn with fear.

'Please go,' she whispered. '*Please!*'

Tears sparkled in her eyes and she could feel she was heading towards a full-blown panic attack if she wasn't careful. One Ear seemed to pick up on his mistress's fear and shoved his wet nose into the palm of her hand and gave a little whimper.

'I'm okay,' she told him, but the big soulful eyes that looked up into hers told her that he didn't believe her.

Orla really wasn't expecting him to be there the next morning. But he was. Had he really spent the whole night in that van of his, or had he gone to a local bed and breakfast and come back at first light? Did he realise that he was trespassing and that she could call the police? Or maybe he innately knew that she wouldn't want that sort of a fuss.

Some of the anxiety of the day before had left her now, to be replaced by anger. Anger that this man was making her feel threatened and forcing her to hide away. Well, she wasn't going to have it.

'Come on, One Ear,' she called to the dog. He pricked up his one ear and followed her out of the great hall, down the spiral stairs to the ground floor. Orla grabbed one of her hats and pulled it over her head and popped a pair of dark sunglasses on. This man – whoever he was – wasn't going to stop her from enjoying her morning walk.

She let herself out of a side door and then sneaked out of her garden via a gate in the wall. It led out onto a narrow footpath that went through the allotments. They were usually quiet so early in the morning, although there was somebody there now. An old man with a shock of white hair. He looked up and nodded and Orla nodded back briefly, sure that her hair was covering her face.

Head down, she crossed into a quiet country lane and then took a footpath which led to the sea. The beach was her special place, her sanctuary, the only place she really embraced other than the castle. Nobody disturbed her there. Not that they disturbed her at the castle, but there was something extra special about the beach. People went there to walk rather than talk. There seemed to be some unwritten rule about that. Anyway, she rarely saw anybody there. The beach was long enough to happily accommodate plenty of walkers, should they be there at the same time. Walkers who seemed content to do nothing more than nod a head in acknowledgement of a fellow walker if you happened to glance their way.

One Ear loved the beach and knew exactly where they were going, his pace picking up as the footpath slowly became sandy and the first breath of salt air filled their lungs.

Orla never tired of the first glimpse of the sea and stood for a moment and inhaled deeply. It was the best cure-all – a doctor of salt water and wind – who could heal you with a wintry blast or summery caress. The sea had a voice that changed with the seasons and the weathers. Its colours and the shapes of its waves were never the same either. Sometimes, Orla walked, head bent into the wind, unable to see anything other than her boots and the sand. At other times, she'd sit on a shingle bank and let her fingers sift through the stones and shells, causing tinkling avalanches in search of more treasure for the deep windowsills of the castle. Today, she walked. She needed to stride out and exercise some of the pent-up angst she'd been carrying inside her ever since Luke Hansard had arrived. And so she let the voice of the sea drown out all the negative thoughts from her mind, the unrelenting pounding of the waves helping to settle her emotions.

Luke had had enough of sitting in his van. He was stiff and uncomfortable after a restless night spent in the back amongst his toolboxes. He'd thought about trying to find a bed and breakfast, but had wanted BB to notice his presence. It had crossed his mind that she could call the police and accuse him of stalking, but he decided to take the chance, half expecting her to knock on his van as soon as it got dark and invite him in. Only she hadn't.

He got out of the van and stretched his arms high above his head. It was a glorious day and he was by the coast so, with that in mind, he thought he'd make the very best of it before deciding what to do. Quickly finding a footpath, he set off, not totally sure where it would lead and pleasantly surprised when it opened out onto a long beach dressed with shingle and sand.

He tried to remember the last time he'd gone to the coast. It had been in early spring sometime and the weather had been pretty awful. He and Helen had almost been blown off their feet and had ended up taking shelter in a scruffy café, trying to make their hot chocolates last as long as possible. He remembered the scene now, how cold Helen's hands had been but how warm her smile. She'd always loved the sea and now he wished that they'd had more visits out to the coast. How easy it was to have regrets when it was too late – to see all the mistakes, all the missed opportunities, all the bits of life you'd overlooked. Now, he wished with all his heart that they'd both skipped work now and then, called in sick and jumped in the car with a picnic and spent the day sitting in the sand dunes and paddling in the sea.

As Luke walked along the beach, he became aware of a woman up ahead of him. She was wearing a hat and had long dark hair and a large dog beside her. He probably wouldn't have taken much notice of her except for the way that she kept glancing back at him and nervously picking up her pace. Luke looked around as if there might be something genuinely scary on the beach, but he was the only one there. It was *him* she was trying to get away from, which meant that she must recognise him. It was the woman from the castle.

'BB,' he said, breaking into a run. 'Hello!'

The woman glanced back as he called out, but he couldn't see her face properly because of all the dark hair and glasses.

'Can I talk to you for a moment, please?' He'd caught up with her now and her dog approached him, pushing his big wet nose into Luke's hand. 'Hey, boy!'

'One Ear – come here!'

Luke grinned. He'd never met a dog called One Ear before. He looked up at BB, but her face was obscured by her hair.

'I'm Luke – I called yesterday,' he explained.

The woman was walking away from him.

'I wanted to talk to you about Helen.'

'I don't know you,' the woman called back.

'I'm Luke. Luke Hansard. Helen's husband. She was your friend on Galleria.'

'You're scaring me!'

'I don't mean to scare you. *Really*. I just want to tell you about Helen.'

'Don't come near me!' Her voice was high-pitched and full of fear.

Luke stopped walking and watched as the woman moved on, clumsily stumbling up a shingle bank away from him. What on earth was she so afraid of? Luke didn't think he was particularly scary-looking, but it was no good. She seemed genuinely terrified of him and he didn't want to go on torturing her like this. He sighed. His trip to Suffolk had been a complete waste of time and yet there was a part of him – the part that was still connected so wholly to Helen – that needed to tell this woman what had happened.

'She died!' he shouted after BB. 'Helen died.'

He swayed a little, shocked by the reality of hearing the words. He hadn't actually had to say them out loud like that before, other than telling his mother on that dreadful night. She had then taken on the burden of breaking the news of Helen's death to their relatives and friends.

'She . . . She died,' he said again.

The woman stopped at the top of the shingle bank but didn't turn around and then something strange happened. Luke felt horribly light-headed. The hateful words he'd shouted into the wind seemed to echo around his head. His vision was blurry now. He felt as if he was slipping away from himself. *Helen died.*

Everything went black.

Chapter 5

Orla wasn't quite sure what she'd have done if Bill Wilson hadn't been walking along the beach at that moment. At first, One Ear had thought that the falling man was some kind of game and had run around him, barking. Orla had pulled the excitable dog back and sunk to her knees in the sand.

'Luke?' she called, not getting too close.

Bill was running down the beach towards her, his little dog following close behind.

'What's happened?' he cried, sinking down beside her.

'I don't know. He just fell. I think he might have banged his head. The beach is so stony here.'

'Do you know him? What's his name?'

'Luke. But I don't know him.'

'Luke?' Bill said. 'Can you hear me?'

'Is he breathing?' Orla asked, panicking now.

Bill leaned in closer. 'Yes, he's breathing. Luke?'

'He just fell. One minute he was talking to me and the next—'

Luke stirred and winced as if in pain.

'That's it,' Bill said, inching forward to help. 'Now, let's see if we can get you up. Nice and easy now.' Bill placed his arms behind Luke to help him into a seated position and One Ear came forward again, whining, which set Bill's dog off barking.

'Quiet!' Bill cried.

'Back, boy,' Orla told One Ear, taking her first proper look at Luke now. He had curly dark hair, slightly longer at the front. His eyes were dark too and his face was horribly pale.

'Helen,' he said. 'H-H-Helen.'

'Who's Helen?' Bill asked Orla.

'His wife.'

'Then you *do* know him?'

'No. He only told me his wife's name.'

'I need to speak to Helen,' Luke said, glancing at Orla and Bill, but only seeming to half see them.

Bill turned to Orla. 'Can we find his wife's number and call her?'

'I don't think so.'

'Why not?'

'Because she's dead.'

'How do you know that?'

'It's what he told me.'

Bill looked even more confused now and Luke was struggling to his feet.

'He's not in good shape,' Bill pointed out. 'His head's bleeding. I think we should get him indoors and out of this sun.'

Bill stood up and linked his arm under Luke's as Orla did the same on the other side.

'Nice and slowly now,' Bill said.

'I need to t-talk to Helen. Sort this out,' Luke was saying, tears rolling down his face.

'It's okay,' Orla said. 'You're all right.'

'He's limping too,' Bill said. 'You're from the castle, right? I recognise your dog.'

Orla nodded.

'Well, it won't be easy, but I think we should try and get him back there.'

'What?' Orla panicked.

'We need to get him back to yours.'

Orla felt the colour draining from her face. 'I don't think that's a good—'

'It's the closest property, isn't it?'

'Well, yes.'

'And we need to get him inside and get that cut looked at.'

'But I . . .' Orla's voice petered out as Luke stumbled and groaned.

'Come on,' Bill said, and Orla found it hard to protest further.

It was a struggle to get Luke back to the castle. Orla really wasn't sure how they did it. The steps up to the front door proved especially tricky but, finally, they made it inside and laid Luke down on the Knole sofa, his face still deathly pale.

'Shall we call a doctor?' Bill asked.

'I'm not sure. Let's just see if he's okay first.'

'Do you want me to stay with you?'

Orla shook her head, turning to Bill now.

'Well, here are my numbers,' Bill said, scribbling them down on a piece of paper and handing it to her. 'Me and Margy are just down the road if you need us. Oyster Cottage. On the way to the quay.'

'Thank you.'

Bill took another look at Luke. 'His wife died, you say?'

'That's what he told me.'

'Poor chap.' Bill tutted and sighed. 'What did he do to deserve that fate?'

When Luke came round, he discovered he was lying on a sofa. A rather hard, lumpy one. His vision was blurry for a moment, but he could see large stone walls surrounding him. They were white and looked rough to his builder's eye and there was a lofty ceiling crisscrossed with impressive beams the size of felled oak trees. Light poured in from three enormous arched windows set with deep, thick windowsills. He rubbed his eyes and blinked hard and that was when he became aware of the smell of the place. It was unmistakable – like the smell you get when you walk into a church – the smell of centuries-old stone. A medieval smell.

Either he was dreaming or he was inside Lorford Castle. He struggled to sit up and, once upright, his suspicions were confirmed. What an incredible place to live, he thought, marvelling at what must surely be the great hall of the castle. There were some large pieces of furniture around the room in some kind of dark wood, but even they looked dwarfed by the dimensions of the castle. He admired a Persian carpet in rich reds, blues and golds and noticed that there were china jugs of flowers everywhere, bringing the outside in. There was also an enormous, hairy dog, who was looking at him from the middle of the room. The dog was sitting on the floor but was still at eye level with Luke on the sofa.

'Wow, you're a big boy,' Luke whispered, noticing that the dog was missing an ear. Something clicked in Luke's memory. '*One Ear!*'

At the sound of his name, the dog was immediately on his feet, trotting towards the sofa.

'Hey, boy!' Luke said, sitting up properly now and giving the dog's hairy head a rub. 'Where's your mistress, then? And what on earth happened to me?' Luke looked around and felt himself sway as he tried to stand up, grabbing at his head in sudden pain, as he saw a woman entering the room.

'Are you okay?' she asked from the doorway.

'Not sure, actually. I feel a bit dizzy and . . .' – he winced again – 'my head hurts.'

'Don't try and get up yet.'

'I'm in the castle?'

'That's right.'

The woman's right profile slowly came into focus as she moved forward and Luke noted how beautiful she was. Her skin was pale and almost luminous against her long dark hair. She reminded him of a heroine out of one of the Pre-Raphaelite paintings Helen had once shown him. Isabella, was it? He didn't have a memory for such things.

As she turned her face towards him, Luke saw her fully for the first time and had to stop himself from gasping.

Something terrible had happened to this woman. Some kind of accident had robbed her of half of her face. Her dark hair obscured a lot of it, but she couldn't hide the red soreness of the skin on the left side nor the eyelid drooping over her left eye. A fire, perhaps, or scalding water, Luke wasn't sure, but it was shocking to behold. Maybe it explained why she lived as she did – on her own in a castle – and why she gave so little of herself away on her Galleria profile. And why she'd been so reluctant to open the door to a stranger, Luke thought, feeling horribly guilty at having scared her so much both in her own home and on the beach when he'd tried to talk to her.

His mouth dropped open as he took it in, but he caught himself in time and looked back at One Ear.

'How did I get here?' he asked.

'It wasn't easy,' she told him. 'But I had some help.'

'Did I black out or something?'

'Yes. We lost you back there for a moment. I think you might have hit your head quite hard when you fell. I've bathed the cut for you. Do you remember anything?'

Luke frowned. 'I'm not sure. I went to the beach. That's where I saw you, isn't it?'

'That's right.'

Luke frowned, trying his hardest to remember. 'I don't remember much else. I don't think I ate much yesterday.'

'I think it was probably more than a lack of food.'

'What do you mean?'

'You – you were saying your wife's name over and over again.'

'No.'

'You were calling for her.'

'That's not possible.'

There was a pause full of awkwardness and she moved closer to him.

'Listen – my name's Orla and I think we got off on the wrong foot.'

Luke sat up straighter. 'I'm Luke.'

Orla nodded. 'I'm sorry I ran away from you on the beach when you were trying to tell me something so important,' she said.

'I'm sorry I scared you.'

She looked up at him and smiled nervously, although he still felt that he was somehow scaring her. Perhaps this visit hadn't been a good idea after all.

'I'm sorry to put you through all this,' he told her. 'I'll be on my way.'

He made to move and found that he couldn't. His head felt as if it was going to explode and he cradled it in his hands.

'Oh!' Orla cried.

'It's okay,' he assured her. 'I'll be fine in a minute.'

Orla shook her head. 'Perhaps – erm – you should rest? Just for a little while.' Her fingers were tying themselves into knots and she'd gone horribly pale.

'No, no – I'll make a move.' But the truth was, Luke found that he couldn't. 'Whoa!' he said as he tried to get up again. He glanced up at Orla, who was looking around the room as if in distress. 'Just give me a moment.'

Orla took a deep breath. 'Look, you're obviously exhausted. Why don't you rest here? Or I can make a bed up for you if you think you'd be more comfortable.'

Luke felt awful at putting her out like this. 'But I can't stay here.'

Orla looked as if she were instantly regretting inviting him to stay.

'I don't think you're in any state to go anywhere,' she said eventually, her voice full of anxiety. Luke felt it was more for herself than for him and felt guilty all over again.

'But I've caused you enough trouble already. First I scare you and then I go and pass out.'

'It's okay,' she said, but she sounded far from sure about the situation he'd put her in.

He shook his head. 'No, it's not.'

'We don't need to talk about this now,' Orla said. 'The important thing, I think, is to get some rest.'

'I should just go home.'

'And where's that?'

'Kent.'

Orla looked momentarily shocked. 'You're seriously thinking of driving to Kent?'

'Sure. Why not?'

'Because you're as weak as a kitten,' she told him. 'You really shouldn't move at all.' She chewed her lower lip. 'Why not just lie back and rest and I'll make a bed up for you?'

'I can't,' Luke said, attempting to get up again and swaying unsteadily once more.

'Still dizzy?'

He sunk back onto the sofa. 'Maybe I'll rest – just for a moment.'

Orla nodded and gave a hesitant smile.

Still feeling anxious and perplexed by the events of the day, Orla made up a bed in one of the castle's many rooms. It was only a small one with simple white walls, a pretty rug thrown over the dark floorboards and a pair of curtains in a heavy navy and gold fabric. The bed at the centre was a fine piece at least two hundred years old, with an ornate headboard in dark oak which Orla had bought at an online auction. It was the only guest room she had in the place and was only ever used when her mother, Bernadette, visited.

As Orla quickly fitted clean sheets, she wondered if she should ring her mother now and tell her what was going on. From past experience, she knew that Bernadette would have something to say about things. However, the more she thought about it, the more she bucked against the idea of ringing her. She just couldn't deal with the deluge of advice her mother would be sure to give on top of everything else that had happened that day. Anyway, she knew what Bernadette would say.

'Get him out of there! What were you thinking, bringing him into your home?'

Yes, Orla thought, Bernadette was of the opinion that her daughter should have nothing to do with the outside world. She'd been only too pleased when Orla had bought the castle and locked herself away inside it.

'It's for the best,' her mother had told her, and Orla had believed her.

Now, she drew the curtains and then returned to Luke, carefully leading him up the stairs, showing him where the bathroom was and leaving a glass of water by the bedside.

'Can I get you anything else?'

'No, thank you,' he said, looking as if he was ready to collapse into a deep sleep at any second.

'Did you want to see a doctor?' she asked.

'God, no!'

Orla was relieved. She felt she had to ask, but the last thing she wanted was another stranger in her home.

'I'll leave you to it, then,' Orla said, backing out of the room and closing the door.

'Thank you,' he called after her.

It was beyond strange, having somebody in the castle with her. Even stranger that the person was a man. That, she thought, was a first.

'You *do* trust him, don't you, One Ear?' she asked the dog when she returned to the great hall. 'And you will protect me from him if you change your mind?' The big dog cocked his head to one side. 'Well, you'd better.'

She still wasn't sure it was wise having this man in her home. She'd spent the last few years hiding away, avoiding people, and then she opened her door to this stranger. Only he wasn't a stranger, was he? He was Helen's husband. That made it only slightly less strange. At least she'd stopped shaking now. That was an improvement. But she still had misgivings about the whole thing. Surely Bill could have arranged something else? He could have called for help by now and had Luke taken elsewhere. But would that have been the right thing to do? What would Helen have wanted her to do, she wondered?

Helen.

She'd only just learned the name of her friend. Her dead friend.

She walked across to the table where her phone was and logged on to Galleria. So, she'd been right to miss her friend's posts, she thought, feeling guilty now for not having reached out more in the past. Now, she scrolled through the photos on her friend's page, reading some of the captions again and feeling all the warmth and humour which had delighted her just as much as the day she'd first seen the photos and read the accompanying words.

As with Orla's own posts, there weren't any actual photos of Helen herself – at least not beyond a hand holding a bunch of flowers or a pair of shiny boots amongst autumn leaves. Orla hadn't known her name nor what she'd looked like, but that hadn't really mattered, had it? She had known that Helen was married, but not her husband's name nor the exact place she'd lived. They hadn't talked about such specific things. Their conversations had been more about thoughts and feelings, hopes and dreams, and a shared love of the beautiful things in the everyday: shadows playing across a lawn, the changing colours of the seasons, the moment when a flower opens or the patterns clouds made in the sky. They'd also spoken about Helen's need for change and how unfulfilling she found her job, and Orla had encouraged her to pursue her passion.

And now she was gone.

Orla could feel a void opening up inside her at the loss of this person she'd never met. Was that crazy? Could you mourn for somebody you'd never met? Tears blurred her eyes and she let them fall as she put her phone down and walked to one of the windows. It was a cold, cruel world that had taken so bright a gem. She could only imagine how Luke was coping with it all. It couldn't have been that long ago either, she realised, and yet one of the first things he'd thought to do was to tell her. And she'd behaved so very badly. She felt awful now. This poor man had driven across the country when he was still in mourning and she'd shut him out and then run away from him. Well, she'd have to do her best to make up for that now.

With that in mind, she headed to the kitchen. It was one of her favourite places in the castle – a large square room on the first floor with two huge windows looking out over the garden. There was a beautiful old butler sink and a massive range that she had been terrified of at first, but which she was now coming to love.

Pulling a pan down from a rack, she started gathering ingredients. Bill had left her some fresh spinach and a spring cauliflower pulled from the garden and she'd got some potatoes left over from her shopping delivery. What was more hearty or heartening than a soup made from all that was good in the season?

Orla had been surprised at how much she enjoyed cooking for herself. In her previous life, cooking just hadn't been feasible with her busy timetable and a hot meal at home had meant buttered toast but, since her move to Lorford, she found that she enjoyed browsing through cookbooks and assembling different ingredients. She'd even bought herself a spice rack, and she always delighted in plucking the little glass jars from it.

Getting to work now, she washed and chopped, inhaling the earthy goodness of her garden ingredients and hoping it would do Luke some good once he was ready to eat. Once the pan was on the range, Orla walked back through to the great hall. The light was just right now, lancing through one of her favourite windows onto a little oak table. It had a wonderfully mellow patina, with chestnut highlights, and was silky smooth to the touch. It made the perfect backdrop to so many of her still lifes and she was going to use it now for this morning's Galleria post.

The day before, a new box had arrived full of china purchased from an online auction. It had been a job lot and some of the pieces were commonplace, but there were a couple of really beautiful Royal Albert cups and saucers that she knew she had to have for her collection. They looked exquisite when she placed them on the table in the sunlight, as she'd known they would when she'd seen them advertised.

Orla had to admit that she'd become rather addicted to online auctions. First, there was the thrill of the chase – of hunting those beautiful items down. Then there was that delicious moment when they arrived at the castle – the weight of the box, the heaps of bubble wrap and tissue paper which made it feel like a little Christmas on a perfectly ordinary day. Then there was the joy of seeing and handling the pieces for the first time, examining the shapes, colours and all the little imperfections that made each piece unique and beloved. Orla never tired of it.

Now, as she chose and positioned one of the Royal Albert teacups and saucers, she congratulated herself on her special find, marvelling at the way the light hit the gold rim of the cup and how gloriously rich the burgundy, pink and yellow roses looked against the dark oak of the table. She remembered reading the description at the online auction and how they had listed all the little chips and hairline cracks, probably believing that these would put people off. Of course, this was the very thing Orla looked for and she gazed at the little chip on the elegant curl of the cup handle. She touched it with a finger, feeling its roughness where it should have been smooth.

Like my own skin, she thought to herself, not for the first time. Briefly, her fingers touched her left cheek, feeling the coarseness of it. It still made her wince, even though it had happened four years ago. But the horror of it would never leave her. Her face – the one her parents had given her – had gone for ever. In its place was an angry-looking, lumpy, bumpy mess. The right-hand side, the side that hadn't been affected, had also lost its beauty, but to fear at the world around her.

Orla closed her eyes and tried to banish all thoughts of herself. She was learning to do that well these days. She was just beginning to control the fear and she was proud of the new life she had made for herself with her photography and her love of rescuing broken things. With that in mind, she picked up her camera and started photographing the teacup. When she'd first started this venture, it had been purely self-indulgent. She could see the beauty in broken things, but would anybody else care? Would she be making a fool of herself by putting her pictures online? That was one of the reasons, although not the main one, for her coming up with the identity *Beautifully Broken*.

At first, things had been slow. She'd gained a few followers, found a few accounts to follow herself, took more photographs and began interacting. It was the beginning of an incredible journey. For somebody who had turned away from the world, she had still managed to find a way back into it, albeit without physical interaction. But that was part of the attraction for her. She didn't need to actually talk to people or be in the same room with them, because she'd really rather not be. But there was a part of her that still craved contact, that sharing of ideas, the exchanging of thoughts.

And how her number of followers had grown. Orla was amazed by it all and, increasingly, felt under pressure to deliver. She found that, if she didn't post daily, messages would pop up asking her when her next post would be. It fascinated her that people were taking notice and were anxious for more of what she had to give them.

Putting her camera down, she took a few more photographs with her phone. She would then compare them and see which looked best and which she would choose to post. Hours could be lost in this simple task, but she was wholly absorbed and never begrudged a second. It had taken the place of the job she no longer did. This was her new work, although it didn't earn her a penny. She'd been approached by several companies, offering her money for product placement because of the number of followers she now had on Galleria, but she had turned them down. She didn't do this because she wanted to make any money from it, and doing so would complicate things. If she worked with people, they would have to know her real name, they would most likely want her address or her telephone number. They might even want to talk to her face to face. No, her art was her own private thing. She might share it with the world, but she was never going to share herself with the world ever again.

The next few minutes were spent looking at the photos she had taken, deleting the less than perfect ones and then comparing the few that she liked the most, making her selection and then uploading it to Galleria. Sometimes, she would take a series of photos in one session, formatting them and saving them in a file for use at a later date. Rainy-day photos, she called them, using them when perhaps inspiration was lacking. Of course, these photos weren't seasonal ones. It would be very poor to use an out-of-season image – for example, one would never post a photograph of a bluebell wood once the bluebells were over. Users on Galleria were very strict when it came to such things. Seasonality was king. But a photograph of a teacup was seasonless and so many of Orla's subjects could be used all year round.

Orla selected a few simple words to accompany her chosen photo. She didn't use the most poetic of language as some Galleria users did, nor did she quote from literary tomes like others. Her words were simple, conveying her appreciation for her subject.

> Mellow light and Royal Albert. A winning combination.

That was enough, she thought.

Hitting the upload button, Orla scrolled through the day's offerings, smiling at her little window on the world, admiring the flowers in people's gardens, the views from their windows and the scenes from the places they lived. Orla sometimes wondered if she could ever summon the courage to take part in normal life again. Could she ever open that great castle door with the intention of stepping out into the world? Could she ever venture further than the beach and go up to strangers again and trust them not to hurt her? Her mouth went dry just thinking about it, and so she tended not to. Galleria would be as close as she got to forging relationships. Even some of those hadn't always felt safe and she'd found herself blocking some of the users who asked her too many questions.

What's your real name?

Where do you live?

Can I visit?

Why did people always try to get close? Orla supposed it was a kind of compliment – that the image she projected was a friendly one. And how miraculous was that? Despite everything she'd been through, there was still a part of her that wanted to reach others, even if that was from the relative safety of a social media site.

Of course, she'd made friends with Helen that way too. If Orla hadn't taken a chance and put herself onto the platform, she would never have had the joy of knowing Helen and that was worth so much to her.

She spent a little more time looking at some of her favourite accounts, then took one more look at *Trees and Dreams*, smiling sadly at the last image of Helen's beloved oak tree, her fingertips hovering over the picture before switching her phone off and sitting in sad silence for a moment, unable to believe that her friend was truly gone, her eyes misting with tears once more.

And that her friend's husband was in her home.

She got up and returned to the kitchen to check the soup, lifting the lid of the pan and sniffing appreciatively. It was just about ready, but she was anxious not to disturb Luke before he was ready to get up naturally. So she took the pan off the heat and returned to the great hall, picking up a book to read.

As with cooking, reading was something which Orla really hadn't had time for in her previous life, and she regretted all the wasted years that she hadn't spent with her nose in a book. It had been her mother, Bernadette, who'd encouraged her to read, during all those long, painful months spent in hospital. At first, Bernadette had read to her because Orla's vision had been compromised. Bernadette had then bought her a Kindle and had loaded it with audio books. It had been the most thoughtful of gifts and had got Orla through some pretty dark days. Those books – those wonderful books – had been a sort of portal out of the pain.

Now, she found that good old-fashioned paperbacks were her favourite way to read and she had stacks of them around the castle. She'd bought three beautiful antique bookcases and was enjoying the process of filling them with novels, autobiographies, natural history and gardening books. As with all her other purchases, Orla sourced them online and had them delivered to the castle. She couldn't help regretting that a little bit, because she instinctively felt that she would find browsing in a bookshop a wonderful experience. But the virtual shelves had to do for her.

Opening the paperback now, she tried to lose herself in the fictional world while painfully aware of the stranger sleeping in her spare room.

Chapter 6

Bill Wilson was still a little shaken up about the incident on the beach. Picking up his daily newspaper from the village store and making his way back to Oyster Cottage with his Jack Russell, Bosun, he wondered if he should have insisted on staying at the castle. He didn't like the idea of leaving Miss Kendrick alone with a fainting stranger. Perhaps he should call the police or a doctor. But she hadn't wanted that, had she? Well, she was a grown woman. She knew her own mind but, all the same, he was glad he'd given her his number.

Arriving home, he opened the neat front door to the little red-brick cottage, kicked his boots off in the hallway and grabbed a towel to give Bosun a quick rub. The little dog was clean and dry, but it was a habit of Bill's just to make sure before Margy yelled at him about the mess the little dog had trailed in.

'Margy?' he called as he walked through to the kitchen to give the dog his breakfast. 'Where are you?'

'What is it?' Margy asked as she came into the room, holding her knitting. Margy never went anywhere without her knitting. It seemed to be a natural extension of her hands.

'I met her.'

'Met who?'

'Miss Kendrick.'

Margy's mouth dropped open and she stopped knitting. This was serious. 'What was she like?'

Bill popped Bosun's food into his bowl and waited for the dog to sit before putting it down.

'Well, we didn't have a conversation or anything. We were kind of preoccupied.'

'With what?'

'Getting that fella off the beach.'

'What fella?'

The two of them went through to the sitting room, although Bill felt too restless to sit down. But sit down he did.

'There was this fella and he just collapsed on the beach. We took him back to the castle.'

'He was with Miss Kendrick?'

'Not really. She knew his name, but I don't really understand any more than that.'

'Is he all right?'

'He was pale. Didn't look too good, but he was resting when I left him.'

Margy seemed to take this information in, her knitting needles working overtime as they always did when she was agitated. 'And Miss Kendrick – tell me about her.'

Bill shifted uneasily on the sofa. He didn't rightly know if he had the words to describe her.

'She's – well – she's got . . .' His voice petered out as his hand did an odd sort of movement in front of his face.

'What?'

'She's – her face is kind of . . .'

'Kind of *what*?' Margy's knitting needles were fairly flying now.

'I'm not sure. Burnt, perhaps. Scarred. It was hard to tell. Her hair covered half her face, and there was so much going on with that lad that I didn't think about what might have happened to Miss Kendrick. But it shook me when I saw it.'

Margy paused in her knitting. 'Poor woman. And is that why she hides away in the castle? Is that why nobody's seen her?'

'I don't rightly know.'

'But she seemed nice, did she?'

'Oh, nice enough, yes. Saw that big dog of hers.'

'I've heard about her dog. Size of a horse, they say.'

'He's big all right. Friendly, though.'

'I think I'd want a big dog guarding me if I lived in that draughty old castle by myself,' Margy said just as Bosun walked in. 'No offence, Bosun, but I'm not sure you'd be up for the job.'

Bill tutted. 'Nonsense!' He bent to scoop up the Jack Russell and plopped him on his lap. 'This little chap is as fierce as they come. He could take on a whole army to keep you safe.' Bill kissed the dog's head and pulled a biscuit from out of his waistcoat pocket to feed him.

'He's just had his breakfast. You spoil that dog, you do.'

'He deserves it. Don't forget the state he was in when we first saw him.'

Instant tears sprang in Margy's eyes. 'How could anyone do that to an animal?'

Bill shook his head. It had been a year since they'd rehomed the terrier and Bill still felt the same raw rage he'd felt when he'd seen the little bag of bones and been told the story of the abusive owner. The dog hadn't even been given a name. Bill had quickly come up with Bosun because the new arrival was soon running their home as if he were captaining a ship, and Bill and Margy were only too happy to be his obliging crew.

'He'll never know anything but love from now on,' Bill promised.

As if he knew he was being talked about, Bosun rolled onto his back on Bill's lap, his furry belly fully presented to his master.

'Your trousers, Bill! Really – you shouldn't let him roll all over you like that.'

Bill laughed. 'What's a bit of fur between friends?'

Margy picked up her knitting again. 'So, tell me what it's like, then.'

'What's what like?'

'The castle, silly!'

Bill puffed out his cheeks. 'I barely noticed.'

'Oh, you're *such* a man!'

'What? I was trying to help that fella, wasn't I?'

'Yes, but a woman would have done that *and* been able to tell you what all the rooms looked like.'

'No doubt,' he said, giving Bosun's tummy one final rub before popping him down on the floor and standing up.

'You going out again?'

'Just to the allotment.'

'Take your mobile. I don't want you late back for lunch like you always are when you go up there.'

Bill suddenly recalled something. 'I gave Miss Kendrick our phone numbers. My mobile and the house.'

For the second time that morning, Margy's knitting fell into her lap. 'Did you?'

'Seemed the right thing to do. You know – if there's trouble with that fella.' Bill shrugged. 'Don't worry. I don't think she's the sort to actually call. But I felt better offering her help in case she needed it.'

'You're a good man.'

Bill winked at her. 'Fancy a couple of fat cabbages?'

Margy smiled. 'You sure know how to spoil a girl.'

It was three in the afternoon when Luke finally surfaced. Orla put down her paperback and looked up as he entered the great hall.

'How are you feeling?'

'Good,' he told her. 'I didn't realise how tired I was. I guess I slept pretty badly in the van last night.'

'You feel stronger now?' she asked him.

'I do, thanks.'

'I thought you might want something to eat.'

'Oh, well – I don't want you to go to any trouble.'

'It's no trouble. It's as easy to make two bowls of soup as it is one.'

She led him through to the kitchen and motioned to the square table in the middle and he pulled out a chair. Orla got to work, warming the soup up and fetching two bowls from a cupboard. She laid the table and toasted some bread. Then, when everything was ready, she served the soup and sat down next to Luke.

'This is really good,' Luke said a moment later.

'Thank you. It's mostly produce from the garden.'

'You made it?'

'Yes.'

'You could go into business.'

She smiled at the compliment.

'Do you mind me asking what you do – I mean, for a living?'

'Yes.'

Luke frowned. 'You *do* mind?'

Orla was gazing down into her soup. 'I'm retired.'

'Oh, right,' Luke said. 'I didn't mean to pry. I'm just curious. I'm a builder. I repair old buildings.'

'Like castles?'

'Nothing so impressive, I'm afraid. Mostly regular homes. Quite a few historic ones. Some date back to the fourteenth or fifteenth centuries.'

'And that's in Kent?'

'That's right, but I work right across Sussex and Surrey too.'

'I used to love Helen's photos of the Kent countryside,' Orla said, and then bit her lip, unsure if she should have mentioned his wife. 'Luke? I'm sorry I didn't listen to you before. I feel awful for not opening the door now. But – well – I don't have any visitors.'

'It's okay.'

'And the beach – I'm sorry I ran away like that.'

He shook his head. 'You don't need to apologise.'

'Perhaps we can talk about Helen later.'

'Yes. I'd like that,' he said, as something strange started to happen. Luke's spoon was knocking the side of his bowl as if it had a life of its own.

'Luke?'

On it went, as if he were a manic drummer.

Orla reached out and put her hand on his.

'Do you want to rest some more?' she asked him gently.

He didn't answer at first but, when he glanced up at her, he shook his head. 'I'm fine,' he said.

'Okay.' Orla removed her hand and Luke continued to eat his soup. His hand was no longer shaking.

They finished their meal in silence and then Luke got up and took the empty bowls from the table.

'You don't need to do that,' Orla told him.

'It's the least I can do.'

Orla watched as he tidied up. His body looked tense, but his face was passive and unreadable. She wanted to help. It wasn't natural for her to have somebody help her around the house; it made her feel uncomfortable. But he obviously felt uncomfortable *not* helping and so she left him to it.

She wasn't used to having somebody sharing her home, but this situation had been forced upon both of them against their will and had come about so strangely that she had to overcome her fears and get on with things.

'There,' he said a little while later. 'All done.'

'Thank you. Can I get you a tea or coffee or something?'

Luke shook his head. 'I'm off caffeine. It's been wrecking my sleep.'

Orla wasn't convinced that caffeine was to blame for Luke's disturbed sleep, but she didn't say anything.

He looked around the kitchen, then walked over to one of the windows and looked out into the garden, his gaze moving beyond the wall towards the allotments, the fields and the windswept coast beyond. Orla watched without speaking, becoming increasingly anxious about him. First, there was the fainting, then the sleeping, then the shaking. Orla didn't know much about losing a loved one. Her father had died when she was two and she really didn't remember him at all, but this man's wife had died – when? He hadn't told her exactly when, but it must only have been a matter of a few short weeks ago. And wasn't that what he was here to talk to her about?

'Luke?' she said softly.

He turned around from the window, his expression a little vague, as if he wasn't fully there in the room with her.

'You said you wanted to talk to me – about Helen.'

A dark shadow seemed to pass across his face and that gentle, vague expression was gone.

'We don't have to – if you don't want to,' Orla added quickly.

'No – no – it's okay. It's what I came here for, isn't it? And I have something for you.'

'Really?'

'Something from Helen. It's in the van.' He motioned to outside. 'Mind if I get it?'

Orla walked to the door with him and unlocked it. One Ear accompanied her and stood on the threshold with his mistress as

Luke walked down the steps and across the driveway towards his van. She watched as he opened the passenger door and lifted a box from the footwell. Carrying it carefully, he closed the van door, locked it and returned to the castle. Orla led the way back to the great hall, where Luke placed the box on a table.

'Helen was going to send it to you, but . . .' He swallowed hard, pausing. 'Anyway, it's yours.'

'What is it?' Orla stepped forward, her fingers touching the sky-blue ribbon.

'Open it.'

Orla untied the ribbon and took the lid off the box, gently removing the layers of bubble wrap and tissue paper to reveal the blue and white vase.

'Oh!' she gasped. 'It's lovely!' She handled it carefully, mindful of how fragile it was and how much care had gone into choosing it and wrapping it. She was deeply touched that a stranger should go to so much trouble for her.

'It's chipped, I'm afraid, but she said you wouldn't mind that. That's what you liked about old things.'

'Yes. That's right.'

'Helen liked that about you – that you saw the beauty in broken things.'

'She did?'

'She said it's easy to love something that's shiny and new, but it takes someone special to love the old, neglected things.'

Orla felt her eyes sting with tears. 'She said that?'

'You were a great inspiration to her. She started her own small collection because of you. I say small because our house is small. But she took so much pleasure in every single piece she found.'

'I didn't know that.'

Luke nodded, and Orla could see that he was becoming emotional too and she couldn't help wondering if he was remembering some special moment with Helen. Maybe he'd been there when she'd bought the vase or maybe he remembered her bringing it home.

'There's a card with it,' he said, pointing to the box.

Orla placed the vase on the table and moved the last of the tissue paper from the box and reached in for the card. She could feel Luke watching her as she opened it and read the words, her eyes filling with tears again.

'I can't believe she did this for me,' she whispered, returning the card to its envelope with shaking hands.

'You meant a lot to her. Your friendship. Your advice.'

'You know about that?'

'Little bits,' Luke confessed. 'She used to talk about you and . . .' Luke stopped. 'I found her journal and – well – she said that you encouraged her. You helped her.'

Orla bit her lip but didn't say anything and then she looked at the vase, picking it up and holding it tightly.

'I'll treasure this always. It means the world to me. It really does.' She noticed that Luke was still standing. 'How rude of me – please sit down.'

Luke nodded and, as soon as he was sitting, One Ear looked up from his basket and then got up, stretching his long body before trotting over to say hello. Luke smiled and patted the dog's head and, after placing the vase on one of the deep windowsills, Orla sat in a chair opposite him.

Luke was perching forward on the sofa as if he were about to be interviewed for a job he didn't want. One Ear nuzzled up against him and Luke continued to make a fuss of the dog, delaying whatever he wanted to say a little while longer.

'Luke?' Orla prompted him. 'You were going to tell me what happened, weren't you?'

He nodded, and Orla realised how very difficult it must be for him.

'It was last month,' he began slowly. 'Helen had a job in London and she'd catch the train in and out every day. She usually got back home around quarter past seven. But she didn't come back. I waited, thinking she'd gone shopping or that there were delays on the trains. It's usually a good line, but you can never tell in this country, can you? A spot of rain or a windy day and the whole system can collapse.' He gave a hollow sort of laugh. 'I wish it had just been rain or leaves on the track that day, but it wasn't. There was some sort of signal failure.' He paused, as if trying to find the right words, and then they gushed out of him all at once as if he wanted to be rid of them. 'There was a train crash. Two trains. Eleven people died and Helen was one of them.'

'Oh, Luke! I'm so sorry.'

He dropped his gaze to One Ear and ruffled his head again.

'Perhaps you saw it on the news? It was everywhere for a while. You couldn't escape it.'

'I don't watch the news,' Orla told him. 'How did you find out?'

'The police called at my house.'

She sighed. 'I can't imagine how awful that must have been for you.'

'I can't remember much about it, to be honest. It's all a bit of a blur. The whole month has been. Cards, phone calls, emails. I've never had to talk to so many people before.'

'And I'm so grateful that you thought to contact me.'

'Helen cared about you. Even though you'd never met.'

'And I cared about her.'

'I felt that. I felt that connection between you. It was as real as any regular kind of relationship.' Luke smiled sadly. 'She used to look forward to your posts so much and she'd miss them if you

76

didn't post. She'd look at them each morning at breakfast before she went to work. I think you put her in a good mood for the day. "Something bright in a sometimes dark world", she'd say of your posts.'

'Really?'

Luke nodded. 'She used to share them with me, reading them out and showing me the pictures.' He gave a faint smile. 'You have a lot of teacups!'

Orla laughed, tears in her eyes. 'Yes. I do.'

There was an awkward silence as some of the darkness seemed to seep back into Luke.

'She sent me a message,' he began again at last, 'just before the train crash. She said she had a proposal for me, but I can't think what it could have been and it's been driving me crazy.' He paused and then took a couple of deep breaths before speaking again. 'I don't suppose she talked to you about it?'

'You mean the night of the crash?'

'Yes. Did she message you, perhaps?'

'What date was the accident?'

'The twelfth of April.'

'Let me check.' Orla got up and went to get her phone.

'Have you got anything? Did she message you?' Luke asked desperately.

'Wait a minute.'

Luke crossed the room and peered over her shoulder as she searched her phone.

'Here,' she said at last. 'The twelfth. She asked me a question.'

'What was the question?'

'"Do you think I can make a living from my photography?"' Orla looked up at him.

'She asked you that?'

'Yes.' She turned the phone round for him to see and he grabbed it in shaking hands before reading the message, taking a moment to digest it. Orla gave him a bit of space as he absorbed each and every word Helen had written. Finally, he looked up from the screen and suddenly seemed to realise that he'd taken the phone without asking.

'I'm sorry,' he said, quickly handing it back.

'It's fine.'

'I only read Helen's—'

'It's okay. Really,' Orla told him.

'Do you mind me asking what you said to her? I mean, if you replied.'

'I told her that I thought she could make a living from it and that she should give it a go.' Orla looked at her phone, reading the words she'd sent to Helen. 'I said, "Go for it! Your gift for photography and your passion for what you do are a recipe for success!"'

'Did she answer back?'

'Just this.' Orla turned the phone back to Luke so he could see the smiley face that Helen had sent in response.

'Was that her last message to you?'

Orla nodded.

'Her last message was a smiley face,' he said.

'Yes.'

'What time did she send it?'

Orla looked at the screen again.

'At 18:26.'

'Oh, my God,' Luke said. 'That was just a few minutes before the crash. She messaged me at 18:15 so you must have been the last person she messaged.'

Orla's fingers closed tightly around the phone as if that knowledge made it all the more precious, and then she looked up at Luke, whose eyes were filled with tears.

'She left the world with a smile,' he said.

Chapter 7

Luke walked along the beach, still feeling shaken by the revelations on Orla's phone. He'd seen the way her hand had closed around it after he'd told her that was probably Helen's last ever message. He knew how she felt because he felt the same way about his phone. There was a little piece of Helen locked away inside it. As well as the texts and photos she'd sent him, there were voicemails too that he was so glad he'd never got round to deleting. They weren't especially endearing messages – one was a reminder for him to pick up a bag of self-raising flour on his way home, and another revealed the Helen that could be just a little bit moody when Luke had forgotten to do something. He couldn't help smiling as he remembered that about her. She was so organised and just couldn't understand his chronic forgetfulness. But even though her message didn't show her in the best light, it was her voice, reaching out to him from beyond the barrier of death, and it was so precious to him. He knew he could never delete that message.

It was funny, Luke thought, but you even missed all the little things that used to annoy you about a person when they were no longer around, like the way Helen would leave the entire contents of her make-up bag all over the bathroom when she was in a rush to catch her train for work. How Luke missed that now.

As he walked, he thought about the message Helen had exchanged with Orla. So, she'd really been thinking about making a living from her art. She'd made noises about it before, but he hadn't thought she was serious. Her photography had always been a passionate hobby. She'd never really said anything about turning it into a job. And now she'd never get the chance. The world beyond her little platform on Galleria would never know how very talented she was.

'Oh, Helen,' he whispered into the wind, an immense sadness filling his heart at the thought of her dreams coming to nothing. The waste of a beautiful life. Unfulfilled potential. What would she have been able to achieve? Had she been very unhappy in her day job? Luke had known she sometimes found it unchallenging, but she'd never been one for complaining about things. She'd known how lucky she was to have a good, safe job. Perhaps that was part of what had held her there for so long – the fear of letting something safe go and leaping into the unknown. Fear, he thought, could be a pretty powerful jailer.

Unless it was something else. Luke knew it had taken him a good few years to get his own business off the ground and that they'd had to make a few sacrifices along the way. Fancy holidays had been out for a while, and he'd had to make do with repairs to his old van because there wasn't any way they'd have been able to afford a new one. Had Helen put her own dreams on hold so that Luke had been able to pursue his? The thought had never occurred to him before, but now he felt it like an arrow in the heart. Had he been so selfish as not to have seen Helen's sacrifice? Had she resented him each morning she'd left for work for that mind-numbing commute to the job she didn't love?

'Oh, God!' he cursed, the sea-blown air carrying his words away so that he imagined them circling with the gulls above, and then he sank down onto the shingle, his head in his hands as the darkness engulfed him again. It came on very suddenly, he'd learned, like a great tsunami. He'd lost whole days to it, and he was utterly helpless to stop it. Then, he'd feel completely drained. He took a moment now as the image of Helen's sweet face sharpened in his mind.

I'm so sorry, he told her silently.

Don't be such a loon!

'Helen?' He looked up, convinced he'd heard her voice and that she'd be standing right before him on the beach. But, she wasn't. He had so many moments like that: hearing her, imagining her, feeling her presence. Was that normal, he wondered? Was it some weird kind of coping mechanism? There was nobody you could ask about it. Nobody he knew had lost a spouse. Perhaps it was a fault in him that only death brought to the fore. Perhaps he was weak; he couldn't face something as big as death so he was trying to somehow bring her back. By imagining that she was still there, however briefly, he was essentially denying death. Of course, those moments were all too brief and the enormity of the truth soon overwhelmed him once more. Helen had gone. She wasn't coming back. Those fragmentary moments when he thought she was there, when he heard her voice, when he glimpsed her in the corner of his eye, were just in his mind, weren't they?

He let his gaze settle on the sea, watching the incessant waves rolling in, blue-grey and beautiful, their rhythm gently soothing his soul and helping his mind to still. He welcomed these brief moments that came in-between the bouts of pain and he would try to cling onto them for as long as possible, knowing that the onslaught of grief was just a thought away.

He wasn't sure how long he sat on the beach for, but it was long enough to start to feel better. Standing up, he brushed himself down and walked into the sand dunes and then along a footpath which led back into Lorford, stopping as he came to the road. He knew his way back to the castle, but there was a grassy track which caught his attention and made him take a little detour. The track widened and he soon saw that it led to the village allotments. He paused for a moment, taking it all in. There were dozens of plots, all neatly fenced with tiny sheds in various stages of dilapidation and chocolate-brown beds ready for planting. Spring greens coloured some of the spaces and there were structures erected in others for the beans and peas of summer. There were compost bins and water butts, and whole cities of canes ready for action. And, rising magnificent above it all was the castle. He took a minute to absorb it all and then he became aware of a white-haired man who was watching him. Luke gave him a brief nod and the older man nodded back.

'Glad to see you're up and about now,' the man said to him as he walked towards the wooden gate at the end of his allotment.

Luke did a double take. 'Pardon?'

'Glad to see you're okay. After . . .' The man paused. 'You don't remember me?'

'We've met?'

'On the beach.'

'But I was alone on the beach,' Luke said, becoming more confused by the minute.

'Earlier this morning.'

Luke swallowed hard. 'Ah.'

'Are you all right?'

'I am. Listen . . .'

'No need to say anything,' the man said.

'I'm sorry,' Luke said nonetheless.

The man opened the gate and stepped forward onto the path, wiping his hands on the front of his cord trousers before extending one towards Luke.

'I'm Bill.'

'Luke.'

'Good to meet you, Luke.'

'I wasn't feeling very well,' Luke told him. 'This morning. I hope I didn't put you to any trouble.'

'Not at all.'

'You've got a nice plot here,' Luke said, keen to change the subject as quickly as possible.

'Thank you. You know I garden for Miss Kendrick up at the castle?'

'Oh, right. I didn't know.'

'I mean, she does a fair bit herself, of course.' Bill pursed his lips together. 'You two getting on all right?'

'Sure. She's made me feel very welcome.'

'Oh?'

'Yes.' Luke was surprised that Bill looked so puzzled by this. 'Today was – well – it was the first time I met her in person.'

'What do you mean?'

'I've never seen her before.'

Luke frowned. 'Never seen her? What – ever?'

'Not so much as a passing glimpse. We do all our communication through written notes.'

Luke took this in. 'She's a bit of a recluse, isn't she?'

'The first one I've ever known.'

'Do you think it's because of what happened to her?' Luke asked.

'What happened?' Bill asked.

'I don't know, but I'm imagining it has something to do with her face. The way she tries to hide it and the anxious way she behaves in general. It kind of makes me think that something happened to make her hide away from the world. Do you know how long she's been in the castle?'

'A couple of years,' Bill told him, 'and, to my knowledge, she's only ever left the castle to walk on the beach.'

'And you've never seen her there?'

'No. We go at different times and I like to respect her privacy. I value my job at the castle and wouldn't want to make her uncomfortable.'

'And she doesn't go into the village?'

'Never. It's a strange thing, isn't it? To come to a place as friendly as Lorford and not to be a part of things.'

'It does seem a shame,' Luke agreed.

'You staying long?'

'No,' Luke said, staring up at the castle now. 'I'd better get back to work. I'm a builder and there's always plenty to do.'

'You don't fancy a spot of work on the castle, then?'

Luke laughed, but then looked back at the great building. 'I've worked on some old buildings in my time, but never a castle before.'

'I dare say there'd be a bit of work for you there.'

'I dare say you're right.'

'Well, it was good to meet you,' Bill said.

'You too.'

Luke watched as Bill returned to his plot, picking up a spade and settling down to some work. It really was time Luke thought about returning to work too. Chippy had been more than understanding over the last few weeks, but Luke knew that he'd have to get back to things at some point.

He returned to the castle. Orla had asked him not to leave without saying goodbye and he wanted to thank her for her kindness in looking after him. It really was an extraordinary place and he almost felt jealous of Orla living there. He felt he could do with something like that at the moment. A huge fortification against the world.

Then something occurred to him as he thought of Bill's words about the castle needing a builder. Perhaps this place needed him as much as he believed he needed it. One thing he knew for sure was that, in the brief time he'd spent at Lorford, he'd come to be very fond of it and he didn't feel ready to leave just yet. And then something else occurred to him. Perhaps Orla needed him too. Perhaps he could help her. Hadn't Helen said Orla had sounded lonely and that she'd wanted to help her? If she spent all her days holed up in a castle, not talking to her neighbours, he could understand why. But perhaps she was scared. Perhaps she needed help reaching out.

Perhaps I can help her.

He rang the bell outside the front door and waited for Orla.

'You okay?' she asked when she opened the door, One Ear by her side.

'Yes,' he said, wondering how he was going to say what he wanted to say. Quickly, he told himself, before he lost his nerve. 'Orla?'

'Yes?'

'I have a proposition for you.'

'Oh?'

They made their way into the great hall and Luke looked around the stonework, noticing the bits of plaster that were flaking away. He'd noticed a lot of other jobs that needed doing as he'd left the room he'd slept in. His builder's eyes meant that he couldn't help making a mental catalogue of all the work needed on the floor, walls, ceilings and windows.

'This place of yours,' he began, 'have you ever had any work done on it?'

'Yes, lots. Before I moved in, I got planning permission for extensive repair work and had a team of builders in for a while.'

Luke frowned. 'There's still a lot to do.'

'I know. I thought I'd better stick to a budget so I was careful in the jobs I chose to tackle first.'

'I see. So you've got planning permission and everything?'

'Yes. It was a bit of a nightmare getting it all signed off with English Heritage, but I've got all the paperwork. Why?'

'Well, there are a few things I wouldn't mind having a go at.'

'I'm afraid I'm not really in a position to hire anyone at the moment.'

'That's okay. I thought we could do a trade.'

'What do you mean?'

Luke ran a hand over the back of his neck. 'I wondered if I could stay here for a while. I don't really want to go home, you see. It's been nice to get away for a bit, if I'm honest.' He stopped, feeling the thud of his heart and the ridiculousness of his request as he looked at Orla's stricken face. 'Look, forget it. It was wrong of me to ask. You've been so kind and I shouldn't impose any longer. I'll get out of your way.'

He turned to leave, regretting having made even more of a fool of himself than before, and then he winced and clutched his head.

'Luke!'

'Yes?'

'Are you okay?'

'Just my head.'

'Where you hit it on the beach?'

'It's fine.

Orla hesitated. 'I don't think you should be thinking of driving anywhere yet.'

Luke sighed. 'You're probably right.'

'I think . . . I think you should come back inside.'

Luke saw the nervousness in Orla's face and instantly regretted having even broached the subject of staying. What had he been thinking of?

'No, no. Really. I should go.' He turned to leave and then Orla said something that surprised him.

'It's what Helen would have wanted, isn't it?'

The mention of Helen stopped him and he looked round at Orla.

'Don't you think? She would want us . . .' Orla paused. 'To be friends, I think.'

'Yes,' Luke said, not needing to think about the answer. 'I think so.'

Orla's hands twisted together in front of her.

'Listen – this is strange for me,' she told him. 'I haven't spoken to anyone other than my mother for months now, let alone lived with someone under the same roof. And I know I've got a pretty big roof, but I think you can guess that I like my own space.'

'I had kind of got that impression, yes.' He smiled.

'So I think you ought to stay.'

Luke blinked. He wasn't sure who was the more surprised: him or Orla.

He laughed. '*Really?*'

'Yes,' she said. 'There's plenty of room, as you can see, and you looked very comfortable in that room you were sleeping in.' She stopped. 'And I want to help and I'm sure – quite sure – that Helen would want me to help you.'

Luke swallowed, but didn't say anything.

'Look, I can't begin to imagine what you're going through but if being here at the castle can help in any small way then I'd love you to stay.'

One Ear came forward and pushed his wet nose into Luke's hand.

'I think he wants you to stay too,' Orla said.

'Then I'd better not say no.'

Orla smiled, her face lighting up. 'Good. Then it's settled. Only, if you truly want to work on the castle, then you must let me cover the cost of materials you need.'

Luke shook his head. 'Don't worry. I get things at trade price,' he told her.

'No, I insist.'

'Well, okay. I'll keep you informed of what we need and you can tell me if that's good with you.'

Orla nodded as Luke hovered awkwardly.

'Well, what do we do now?' he asked with a nervous laugh.

'How about a cup of tea?'

'Sounds good.'

They went into the kitchen and Luke put the kettle on as Orla got mugs from a cupboard. Looking out of the window down into the garden, Luke suddenly remembered his meeting in the allotment.

'I met Bill.'

'Bill?'

'Your gardener.'

'Oh, right, of course.'

'He has an allotment over there.'

'Does he?'

'You've never seen it?'

'No.'

'It's a lovely spot.' Luke paused. 'He said . . .'

'What?'

'He said you only ever leave the castle to go to the beach with One Ear.'

'Did he?' Orla's back was to him as she made the tea and he wondered if he'd overstepped the mark already and possibly endangered his invitation to stay at the castle.

'You should take a look some time – at the allotments, I mean,' Luke continued awkwardly. 'You obviously enjoy your garden. I think you'd like it.'

Orla didn't respond at first, but moved to the kettle to finish making the tea, presenting Luke with his mug a moment later.

'Luke,' she began, 'if you're going to stay here, I'd appreciate it if you didn't question the way I live my life.'

Her eyes held his and he noticed that they were green, only her left one was more opaque than the right. As if sensing the intrusion of his gaze, she turned away.

'Sorry,' he said, both for overstepping the mark and for staring at her. 'I just – I think you'd like it there.'

She paused by the sink for a moment and then made to leave the room.

'I've got some work to be getting on with,' she told him without turning around. 'You have everything you need to make yourself at home here?'

'Yes, thank you,' Luke said, cursing himself for having riled her and hoping she'd forgive him. But it did make him wonder about her situation and why it was that she chose to shut herself away from the world. Helen had been anxious about that too, hadn't she?

Once Luke had brought his few things in from the van, he opened his bag and reached inside for Helen's journal, which he'd brought with him like some kind of talisman – a little piece of her to travel with him – and he turned to the page where he thought he'd read about BB. Orla. And there it was: Helen's concern about her friend.

I wish there was something I could do to help her. She sounds so isolated. So alone. And scared too, although she won't tell me why. That's no way to live, is it? I wish she'd confide in me. I'd love to help.

Luke read Helen's words again, making a silent promise to her that he would try to help Orla. Luke knew that he had failed to help Helen realise her dreams, but perhaps there was something he could do to help Orla reach hers.

The first morning after Luke's arrival at the castle was particularly difficult for Orla. She'd slept badly the night before, wondering if she'd made a dreadful mistake in agreeing to his staying there and, several times during the night, she'd been on the verge of ringing her mother for advice. However, a cup of herbal tea, a walk around the great hall and a cuddle with One Ear had calmed her down on each occasion.

Now, though, as Luke got up from the kitchen table and walked to the worktop where the kettle was, she found herself feeling agitated in a way she couldn't explain. He was babbling about something – a nervous kind of chatter, probably to fill the void of silence between them which she was doing nothing to alleviate.

Orla felt herself nodding, possibly in the wrong places because she wasn't sure what he was saying. Her head was full of a sort of white noise and that awful panicky sensation filled her.

Luke had put the kettle down and was now standing in front of her. In her space.

'Are you okay?'

She took a step backwards.

'I – I need some air,' she said, and ran out of the kitchen into the green serenity of the garden. She could breathe more easily there. It was just her and the plants. Her little haven.

The next day was just as bad, with Orla seeming to trip over Luke every time she turned around. Perhaps she was overreacting. It was highly likely that she was. She knew she was more susceptible to nerves than most people. But, all the same, she couldn't help her reaction.

The only cure for her seemed to be long walks on the beach to calm herself, inhaling the salty sea air and finding a space to call her own.

When she got back to the castle, Luke was unloading his van.

'Just been into town to get some clothes and toiletries,' he explained.

'Do you have everything you need?' she asked, knowing that the guest bedroom was small and fairly basic.

'Yes, thank you.'

Orla nodded and scuttled inside.

There was another very awkward moment that first night. The castle had two toilets, but only one of them had a shower and bath and Orla had just wrapped herself in her towel after getting out of the bath when Luke knocked on the door.

'Orla? Are you in there?' he asked gently.

'I'll be out in a moment.'

'No rush, please!' he called.

But she hadn't been able to relax after that and found that she was feeling panicky again, her personal space violated.

When she'd got dressed and summoned up the courage to face Luke, she found him in the great hall, his hair covered in dust and cobwebs.

'Thought I'd better take a shower after rummaging around the basement,' he'd said with a grin, and Orla couldn't help but smile.

The big thing on Luke's agenda, he told her, was to assess what work needed doing to the castle. It was a long list which could have taken several builders and decorators many years, so he had to prioritise, asking Orla's advice as he went. Together, they decided to focus on the rooms that were used the most: the great hall, the great chamber, one of the passageways and another room which Orla had been hoping to use for her photography. Luke looked like he was enjoying the slow process of getting to know the castle and Orla began to enjoy her role as a guide to it, taking him down into the dungeons, where the stonework was rough hewn, and then up onto the turreted platform where the views across Lorford's coastline could be seen in all their glory.

Luke was obviously impressed.

'I just hope I can do justice to all this,' he told her.

She watched as he left each day to gather more materials, observing the careful way he handled everything.

'The thing to remember is that you have to use natural materials in these old buildings,' Luke informed her. 'They have to be able to breathe, you see? So no dreadful man-made products like cement or emulsion. It's all got to be natural.'

'Good to know,' Orla agreed.

Once they'd decided which rooms to focus on, Luke got to work, setting up his equipment in one of the many disused rooms in the castle. One Ear was as curious as Orla was and frequently kept Luke company while Orla let him get on with things.

'It's so good to be working again,' Luke told her one evening.

Orla was pleased he was happy, but she couldn't help remembering what she'd lost giving up her own work. That comforting routine – to have a project to focus on, to have something solid like a full day's work ahead of you. It gave the mind clarity and took one out of oneself, didn't it?

Orla couldn't help envying Luke that.

For that first week, Orla pretty much left Luke to himself, giving him the space he needed for the work he had planned. Slowly, she found herself spending more time in his company. She found it fascinating to watch him bringing in all the equipment he needed. She had pointedly not been around while the workmen had done some of the major repairs on the castle after she'd bought it. The thought of all the noise and dust and dirt was too much to even contemplate but, more than that, she hadn't wanted to be stared at. Business had been conducted over the phone with a project manager who'd made sure everybody knew what they were doing. To be honest, Orla didn't really know if they'd done a good job or not. It was hard to tell with so ancient a building and she'd only had a limited budget. So it was nice to be more involved this time. And there was something else about Luke working on it – she didn't seem to feel so self-conscious around him. She had felt a little anxious at first to have a man staying in her home and it had been awkward to wake up, knowing he was just a few rooms away and that, during the day, he might disturb her peace at any moment by entering the room she was in.

Perhaps it was because he was as vulnerable as her in his own way. The loss of his wife had injured him in just as devastating a way as she had been injured physically. Maybe that's why she'd let him into her life so easily. Even though Orla hadn't shared her home with anyone in many years, she found that she quickly became used to Luke's presence and they soon learned how to move around each other's routines, respecting one another's time and personal space. Perhaps it was that special link they shared together. Helen.

But there were still awkward moments, such as when she'd been watching him from one of the windows of the castle as he was unloading various pots and boards from his van. He'd turned around and nodded up at her and she'd flung herself away from the window just as she did if somebody ever so much as glanced up at the castle. It was instinct. She was so used to not wanting to be seen. Only this was Luke and he *had* seen her fully because she had let him into her home. But she still felt like she might have made a terrible mistake letting him stay with her and she knew that the transition would be a difficult if not painful one.

It was one evening at the end of May when Orla asked Luke something that had been preying on her mind. He'd been cleaning and plastering a section of wall in the great chamber that day and had taken a shower before joining her in the great hall.

'Something's been bothering me,' she told him as they sat down on the sofa together.

'What's that? Am I making too much noise?'

'No – nothing like that.'

'What is it, then?'

Orla took a deep breath, nervous about asking him this question, but anxious to know the answer. 'How did you find me? I mean, I never actually told Helen where I lived.'

'No. I didn't think you had.'

'So how did you find me?'

Luke cleared his throat. 'I – erm – looked at clues in your photos.'

'What do you mean?'

'On Galleria.'

'But I don't photograph the castle and I'm very careful with taking shots inside.'

'Yes, I noticed,' Luke agreed, 'but there were some clues if you look closely enough, which I'm sure most people don't.'

'Where?' Orla asked in panic. 'Where are these clues?'

'Do you have your phone nearby?'

Orla picked it up from the table and called up Galleria before handing it to Luke and watching as he scrolled through her photographs.

'You see this church?'

'Yes.' It was St George's in Lorford and was a favourite subject of Orla's.

'It was one of the first things I noticed about your feed.'

'But I never photograph the whole building – just bits of it.'

'I know, but it's a very distinctive building. See here?' He turned the phone round to her again. 'You've got the round tower featured.'

'Doesn't it look like most churches, though?'

'No, I'm afraid not. Round-towered churches aren't commonplace and are quite distinct to East Anglia.'

'I didn't know that.'

Luke took the phone again. 'You also photograph the sea a lot. Now, that could mean you have a holiday home by the sea or take a lot of day trips, but it does help when trying to locate someone.'

'I never thought of that,' Orla admitted. 'I mean, I was aware I was photographing the sea, but we live on an island, right?'

'Yes, but it's when you start putting all these things together.'

'And that's what you did?'

'Yes.' She saw Luke's face colour slightly at the admission. 'And then there was the castle. The windows. The windowsills. You might not have photographed the exterior or anything obvious like the turrets, but the interior backgrounds are very revealing. Not in all your pictures, of course – I had to search carefully, but that was what I needed to do to find you.'

Orla didn't say anything. She was too stunned. How could she have been so stupid? She'd thought she'd been so careful never photographing the whole of the church and only showing little corners of her home, but that had been enough for Luke to find her. And, if he could find her . . .

Suddenly, she grabbed her phone off him and started tapping furiously.

'What are you doing?' Luke asked.

'Deleting.'

'Your account?'

'No, but perhaps I should.'

'No! Don't do that.'

Luke got up and stood over her, watching as she deleted photo after photo.

'That seems a bit drastic.'

'You found me, didn't you?'

'Well, yes.'

'Nobody should be able to do that. I've been too careless.' Orla could feel her heart pounding as she went through her photos. What had she been thinking, posting all those church pictures? And the beach ones too. She'd thought she'd been clever in her obscurity and that quirky angles and incomplete images were enough to hide behind, but it was obvious that they weren't.

'Orla,' Luke whispered, sitting down next to her again. 'It's okay.'

'No, it's not. I've got to get rid of them.'

'But what about all your lovely comments?'

She paused. She hadn't thought about that. He meant from Helen, didn't he? She wasn't just deleting photographs, but Helen's voice from the past.

She could feel hot tears rising now. She felt helpless. 'I don't know what to do,' she said.

'May I have a look at the phone?' Luke gently held out his hand. 'Is there a way of saving the photos and comments? We could store them somewhere else so they're not visible to anybody but yourself.'

Orla nodded and handed him the phone. 'I think we can do that.'

'Okay, good. Let's do that, then.'

'But I've already deleted so many.'

'Don't worry about those.'

'But Helen's comments—'

'It's okay. We'll save the other ones.'

The two of them worked together. It took some time, opening each photo and saving the images and comments to another place, but they finally managed it.

'I've lost a lot of content,' she said once they'd finished.

'You'll make it up again.'

'With more care next time.'

'Yes,' Luke agreed. 'If you think that's a good idea.'

'I do,' she said. 'I'm just glad it was you who found the clues and not . . . somebody else.' She bit her tongue. She'd said too much, and she could see the questions rising in Luke's face so she got up and turned away from him.

'Orla?'

'Yes?'

'I think you're worrying too much.'

Orla didn't say anything, but she knew that Luke was wrong. As far as she was concerned, she hadn't been worrying enough.

Chapter 8

The nightmare was always the same. She was walking down a long corridor, clinically white, the lights bright and harsh. Some kind of hospital. She should have been safe in a hospital, but she instinctively knew that she wasn't. Her whole body felt cold with fear and she could feel her heart racing as she passed each open doorway. Why were they always open? Anybody could leap out of them as she passed. Or maybe that was a distraction or some kind of trick. Maybe they would come from behind her? She turned around, just in case, but there was nobody there, and so she walked on, her speed quickening until she was running. And the corridor just kept getting longer and longer, never ending, stretching, elongating, reaching out until . . .

Until she woke up.

Bolt upright in her bed, Orla took some deep breaths as she chanted to herself, *I'm awake, I'm awake, I'm awake*. It took a little while to convince herself and for her trembling body to catch up with her mind but, finally, she felt safe enough to leave her bed.

The nightmares were becoming rarer now, but they still had the power to shake her to her core when they struck. Swinging her legs out of bed and turning on her bedside lamp, Orla knew it would be a while before she'd be able to fall asleep again and so she pulled on a cardigan and got up. The room she'd chosen for her bedroom was one of the smallest in the castle and was painted a warm cream with a small deep-set window which looked out over the flower garden she loved so much. She'd decorated it with thick tapestry drapes in burgundy and gold with a bedspread to match. There was a single wardrobe in one corner and a Lloyd Loom chair with a big red velvet cushion, and that was it. There was no dressing table and no mirrors. It was a safe, protective space and yet, as much as she'd made it a cosy, comforting place, it couldn't protect her from her nightmares.

Perhaps she was responding to having somebody staying with her in the castle, she thought. Maybe her subconscious was fearful even though – consciously – she wasn't afraid of Luke. She genuinely liked him. One Ear liked him. He was the husband of her dear friend, Helen, and she truly believed that he wasn't a threat. Yet maybe there was a part of her that didn't trust him. That little part of her that kept her hidden from the world because she was fearful of being hurt again.

Padding quietly through the castle corridors towards the kitchen, she determined to make the most of being up at so ungodly an hour and have a cup of herbal tea. Something warm and soothing to chase every last remnant of the nightmare away.

She was just about to turn the light on in the great hall when she became aware of a presence. There was a change in the air around her and she instinctively knew that somebody else was there. At first, she stood paralysed. When she'd moved into the castle, she'd been terrified of the long dark corridors at night and had wondered if she'd made a huge mistake in moving there, but she'd gradually got used to the place and she knew her security was tight. Still, the thought of somebody breaking in was one she dreaded.

Of course, it could have been Luke but, if he'd got up, wouldn't he have turned the lights on? Possibly not. Maybe he hadn't wanted to disturb her or maybe he had excellent night vision.

'Luke?' she called into the darkness as she entered the great hall. Surely he wouldn't be up in the middle of the night. 'Luke – is that you?'

One Ear was immediately out of his basket at the sound of his mistress's voice, and Orla took comfort from having the animal by her side. If he wasn't growling, then perhaps the threat she felt was imaginary. She switched the light on.

And there he was. He'd been sitting there in the dark. His eyes were open, but he didn't seem to see her as she walked into the room.

'Luke?' she whispered. 'Luke!' She reached out towards him, but then something occurred to her. Maybe he was sleepwalking. You weren't meant to wake sleepwalkers, were you? She didn't know if that was a myth or not, but she thought she'd try something else because she really didn't want to distress the poor man, and so she gently took hold of his arm and encouraged him to stand.

'That's it. Nice and slowly. We're going to get you back to bed,' she told him as she guided him out of the room. One Ear walked behind them, taking this new phenomenon in his stride as Orla became anxious that Luke might actually wake up, and then what would she do? Would he be angry or upset or just embarrassed at being caught in his T-shirt and boxer shorts? But she needn't have worried because they made it back to the bedroom. Indeed, Luke seemed to know where he was going now and got himself into bed.

Orla watched him for a few minutes, making sure he was going to stay in the safety of his bed before leaving the room. She was wide awake now and so, after making a cup of tea, she took the opportunity to look up sleepwalking online. The most likely cause for Luke, she believed, was sleep deprivation. She had the feeling he hadn't been sleeping properly for some time now. What a pair they were, she thought – him sleepwalking and her with her nightmares.

The minutes ticked by as Orla began researching bereavement on the internet. She soon realised that there was a lot of confusing information. Some sites said that there were five stages of grief, but there was another that stated there were seven. Another article she found agreed that there were five: denial, anger, depression, bargaining and acceptance, but that they weren't always neat and consecutive, but muddled and messy. But did anyone really know for sure? And did a grieving person know that there were all these neat stages to get through? Did they feel them instinctively? Orla somehow thought not and soon came to the conclusion that, because each person was different, it stood to reason that they would work through grief differently and that there was no one-size-fits-all pattern or solution. Some people might eat their way through their grief whilst others would starve themselves. Some people found talking to others about their grief helpful whilst others shunned company and grieved alone. There was no right or wrong way.

She yawned, her eyes sore from looking at the bright laptop screen in the middle of the night. Sleep, perhaps, was beckoning her at last and she switched the computer off. One Ear, who'd been snoring in his basket, raised his one ear and opened an eye as she got up to leave the room.

'I'll see you in the morning,' she told him, switching off the light and making her way to her bedroom, pausing briefly outside Luke's room. Was he still asleep, she wondered? And were his dreams as troubled as her own? She made her way to her bedroom, crawling under the duvet and switching the light out. The first rays of morning light were creeping under the curtain and Orla welcomed it. The night had been long enough and, although she felt she could sleep for at least a couple of hours, she would be glad when the time came to get up and greet the day properly.

Sure enough, Orla managed to sleep and, when she awoke, she whistled for One Ear and they left the castle together. A walk on the beach always restored her spirits after a rough night. There was something deeply comforting about the sea and, for some time, her world would be focused on the waves, the sand and the stones. Nothing else existed.

Every so often, Orla would bend to pick up a particular stone that had been waiting, hundreds of thousands of years, just for her to find it. Maybe its perfectly round shape appealed to her eye or its elongated body fit snugly in the palm of her hand, or perhaps the flat surface was fingertip friendly and perfect for skimming. Her favourite stones were the ones that simply *felt* right. She thought of them as good *holding stones* – companions for her seaside walk. She'd pick them up and dance her fingers around them while she was walking or quickly drop them in favour of another, prettier, stone, her affinity to the previous one quickly forgotten. Nature's gift was a pocket full of pebbles.

One Ear wasn't interested in stones. He preferred a bit of drift-wood to carry or half a crab's shell to crunch into splinters, or simply to chase the seagulls, scattering them seawards to a chorus of delighted barks.

Orla took it all in – walking, breathing and emptying her head of the assaults of her nightmare. The salty sea breeze was a great balm to a troubled mind and she refused to let the fears of the night carry over into the day. But there was another darkness filling her mind that morning – the loss of Helen. She was still in shock at having been told that her friend had been killed, and she could only imagine what Luke must be going through. Orla only wished now that she'd got to know Helen better. They'd exchanged many messages, but they'd always been so guarded. Or at least Orla's had been. That had been deliberate on her part. It was a miracle at all that she'd connected with Helen in the way she had. She hadn't talked to anybody else on Galleria in the same way, and yet there'd always been that part of her that hadn't revealed itself. She kind of regretted that now because the opportunity to really get to know her friend had been taken away from her.

She looked out at the sea again, knowing that regrets were useless and that the past could never be changed, but how she wished she could go back and reach out just that little bit more. Luke had told her how much her words of encouragement had meant to Helen and the sweet gift that Helen had chosen for her meant the world to her, but she couldn't help feeling that there was more she could have done and more that she could have shared.

Luke was up when she got back to the castle.

'How are you?' Orla asked.

'Good,' he said. 'I slept well.'

Orla took this in, wondering if sleepwalkers ever knew they had been sleepwalking. She thought it better that she didn't mention it. He certainly looked okay.

'Been to the beach?' he asked her.

'Yes.'

'I thought I'd pop out later. Get to know the village a bit.'

Orla nodded. That was, after all, normal behaviour, wasn't it?

'Can I get you anything?'

'No, thank you.'

'Nothing from the local shop?' he asked, and she shook her head. 'You want to come with me?'

'No.' Her answer was blunt, but she needed him to know that there was no compromise to be made here. She'd already asked him, politely, not to question the way she chose to live.

'I'll get a bit of work done first and then take a breather later. Let me know if you change your mind.'

'I won't. Change my mind, I mean,' she said, feeling flustered.

'Okay.' Luke nodded, smiled and then left the room, and Orla immediately felt guilty for sounding so rude. But better to be rude than unsafe, she told herself.

Luke walked down the little hill towards the market square he'd driven into when he'd first arrived in Lorford. It was a beautiful June morning, with a clear blue sky, and the swifts were at play, screeching high above the rooftops. Luke took some good, deep breaths of summer air. It felt good to be out of the castle. He hadn't been completely honest with Orla; he'd felt a little rough that morning, as if he hadn't slept well, and yet he had no recollection of having woken in the night. He just felt unrested somehow. It wasn't an uncommon feeling. Ever since the night of the train crash, Luke had found his relationship with sleep had become patchy at best. Sometimes, he was able to lose himself in a heavy and deep sleep, only to wake up feeling even more exhausted than before, and other nights he'd be restless, getting up every hour or so and then waking red-eyed and thick-headed in the morning. Maybe more walking would go some way to helping him sleep better, he thought. He was certainly in the right place, with the beach and the footpaths he'd spotted which led out across the fields and reed beds. Although a little voice told him that you couldn't outwalk your grief.

He paused for a moment, glancing back at the castle. He'd been hoping that Orla would feel some sort of obligation towards her guest and come with him to show him around Lorford, but he was beginning to realise that it was more likely to be the other way around because she obviously didn't venture into the village. She only ever seemed to go to the beach, although she did occasionally photograph the church. But that was set back from the village and he could see how she could walk there easily without too many people seeing her.

It seemed such a shame that Orla had decided to live in a place like Lorford and not choose to be a part of things. As Luke walked through the village that morning, he could see that it was the sort of place one should move to if one wanted to be a part of things. There was such a feeling of community, with the little shops, the sweet rows of cottages and the people out walking their dogs. There were a few tourists down by the quay. The café was open and there were people lining up for one of the boat trips along the river, and what a perfect day it was for that too, with the sun sparkling on the water. It might not be as bustling as Aldeburgh or Southwold further up the coast, but Lorford had many charms and Luke felt sad that Orla shut herself away from them all. What was it she was so afraid of? He instinctively felt that these people would be nothing but kind and welcoming to Orla, but she had to meet them halfway. He wanted to find out what it was that kept her hidden away from the world, and he knew that Helen had been intrigued too. She had wanted to reach out to Orla, but raising the subject would be tricky. After all, it was a miracle that he was staying there at all. He couldn't expect her just to open up to him after knowing him for so little time.

He wondered what Helen would make of it all – of him coming to Lorford and finding Orla and staying at the castle with her. He guessed Helen hadn't known about the castle and he couldn't help imagining her response at finding out about it and seeing it for the first time. She'd have loved it; he knew that much. She had a special appreciation for England's ancient buildings and Luke so desperately wanted to share it all with her.

But you wouldn't be here if she hadn't died.

He sighed, knowing it was true, but not wanting to hear that horrible little voice telling him.

He looked down at his hands. He didn't wear a wedding ring. Helen hadn't put any pressure on him to do so. It was dangerous in his line of work, she realised that, but she did often tease him about that just being an excuse. Now, he wished he had that link to her. He wouldn't care if it put him at risk. At least he'd have that connection.

His memory rolled back to the moment when he'd slid that slim band of gold onto Helen's finger. Theirs had been a simple wedding. They hadn't had much money for anything fancy. The local registry office had been good enough for them, with a reception at Helen's parents' house afterwards. Helen's mother had gone all out with the flowers. Luke still remembered Helen's face when she'd seen them all: great towers of flowers, completely disguising the modest semi-detached. It had been so beautiful. And Helen. She had taken his breath away with her hair swept up and her long lacy dress in the softest of creams. When he'd placed the ring on her finger, she'd whispered to him that she'd never take it off, and she never had.

She was still wearing it now, he thought, in that other dimension, wherever she was. She had taken it with her. Helen's mother had asked him if he wouldn't rather have it as a keepsake, but it hadn't been his to take. It was Helen's ring and he had respected her wishes to wear it always.

Closing his eyes for a moment to regain his composure, he got up from the bench before leaving the quay at a fast pace. Walking helped to calm him down. That steady, simple rhythm of putting one foot in front of the other really helped to ease the grip of grief, he found. The only trouble with Lorford was that it was so small, and he soon found himself back in the market square. He paused, looking around as if reminding himself of where he was, and then he saw the small village store and walked towards it, picking up a basket and filling it with groceries. It was one of those mindless, everyday tasks that was proving to be a little lifesaver in its own way.

'You on holiday?' the lady behind the counter asked him as she took his money a few minutes later.

Luke was surprised by her question. 'Kind of, I guess.'

'Staying locally?'

'In the castle.'

Her mouth dropped open at this declaration. '*Lorford* Castle?'

'Yes.'

'You're a friend of . . .' her voice petered out.

'Miss Kendrick, yes,' he said.

'Well, that's . . . very nice.'

Luke nodded, not knowing whether to add anything. After all, Orla didn't have anything to do with the village.

'I'll see you soon,' he said as he left the shop, thinking that word of his arrival would soon get around the village.

Crossing the square, he took a quick look at the menu outside the pub, and then he saw it. The noticeboard. Set on the wall by the bus stop, it was full of the usual village stuff: when the next council meeting was to be held, what Lorford was doing to become more green and – Luke blinked – a horticultural group. New members welcome. The people of Lorford, Luke had noticed, loved their gardens, so it was no surprise to him that there was a horticultural society being advertised. The next talk was that very week and was entitled 'Herbs: why you should grow them and how you can use them'.

Luke read the poster again, taking it all in, and something in it linked with the voice he heard in his head, Helen's voice, and the words she'd written in her journal. He recalled them now.

BB has been so kind helping me to discover what it is I really want. I wish there was something I could do to help her. She sounds so isolated. So alone. And scared too, although she won't tell me why. That's no way to live, is it?

Luke agreed. That was no way to live.

He looked at the poster again. His knowledge of herbs was limited to the sort in a bottle on his spice rack. Other than mint, rosemary and basil, he wasn't even sure if he'd met any real-life herbs. But that didn't really matter because he wasn't going there for the talk about plants. Luke had a plan, and he was going to need to get the locals on board with it in order to help him.

When Luke arrived back at the castle, he noticed a small van had pulled up in the driveway and he watched as a man got out, opened the van door and retrieved a large box. He nodded to Luke as he saw him.

'Delivery for Miss Kendrick.'

'I'll take it,' Luke told him, putting his shopping bag down. 'Does it need a signature?'

'No. She never signs for anything. Instructions are to leave it by the back door.'

'I'll take it in.'

The man scratched his head. 'You a friend?'

'Yes.'

'What's she like?'

Luke was a little reluctant to answer as he knew Orla valued her privacy.

'She's nice,' he said, and the delivery man nodded.

'I've been delivering these boxes for two years now and never seen her.'

'Does that matter?'

The man shrugged. 'I guess not. Odd, though, ain't it?'

Luke watched as he got back into his van and drove away, and Luke acknowledged once again that, although Orla might not want anything to do with the outside world, the outside world certainly knew of her presence and felt its absence.

Doing his best to carry both the box and his bag of groceries, Luke negotiated the castle steps and rang the doorbell. As usual, One Ear sounded his arrival and, a moment later, Orla opened the door to him.

'You have a delivery,' he told her unnecessarily. 'Where do you want it?'

'Follow me,' she said, taking his bag from him.

Luke followed Orla into a part of the castle he hadn't seen before. She opened a door and led him into a light and airy room that was full of tables on which sat row upon row of crockery. He'd never seen so many plates, cups, saucers, bowls and jugs in one room before. It was crammed full. There were at least twelve tables in there, of varying heights, and each was smothered in pieces, as were the deep windowsills and a shelving unit against the far wall.

Luke stood in wonder, taking it all in. There was the Victorian jug he recognised from Orla's Galleria avatar and there was the pretty dish covered in golden pheasants which Helen had recently admired. He dared to reach out and touch it, as if his closeness to a thing Helen had loved would bring him a little closer to her.

'You have very good taste,' Orla said, noting his interest.

'Helen' – he paused – 'she liked this piece when you posted a photo.'

'Yes, she did, didn't she? I remember we talked about it.'

'What did she say?'

'Oh, the usual – where had I found it. And that's the tricky thing with vintage pieces – it would be hard, if not impossible, for anybody else to find them.'

'I remember Helen saying something about that,' Luke told Orla. 'How that made the pieces all the more special.'

Orla smiled. There was something in that smile and in sharing their memories of Helen in this way that made him feel both happy and sad at the same time.

'Helen was right,' Orla went on. 'That's why I buy boxes like this.'

Luke watched as she opened the box he'd carried in for her, a huge smile spreading across her face. He'd never seen her smile quite like that before and it charmed him.

'What is it?' he asked. 'What's in there?'

'Why don't you take a look?'

He stepped forward and peered into the depths of the box. 'More china?'

'Of course.'

'But you have so much already.'

'Yes, but you're always looking for that extra-special piece.'

'Do you think you'll ever find it?'

'I hope not, because I wouldn't like to think the search was over. That's part of the fun, you see. The search. Of course, when you buy online, you often have to wade through a lot of tat. This was a job lot, you see, and I only wanted a couple of pieces so I'm now stuck with this nineteen-eighties rabbit ornament.' She pulled the heavy lump of rabbit out of the box and grimaced, then reached back in to retrieve a very average-looking teapot.

'So what was it that was special in this lot?'

Orla's hands dived back into the box and she pulled out a round object smothered in bubble wrap.

'This,' she said as she placed it on a corner of the only free table in the room and began to unwrap it. Luke watched in anticipation as she removed layer upon layer of wrapping. What was inside?

When the final piece of bubble wrap was removed, he found himself staring at a teapot.

'Oh,' he said, unable to hide his disappointment.

Orla frowned at him. 'It's Coalport. Quite rare. Look!' She held it up to the light and Luke saw the delicate creamy white of the china and the pretty sprigs of blue flowers. 'It's early nineteenth century.'

'But it's chipped,' he pointed out, reaching to touch the chip at the edge of the spout.

'I know, and there's a hairline crack here,' Orla told him, running her finger across it at the base of the handle. 'And here.' Her finger journeyed to the other side of the teapot to trace the thin imperfection there.

'Ah, yes! That's part of their charm for you, isn't it?'

She nodded. 'Nobody else would want these things or really value them. But, to me, they're special.'

'A bit like One Ear, eh?'

'Exactly! I told you he'd been in the rescue home for months?'

'Yes.'

'Nobody wanted him until I came along. But I knew he was the one for me. We had . . .' – she paused – 'things in common.'

Luke finally made the connection, because Orla was missing her left ear. It wasn't always obvious because she managed to hide her loss with her long dark hair, but he couldn't help wondering if that was why she'd been drawn to the disfigured dog.

'Orla?'

'Yes?'

'What happened to you?'

She looked up, lowering the teapot carefully to the table. 'You can't ask me that.'

'Why not? You know what's happened to me.'

'That's different.'

'How?'

'You came to me with that; I didn't come to you.'

Luke sighed. She was right. 'But I'd like to know. I mean, if you don't mind talking about it.'

'I do mind.'

'Okay.' He backed down, seeing that she was upset. The last thing he wanted to do was to upset her. Helen would be furious with him if she knew he'd upset her, wouldn't she?

Orla's gaze dropped down to the teapot again. Teapots and cups and saucers were safe, weren't they? He could see why she surrounded herself with them. They didn't ask questions.

'I'll leave you to it,' he said, feeling awkward and backing out of the room.

'Luke?'

He stopped in the doorway and turned back to face her.

'It's not that I don't want to tell you. It's that – I can't . . .' Her voice caught in her throat and her eyes sparkled with sudden tears. 'I can't talk about it.'

'It's okay. Really.'

She nodded, reminding him of a scared little girl standing in the middle of that room surrounded by all that china. The pieces were like grown-up toys, he thought. An adult's version perhaps. Beautiful distractions from whatever horror she was trying to shut out.

Chapter 9

Despite Orla telling him that she didn't want to talk to him about her past or the way she chose to live her life, Luke couldn't help thinking of ways to reach out to her. The thing he kept coming back to was the horticultural group he'd seen advertised in the village. He was so sure that he could help her and he couldn't help feeling that Helen was somehow guiding him in this. So, the next day, after a good couple of hours working on repointing one of the walls in the great chamber, Luke walked into the village and reread the poster on the noticeboard.

'New members welcome,' he read again. There was a telephone number and an address. Oyster Cottage, Quay Road. Luke looked up into the sky and decided to walk down towards the quay. The red-bricked cottages that lined the narrow street looked resplendent in the sunshine and gardens were colouring up with the bright purples of alliums and the first roses of summer. As he approached the quay, the sound of gulls pierced the sky and he started to look out for Oyster Cottage. It wasn't hard to find and he was soon knocking on the door. As with his arrival at the castle, the sound of barking was heard, but this sounded like a much smaller dog than One Ear. Mind you, weren't *all* dogs much smaller than One Ear, Luke thought?

The door was opened by a pretty woman whose long white hair was swept up in a messy bun. She was holding a pair of knitting needles in her hand from which a long project in purple and green dangled.

'Hello,' Luke said. 'I'm Luke Hansard. I've come about the horticultural club.'

'You'll want to speak to my husband,' she said. 'Come in.'

Luke stepped into a narrow hallway. The sound of barking was louder now, coming from behind a door which had been resolutely closed on the anxious animal.

'He's in the garden,' the woman explained.

'Appropriately enough.'

'He lives outdoors at this time of year. Well, at all times, really.'

They reached the back door and Luke saw a garden with neat borders full of colourful blooms, a small pond and a tiny blue shed. And in the middle of it all was a white-haired man wearing a tweed cap, bent over as he deadheaded a rose bush.

'Someone about the horticultural club,' his wife announced, and the man looked up.

Luke did a double take. 'Ah, Bill, isn't it?'

'Luke?'

'Yes.'

'How are you?'

'Very well.'

'You two know each other?' Bill's wife asked.

'Sort of,' Luke said. 'Met each other at the allotments the other day.'

'Still in Lorford, I see.'

'I'm actually doing some work on the castle now.'

'Are you?'

'Your suggestion was a good one.'

Bill removed his cap and scratched his head. 'I'm glad to hear it. So, you wanted to talk about the horticultural club?'

'Yes.'

'Margy – how about a cup of tea, yes?'

Luke nodded. 'Thank you.'

'I'll get the kettle on,' Margy said, disappearing back inside as Bill gestured towards a bench.

'This is a nice garden you've got here,' Luke told Bill. 'Like your allotment. I can see it's a passion of yours.'

'You could say that.'

Luke looked around in admiration, thinking of how Helen had adored their tiny garden in Kent.

'Luke – come and see this peony! Isn't it a beauty?'

Luke flinched and he looked around in confusion. He could have sworn . . .

'Are you okay, son?' Bill asked him, leaning forward.

'Erm – yeah.' Luke blinked and focused on the man sitting next to him. He'd heard her, hadn't he? It had been Helen's voice. Nobody else's.

'You wanted to talk about our little club?' Bill prompted.

'Yes. I'd like to come to the next meeting.'

'This Friday? You'd be very welcome.'

'It's here, right?'

'In our front room, such as it is. We tried the village hall, but it's just too draughty.'

'I'm hoping to bring someone with me,' Luke went on.

'Oh, yes?'

'Orla.'

Bill looked stricken by this news. 'Miss Kendrick?'

'Yes.'

'She wants to come?'

'Not exactly. She doesn't know anything about it yet.'

'Then what makes you think—'

'Look, it's a long shot, I know, but I think getting out into the community will do her some good.'

Bill shook his head. 'I don't disagree with you, but she's lived in Lorford for two years. I think she'd have joined in with village life by now if it was ever going to happen.'

'I know. I might have a battle on my hands, but I really think I might be able to help her. I want to try, at least. It's kind of a – well – a challenge I've set myself.'

'Well, that's admirable, son, but how are you going to do that?'

'I'm not sure. But it's got to be worth a try, hasn't it? I mean, she can't be happy shut away like that all day.'

Bill sighed. 'I can't imagine she is. But it isn't your everyday sort of person who buys a castle, is it? I mean, if she'd wanted to be a part of things, she wouldn't have put a tower of stone between herself and the community, would she? It's a wonder she let you in. I have to say, I'm still surprised by that.'

Luke nodded. 'Me too. I don't think it was an easy decision for her, but we kind of connected.'

'And you think you can use that connection now? To bring her out of herself?'

'I do. I really do.'

Margy arrived then with the tea things, neatly presented on a floral tray together with a plate of chocolate chip cookies.

'Thank you!' Luke said. 'It looks wonderful.'

Margy smiled and left them to it. The two men picked up their teacups and drank in silence for a moment. Bill was the first to speak.

'Are you sure it won't be too overwhelming?' he asked. 'Our club meeting, I mean. Our front room is on the small side. She's going to be in close proximity to a lot of people.'

'She got used to me pretty quickly. And she already knows you.'

'Well, I wouldn't say she *knows* me. I only met her for the first time the other day and we didn't exactly have time to bond.'

'No,' Luke agreed. 'But you're all a friendly bunch, aren't you?'

'Well, of course.'

'How many of you are there?'

'About fifteen altogether, but not everyone shows up at once. There are usually seven or eight at each meeting.

Luke nodded. 'That doesn't sound too scary.'

'Not for you maybe, but what about for Miss Kendrick?'

Luke didn't reply. The truth of the matter was that he hadn't really got beyond the initial excitement of coming up with the idea. But he couldn't help admitting he was becoming more nervous now.

'I guess we'll soon find out,' he said bravely.

Bill took another sip of his tea, keeping his thoughts to himself, but doing a pretty bad job of hiding his scepticism.

Orla had watched as Luke left the castle. He hadn't said anything about where he was going and she didn't think it was her business to ask. But it seemed that he wasn't going for tools or equipment for his work because he hadn't taken the van. She'd looked down from one of the high windows as he'd walked along the driveway and opened the gates, closing them behind him a moment later. He'd briefly glanced up at the castle then but, to her relief, hadn't shown any signs of seeing her. She didn't want him to think she was spying on him.

After she was sure he wasn't coming back immediately, she went to look at the area he'd been working on, smiling at his progress.

It was still strange having him in her home, but she had to admit that there was something rather comforting about it too, and it felt strange now that he'd left for a while. The atmosphere had changed somehow. She couldn't quite explain it to herself, but she felt it as a kind of loss.

Was she slowly getting used to having people around her again? Was she beginning to trust once more? Perhaps it was still too early to say, but one thing she was sure of – she liked Luke.

A little later on, the front doorbell rang. One Ear raced towards it, barking in warning as he usually did.

'It's just me, Orla!' Luke called from the other side, and Orla smiled and let him in.

'You'll never guess where I've been,' Luke said as they walked across the great hall. He sounded excited and anxious too and Orla couldn't begin to guess what he'd been up to.

'Tell me.'

'Oyster Cottage.'

'Where's that?'

'On the way to the quay. It's where your gardener lives.'

'Oh?'

'And we have a lovely invitation for Friday night.'

Orla frowned, not understanding. 'What do you mean?'

Luke smiled. 'Did you know Bill hosts Lorford's horticultural club? Well, there's a meeting on Friday. All about herbs. I think you probably know more about herbs than I do, but I thought it would be fun to go along. You know – get out of the castle for a bit and get to know a few people. What do you think?'

Orla stared at him, unable to believe that he was even suggesting such a thing.

'Are you serious?'

He swallowed hard, but then nodded. 'I think it will do you good. They're wonderful people here in the village and they're bound to be friendly and welcoming. And you've only to walk a little distance. It's not really far at all.'

Orla didn't respond for a moment because she really didn't know what to say.

'It's just a little meeting of friends at Bill's,' Luke went on. 'You've already met Bill. He's a really decent bloke. His wife's lovely too. She makes these cookies – they're amazing. Chocolate chip. She'll probably make some more for the meeting.' Luke paused.

Again, Orla didn't respond.

'What do you think, Orla?' he asked.

At last, she found her voice. 'What do I *think*? God, Luke! I can't believe you thought I'd go with you!' she cried. 'What gave you the right to make that decision for me?'

'Orla – listen to me.'

'No, Luke! *You* listen to *me*! Ever since you got here, you've done nothing but pry and ask questions about my past and the way I live. *You're* the one who came here to tell me about *your* life, and I'm truly sorry for what's happened to you, and to Helen. It breaks my heart that it happened, but that doesn't automatically give you the right to expect me to open up to you! I like you – I really do – but I'm finding all this very stressful. And this – this *plan* of yours to get me out of my own home – well, it feels like a horrible betrayal,' she told him. 'Just when I was beginning to trust you too!'

'Orla!' Luke took a step forward, but Orla backed away. 'Please, Orla – I didn't mean to upset you, although I seem to be doing nothing but that.'

She looked at him, her eyes full of tears. 'Maybe it's time for you to go.'

Her words hung in the air for a moment.

'Can't we talk about this some more?' Luke asked, but Orla felt as if she had nothing more to say to him. 'Okay.' He nodded, and she watched as he backed out of the room.

Orla couldn't believe what Luke had suggested. She felt stunned. Stunned and betrayed. How dare he make assumptions about her willingness to attend social events. Didn't he realise how truly terrifying that was for her? It didn't matter if it was the home of her gardener or if the members of the club were all nice people. They were still strangers and strangers were always dangerous, weren't they?

Orla took a deep breath in order to try and calm herself down, knowing that her heart raced wildly when she felt threatened like this. It was a feeling that was hateful to her, but she couldn't control it. Anything outside her comfort zone made her feel threatened and Luke obviously didn't understand that, did he? She'd thought he had, but how could he? He could only imagine what it was like being her. He didn't really know. He'd probably thought he was trying to help her, only he was doing the very opposite of that, and she just couldn't handle that. Not yet and maybe not ever. So that meant only one thing – Luke had to leave, didn't he? As much as it pained her, and it really did, he had to go.

Luke made the slow, painful walk to his bedroom, silently cursing himself for having upset Orla yet again. He couldn't blame her for throwing him out. He'd brought nothing but bad news and trouble with his arrival and he'd caused her so much upset. It was a wonder she hadn't set One Ear on him, although he had a feeling that the dog was a gentle giant and didn't really have what it took to be a decent guard dog. Still, he wouldn't like to put him to the test and so he quickly packed his few belongings.

After stripping his bed, he took a moment to look out of the arched window of his bedroom, out towards the red rooftops of the village. He'd sincerely thought that his idea for Orla to attend a gathering in the village had been a good one and certainly something that Helen would have encouraged. He'd so wanted to help her build a metaphorical drawbridge from her castle out towards the community and he knew in his heart that that was what Helen had wanted for her friend too. He was so sure the villagers would be good for her and that she had so much to offer them. It bothered him that she was so closed off from the world and the lovely little community on her doorstep. But perhaps it had been naive of him to think he could charge in and change her habits overnight.

Leaving the bedroom, Luke walked through to the great chamber to collect all his work tools and fold away the dust sheets. He reached out to touch the cold stone wall he'd been repointing and looked down at the floorboards, regretting that he wouldn't have the chance to repair them now. He was going to miss this castle and his work here. He hadn't realised how much it meant to him until now, but he'd come to love the castle. He could see why Orla had bought it and how easy it would be to cocoon yourself away in such a place. It was a unique home and, alas, it was one he had to leave.

His van was parked in the driveway and it depressed him to think that he would be driving it home now. He didn't feel ready to face home. But maybe he didn't have to. Maybe he could stop off somewhere on the way – just find some random hotel and hide away for a few days. If he'd learned anything from his time at the castle, it was that the outside world was pretty easy to shut out if you were determined.

Reaching his van, he opened the back doors and placed his toolbox and bag in there before returning for the rest of his equipment. He'd probably never get to work on another castle again, that was for sure, but he was going to miss more than the castle. He was going to miss Orla. He sighed as he remonstrated with himself again for having made such a mess of things. He'd blundered into her life and tried to make changes to it that simply weren't welcome. Well, he'd learned his lesson. Some people couldn't be changed or, at least, didn't want to be.

It was as he was packing the last of his things that he heard her voice.

'Luke!'

He turned around and stared in surprise as he saw Orla running down the steps of the castle, followed by an excited One Ear. He'd never seen her in this part of the garden before – so near the front gates. Whenever he'd seen her leave to walk One Ear on the beach, she went through a gate in the back garden which took her down a secluded path. Here, she suddenly looked more exposed than he'd ever seen her and, as she stood there watching him, she too seemed to realise the fact.

'Can I talk to you? Inside?'

He closed the van door and followed her and One Ear back into the castle.

'If you're worrying about my bill, please don't,' he said. 'There's nothing to pay.'

'It's not about your bill.' She was looking down at the floor, but then turned her gaze towards him. 'I was a bit rash, telling you to go like that.'

'I understand. It isn't my place to tell you what to do.'

'No, it isn't.'

'But I hope we can part as friends?'

'Well, I have a problem with that,' she told him.

'Oh, I see,' he said. 'Well, listen – don't worry. I wish you well, Orla.' He turned to leave, hurt that she didn't want to keep in touch, but understanding her decision nevertheless.

'No, Luke – you don't understand. I want us to be friends. The thing I don't want is the parting bit.'

Luke was confused now. 'I don't understand.'

'I don't want you to go.'

'But I – you – I . . .'

'I know I did. But I've changed my mind. Please stay.'

Luke stared at her, shocked into silence by her for the second time that day. 'You want me to stay?'

'Yes. I think I overreacted and I'm sorry. I really don't want you to go, especially not like this. I . . .' she stopped, seemingly struggling for words. 'I haven't had much company in the last few years. I've forgotten how to be around people, and you've been nothing but kind and thoughtful.'

Luke shook his head. 'I've been a blundering idiot.'

'No – you haven't. It's just that we're both coming from different experiences and – well – you don't know what's happened to me and, without knowing, you can't possibly understand why I am the way I am. I know what you must think – that I'm odd and eccentric – the village must too, and that's okay.'

Luke swallowed hard, seeing that it clearly wasn't okay with Orla, who was horribly pale and on the verge of tears again.

'Orla – I'm sorry. I do nothing but put my foot in it and upset you. I promise I won't do that again. I mean, *really* promise this time! I thought I was doing the right thing. Helen – it's going to sound odd – but I thought I heard Helen's voice. She wants to help you. She even wrote about it.'

'She wrote about me?' Orla said, her gaze softening.

'She kept a journal, and I'm ashamed to say I read it. I couldn't help it.' Luke gave a hopeless shrug. 'I needed to hear her voice, even if it was just through her writing. But she was worried about you. Being alone. She wanted to help.'

'She wanted to help me?'

'Yes. Very much. And I do too.'

There was a weighty silence between them and Luke couldn't tell which way things were going to go.

'Orla? Are we good?' he asked at length.

She looked up at him and gave the tiniest of smiles. 'Yes! We're good.'

'I can come back in?'

She nodded.

Luke sighed, feeling both relieved that he wasn't going to have to face home just yet and also nervous at starting again with Orla. There was no blueprint for this, was there? They were two lost souls who had somehow managed to find one another and who were still navigating their way around each other. It would take time, care and patience, Luke understood that now.

'Luke?' Orla called as he started to head back out to the van.

'Yes?'

'I think it's probably time.'

'Time?'

'Time that I told you about what happened to me.'

Chapter 10

When Luke turned up at Oyster Cottage without Orla, he couldn't help feeling like a failure. Bill greeted him at the front door and placed a consolatory hand on his shoulder.

'I can't say I'm surprised, lad.'

'I tried.'

'You did. Don't take it personally,' Bill told him. 'She's only just beginning to get used to *you*, by the sound of things. You can't expect her to want to mingle with the whole village.'

'She threw me out when I told her about the meeting.'

'She did?'

'I packed all my stuff and was about to leave when she changed her mind.'

'Well, I'm glad to hear that at least.'

'And she's going to tell me what happened to her.'

Bill looked as stunned as Luke must have when Orla told him, but they didn't have time to talk any more because the rest of the horticultural club were arriving and Bill and Margy were kept busy ushering everyone into their living room.

It would have been a fun meeting under normal circumstances and Luke genuinely would have enjoyed himself. The talk about herbs was interesting, with Bill leading the discussion, but everyone chipping in with their own experiences. It was a lovely, friendly group – just as Luke had imagined – with a good mix of ages. Yes, most of the group were retirement age, but there was a couple in their early thirties and a man in his mid-forties.

But, however interesting the talk and however good the company, Luke was finding it hard to concentrate because he was thinking about Orla. Since asking him to stay again and telling him that she'd reveal what had happened to her, Luke had been on tenterhooks. He'd brought his things back in from the van, set his toolbox up in the great chamber, remade his bed and then gone in search of Orla. He'd found her in the china room, dusting and primping. She'd turned round to face him and smiled briefly before turning back to her task. He'd left her to it. When she'd said she'd tell him about what had happened to her, maybe she hadn't meant at that precise moment.

When evening came, they'd shared a meal at the kitchen table and then took cups of tea into the great hall. He'd wondered then if she'd say something, but she hadn't and he hadn't felt it was his place to bring it up – having overstepped the mark so many times with her already.

Then, as he'd got ready to leave for the horticultural club meeting the next day, she'd walked with him to the door.

'After you come back, we can talk then,' she'd said, her face pale and anxious.

'Okay,' he'd told her.

He'd left for the meeting feeling utterly frustrated. How was he meant to concentrate on herbs with Orla's promised revelation hanging over him?

Now, as Bill talked about the medicinal and culinary uses of herbs, Luke's gaze drifted over the assembly. These, he thought, were Orla's neighbours. Good, kind people whom she didn't know at all. He smiled as he glanced around Bill and Margy's living room. It was a cosy space with two small sofas and a couple of armchairs.

Their Jack Russell was asleep on Bill's knee as he talked and Margy's knitting needles hadn't stopped since the meeting had begun, but Luke hadn't taken very much in at all. At the end, everyone started rummaging in bags and pockets and Luke wondered if a collection was being taken, but he soon discovered that it was a seed swap. And then it was time to go. Luke was glad but didn't want to seem in a rush to leave and so hung back.

'So, what did you think?' Bill asked once the last guest had left.

'Good! I never knew there was so much to learn about herbs.'

Bill chuckled. 'Tempted to grow some yourself?'

'Well, I'll do my best to recognise the few we've got in our garden at home,' Luke said, and then flinched. *Our garden*. Only it wasn't any more, was it? It was *his* garden. How suddenly such moments ambushed you. He wasn't sure if Bill had caught the fleeting moment, but he laid his hand on Luke's shoulder.

'I'm glad you came. And I hope it goes well with Miss Kendrick.'

'Thanks. Me too.'

They shook hands before Luke left Oyster Cottage for the short walk back through Lorford to the castle. The sky was an inky indigo now, studded with stars, and the uninterrupted view of it above the castle's turrets was mesmeric. Luke took a moment to drink it all in and then he climbed the steps and rang the bell.

Orla had watched as Luke left the castle without her, a part of her crying out to go with him – that tiny part she'd tucked so deeply away from everybody because she was afraid, if she showed it, she would be hurt again. But it was there all the same; she'd just been so afraid to acknowledge it.

She felt terrible about having thrown him out and hoped she'd gone some way to regaining his trust. Then again, there was a part of her that was still upset at him having betrayed *her* trust. He'd been her guest for such a short space of time and was trying to implement major changes in her life. That, she believed, wasn't fair. She'd let him into her home, but he had no right forcing such massive life changes upon her. He had no idea how she felt about being around people – *any* kind of people – let alone strangers. Well, perhaps he'd have a better understanding when she told him about what had happened to her.

But, as the clock slowly ticked around, Orla began to feel her courage slipping away from her. Was she really ready for this? She wasn't at all sure. She'd never spoken about it to anyone other than her mother. Her friends and colleagues had only ever been informed; they'd never been contacted by Orla directly. She hadn't been able to do it. She'd quietly withdrawn from her life, slipping deeper and deeper into herself.

Looking out of the window as the summer sky deepened from a pale turquoise to a deep indigo, she found her way towards a dark oak cabinet in the great hall, her hand hovering over the little latch that kept it closed. It had been closed for months now, but she needed to open it tonight. Taking a deep breath, she lifted the latch, opened the door and reached inside, her hand settling on the cool neck of a bottle of wine.

Just one glass, she promised herself. One glass to help ease her into things, to gently smooth the passage to her recent past. That would be all she'd need.

By the time she heard the bell ring at the front door, Orla was feeling softer, gentler. Luke seemed to notice straight away and watched her as they walked into the great hall together, One Ear between them.

'Orla, have you been drinking?'

'Just a couple of glasses of wine,' she told him. At least, she thought it was two. But maybe it was three. Or four.

She noticed him clocking the wine bottle on the coffee table. Yes, Orla thought, it looked as if more than a couple of glasses had been drunk.

'Can I get you a glass?'

'Please.' He watched as she poured him a glass and then she topped up her own. 'Are you okay?'

'Of course.' She didn't look up at him. She couldn't bear to see those curious eyes gazing at her.

'Because we don't have to do this, you know.'

'Yes, we do,' she told him. 'I feel I should. You've shared with me and now I should share with you, and . . . it's time. I feel it's time.'

She took a moment, aware that she was beginning to feel a little warm but, whether it was the wine or the knowledge of what she was about to reveal to Luke, she couldn't be sure.

'All right, then,' Luke said.

Orla nodded. It was the strangest conviction, but she did – at last – feel ready to be rid of the burden of carrying this great hurt around.

They sat on the sofa together with One Ear lying down by his mistress's feet as if in support of the decision she'd made, and they both sipped their wine. Orla had lit a small fire and the lamps she'd switched on did their best to banish the shadows and dark corners of the cavernous room. It was a cosy, intimate setting and it went a little way towards calming Orla as she began her story.

'I was a photographer in London,' she began quietly. 'For quite a few years. I loved my job. I worked in a studio for a while, mostly photographing families or being hired for corporate events or portrait photography – that kind of thing. No two days were ever the same and I liked that. But then I was sent to a fashion shoot and my life changed for ever.' Orla paused and Luke waited as she took another sip of her wine.

'I'd never done a fashion shoot before. My partner usually covered them. It's a different kind of atmosphere and it never really appealed to me, but my partner was ill so I stepped in. It was for some high-end magazine. Some of those silly clothes that nobody ever wears in real life. You know the sort – lots of net and trains and feathers and things.' Orla shook her head as she remembered. 'But I wasn't there to judge. Anyway, there was this model. She was beautiful – the loveliest hair and eyes I'd ever seen – but she was a real diva and she was fighting with the director all the time. They just weren't seeing eye to eye. I was doing my best to stay in the background and was counting down the minutes until I could leave. But I never got to leave, because the model did.'

'But how did you shoot without the model?'

Orla gave a wry smile as she replayed what had happened in her mind. 'Because I became the model.'

'What?'

'The director was frantic. He had to get the shoot finished and he was looking around the room for someone to step in and picked me. I really don't know why. I'd never modelled in my life but, before I knew it, I was having my hair and make-up done and I was on set, only, this time, I was in front of the camera.'

Orla remembered the chaos of the day once again and how every fibre of her being had screamed against it, knowing that the role of model simply wasn't her. But she hadn't protested loudly enough, had she? If she had, her whole life would have been different.

'But who took the photos?' Luke asked.

'The director did. He used to be a photographer and he knew how to handle a camera.' Orla took a deep breath. 'So, the photographs came out and the shoot was deemed a huge success by the magazine. I even got fan mail, can you believe it? The editor of the magazine was thrilled and asked for me again. Well, I said no, of course. I was a photographer, not a model. But they made me an offer. It was ridiculous really. More than I made in a year as a photographer. What could I say? I had bills to pay on an expensive London flat.'

'So you said yes?'

She nodded. 'Anyway, I got quite a bit of work after that and, one day, I found myself working with the model who I'd replaced that day. Her name was Kelli and she'd seen the photos and congratulated me, but I couldn't help worrying that she might be mad at me for having got her job and all the subsequent jobs that came my way. But she was always polite to me and I didn't worry about it because I had other things to worry about.'

She paused again, looking into the fire as she finished her wine and stood up to find another bottle and pour herself a glass. She motioned to Luke.

'No, I'm good,' he said. His glass was still half full. 'So what happened next?'

She sat back down next to him, took another sip of wine, wishing with all her heart that she could rewind time and make different choices.

'I started getting a lot more fan mail,' she went on. 'Bags of the stuff. Silly, really, because I certainly wasn't the youngest or prettiest model around. Some of it was lovely, but some of it was really disturbing. I had to stop reading it after a while. I couldn't cope. I had to hire somebody to deal with it all and they were the ones who spotted the letters from . . .' She paused.

'Who?' Luke asked gently.

'Brandon.'

Orla swallowed hard after saying the name aloud and she felt Luke watching her as she drank her wine.

'You okay?'

She nodded and wondered if she could go on. She didn't have to, she knew that. She didn't really owe Luke an explanation, yet she had promised him one and so she continued.

'He started with the odd letter via my agent. The odd *odd* letter. I'm told it's usual in the business to receive marriage proposals and personal questions from strangers, but it felt so weird. Just a few months before, I'd been an unknown photographer, hiding behind the camera, and now, all of a sudden, I seemed to belong to the public. I hated it. Then the letters became more frequent. My agent told me to stop reading them and started keeping a separate file of them. I told Kelli about them and she said she got letters like that all the time. Emails, too, and tweets. She told me to ignore them, and I did, but then he showed up.'

'Oh, my God! Where did he show up?'

'At one of my modelling assignments.'

'How did he know where you'd be?'

Orla shrugged, feeling again the cold terror she had felt at the time. 'How do these types of people find anyone? Because they want to! Anyway, he started showing up wherever I went, calling out to me. "Orla! Did you get my letters? Why haven't you written back to me?" I did my best to block him out, but it was pretty hard. He had a way of getting in my eyeline and I'd have to think of more and more elaborate ways of evading him, getting my taxi driver to go miles out of the way until we lost him. I was terrified of him following me home.'

'And did he?'

'He found out the block of flats I lived in, yes. I used to see him hanging around the corner of the street by a lamppost. But I don't think he knew the flat I was in and I was lucky to move shortly after that. I got a flat where there was a porter and a code for the lift. I felt safer there. But the letters via my agent continued.

Flowers too sometimes. And he always managed to find out where I was working and be there – hanging around studio car parks and shouting over at me. Kelli told me to report him to the police, and I managed to get a restraining order.'

Orla took another sip of her wine.

'I've often thought how scarily quickly a fan can turn. One minute, you're their favourite person on the planet and they're singing your praises and then, the next, they want to destroy you.'

Luke puffed out an anxious sigh. 'What happened?'

'I turned to Kelli. We'd been working on the same project together. It was funny but, since I got that job she'd walked out of, we'd become something of a pair in the industry. It felt good having an ally and I learned a lot from her, but she was becoming more reckless. I think she was drinking or doing some kind of drug. I'm not sure. Anyway, she didn't seem completely *there* most of the time. She had this sort of glazed look and her behaviour was erratic. I tried to reach out to her, but she kept pushing me away, denying that there was a problem, even though she was constantly late for assignments. It was so sad to see her going downhill so rapidly. She was a really beautiful woman. Far more beautiful than I ever was, but I ended up getting more jobs than her simply because she was getting a bad reputation in the industry and was either turning up late or not at all. Anyway, I shared my fears about Brandon with her.' Orla paused.

'And what did she say?'

'"Get used to it, honey. It could be a lot worse."'

'Ah, so not exactly helpful.'

'No.' Orla stopped again, her vision fixed on her now empty wine glass.

'And I'm guessing it got a lot worse?'

'Yes,' she said, her voice barely above a whisper now. 'I was walking home one day after a shoot. I usually got a taxi, but the weather was so glorious and I wanted to walk through the park. It was warm for March and I was wearing this big heavy coat because the week before had been so cold. I remember stopping to take the coat off, but my phone went and I was trying to get it out of my bag when I heard these footsteps running towards me. I thought it was a jogger and I went to scoot out of the way but, when I looked up . . .' Orla stopped, her eyes gazing straight ahead as if seeing into the past at that very moment. Her heart was hammering and her palms felt sticky with sweat.

'Orla? Are you all right?'

She nodded, but tears pricked her eyes.

'I haven't talked about any of this. Not since . . .'

'It's all right,' Luke told her. 'Just take your time.'

She was shaking now, and One Ear came forward, licking her hand and sticking his wet nose into her face and whining.

'When I looked up, I saw a man wearing a dark jacket. The hood was up and I didn't pay much attention, to be honest, because I was still trying to find my phone, so I looked down into my bag, and that's when it happened. He threw something at me. I thought it was water at first, but then it started to burn. Really burn.'

Luke cursed. 'It was acid, wasn't it?'

Orla nodded. 'If I hadn't turned slightly at the precise moment he threw it, the damage would have been a lot worse. The doctors say I would probably have lost my left eye completely. As it was, I just lost my vision for a few months. And my ear. Well, you can see I lost that. My hair, too, and half my face, the skin on my neck. If my phone hadn't gone and I'd taken my coat off, it would have been much worse. I was just wearing a cotton dress underneath. But the acid ate right through the coat. I managed to get it off in time and a passing jogger doused me with her water bottle before the ambulance came.'

'God, Orla!'

'I never knew a pain like that could exist. There was no getting away from it. It just seemed to go on and on for ever. And I couldn't stop screaming. I wondered what it was at first – this inhuman sound – and then I realised that it was me.' She closed her eyes for a moment. 'Have you ever smelled burning flesh?' she asked him. 'No, of course you haven't. I hope you never will because, once you do, you can never forget it. It never quite leaves you. It's like nothing else. I think it was the smell that scared me the most. I mean, the pain was bad. Indescribable. But the smell – that was truly terrifying. I couldn't get away from it.'

She got up and picked up the wine bottle, motioning to Luke, who shook his head.

'Please tell me they got him?'

'Oh, yes. CCTV caught him leaving the park and the idiot had managed to spill acid on himself so there was no question it was him.' She came back to the sofa, where she quickly drained her glass of wine. 'I don't feel so good.' She swayed forward and gasped. 'Oh, dear.'

One Ear, who'd returned to his basket at some point, was now back by Orla's side, and she gave a choky sort of laugh and stroked his head.

'He's my prince,' she said softly. 'My knight in furry armour.'

Luke smiled. 'Come on. Let's get you upstairs.'

As she had helped him into bed on that first meeting, so he helped guide her now. She didn't say anything else as he gently led her to the bedroom and went to get a glass of water for her, placing it on her bedside table.

'Is One Ear here?' Orla asked.

'He's right behind me.'

Orla put her hand out and One Ear came forward to give it a soft nudge before making himself at home on the floor by the bed, as if knowing his mistress needed him tonight.

'Leave the hall light on, won't you?' she said, aware of how like a child she must sound to him.

'If you want me to,' he said. 'Let me know if you need anything,' he told her. 'You know where I am.'

She nodded, her dark hair hiding her face as she sat on the edge of the bed.

He paused before speaking again. 'And I'm so sorry. What Brandon did to you was unforgivable.'

Luke turned to leave the room.

'No,' she said, her voice thick with sleep now. 'You don't understand.'

Luke frowned. 'What don't I understand?'

Orla took a deep breath before she answered. 'It wasn't him. It wasn't Brandon.'

Chapter 11

As Luke stared up into the darkness of his bedroom, he couldn't begin to imagine what Orla must have gone through. How did you get over something like that? Well, he saw how – you hid yourself away in a medieval castle – and he couldn't blame her. There was nothing to adequately describe the fear and the pain she must have endured and he'd never forget her distress when telling him her story.

Although Luke wasn't a great one for keeping up to date with the news – and he'd certainly never heard about Orla's attack at the time it had happened, even though it must have been a big story – he knew enough about acid attacks to know that it was a crime which was on the rise. A disturbing fact. How could anyone do something so destructive and inflict so much physical and emotional pain on somebody? Luke just couldn't imagine how anyone could arrive at such a decision, and he hoped – whoever it was – they were locked away for a very long time.

But, if it hadn't been Brandon who'd attacked her, then who could it have been? She'd said it was a man wearing a hood. Was it just some random mad person? Had Orla been mistaken for somebody else? Or had she had another mad stalker fan who had managed to hide in the shadows behind the massive presence of Brandon? It had crossed Luke's mind that he could do an internet search to find out more – if she'd been well known as a model, there was sure to be press coverage about the case. But it would feel like a kind of betrayal if he did, so he didn't. Perhaps she would continue her story in the morning. One thing was for sure, Luke didn't think he was going to be able to sleep tonight – not after what Orla had told him. He kept playing it over and over in his mind. The beautiful young woman who'd been enticed to follow a career which so obviously wasn't a good fit for her. Now he understood why she hid behind a camera these days and how she regretted the day she'd stepped out from behind its protective shield.

As predicted, Luke slept pretty badly, but at least he got a couple of hours at one point. Somewhere between three and four, he thought he heard crying and got up to check on Orla. The landing light was still on and he walked towards her bedroom, gently knocking on the door so as not to disturb her if she was asleep, which he saw she was when he quietly entered. Perhaps she'd been crying in her sleep, he thought, giving One Ear a nod as he backed out of the room.

He'd slept on and off after that, waking at first light before drifting off an hour later. By the time he got up and went downstairs neither Orla nor One Ear were about so he went into the garden in search of them and, when it was obvious they weren't there, decided that they must be at the beach.

It was a perfect morning to be by the sea. There was a freshness to the air which made his bare arms tingle, and the sky was a bright aquamarine dotted with friendly white clouds. There was a young mother with a couple of toddlers in bright yellow wellies paddling in the sea and, in one of those flashes of the imagination, Luke saw a future that he and Helen wouldn't ever share. He closed his eyes for a moment, grief and anger surging through him at the thought of their future having been stolen from them. So many things, so many moments, had been cruelly snatched away when those two trains had collided, and Luke realised he was only just beginning to process it all. It would take months, years, to truly understand what had happened that night.

He opened his eyes and soon spotted Orla. She was a dot in the distance on the beach and it took a while to catch up with her.

One Ear saw him first and started barking and leaping across the sand towards him.

'Hey, boy!'

Orla turned around and Luke waved to her and she stopped, waiting for him.

'How's your head?' he asked her, noticing her larger than normal sunglasses and wide-brimmed hat.

'Sore!'

'Oh, dear. Did you sleep okay?'

'No, not really. You?'

'No, not really.'

'Sorry. I mean – if that was my fault.'

'Don't worry. Me and sleep haven't been on the best of terms recently.'

She stopped walking and turned to look at him, slowly removing her sunglasses.

'You should really think about taking something to help you sleep,' she suggested.

'Nah! I don't want to get into all that. It might prove addictive.'

'Just for a little while. It might help.'

'It's not for me.'

They continued walking, the sound of gulls screeching high above them as One Ear galloped ahead.

'Orla?'

'Yes?'

'Can I ask you something? Last night – you said it wasn't Brandon who attacked you. Then who was it?'

Orla stopped walking and then she did something unexpected. She sat down, right there on the sand in the middle of the beach. Luke joined her and they both stared out at the blue-green waves.

'It was Kelli,' she said at last.

'The model?'

'Yes.'

'But I thought you said it was a man.'

'Yes. It was a man. But it was Kelli who paid him to do it.'

'You're joking! I thought she was your *friend.*'

'I thought so too. Turned out I was wrong. Horribly wrong.'

'But why would she do something like that?'

Orla sighed. 'Kelli blamed me for taking what she saw as her career.'

'But that's crazy! You said she was out of control and couldn't work.'

'And that's true, but she obviously didn't see things that way. She saw me as a threat, some interloper who shouldn't even be in the business, and she was right because that's exactly what I was. I should never have been in that line of work. In fact, I've come to believe that the acid attack was a kind of punishment.'

Luke's mouth dropped open. 'What do you mean?'

'For my vanity.'

'No, Orla! You *can't* mean that!'

'I do. I really do. I should never have taken that first job or been tempted by the offers that came in after that. I let my colleague down at the photography studio, I walked out on a job that meant something to me, and all for money.'

'But that's only natural. We all have to do things to make money. That's life! There's no getting away from it.'

'But I was so unhappy in that job. I went on taking all those assignments, even though I knew it was all wrong for me.'

'Not as wrong as someone attacking you and leaving you scarred for life. God! I can't imagine what you went through. How do you begin to recover?'

'Slowly!' She took a deep breath and stared out into the waves. Her glasses were still in her hands and Luke could see the terrible scars left by the acid attack as her dark hair blew back from her face. 'It took months of hospitalisation,' she told him. 'There was so much damage. Half of my face and my neck had melted away, and part of my arm, where the acid had dripped down my hair and burned into the skin there. I lost my ear and – well – you've seen my eye, haven't you? I'm lucky that it functions at all. My own reflection horrified me. I made the mistake of looking shortly after the attack. I really shouldn't have done that. And I don't any more. You must have noticed that there are no mirrors in the castle. I can't even bear the windows sometimes if they dare to throw my reflection back at me.'

Luke shook his head. He was truly appalled at what had happened to her, but he was equally frustrated at the effect it still had on Orla even years later. She had no idea how beautiful she was. The scars were just superficial and her damaged eye did nothing to detract from her inner beauty. Did she not know that?

'Do you know how terrifying it is to look in a mirror and not recognise yourself? I saw this strange, red monster of blood and bone staring out at me.' She closed her eyes and Luke rested a hand on her shoulder. 'They made me wear this mask for twelve hours a day so that my scars didn't heal bumpy. It should have been a breeze after what I went through, but it made me feel so claustrophobic – like I was being held in a vice. I lost count of the number of operations I had to have. It was in the high forties, I think, and they advised more, but I couldn't bear it. They told me about a special clinic I could go to, but the whole hospital thing left me traumatised. I just wanted to be left alone and I needed to get out of London. I couldn't bear being there any longer. I had to get away.'

'And that's when you came here?'

'It seemed perfect. I'd never been to Suffolk before. I was just vaguely aware of it from my school days and all the fuss about some Anglo-Saxon treasure.'

Luke smiled. 'I remember that too. Maybe we should go and see the place. I don't think it's that far from here. Sutton Hoo, right?'

'I'm not sure.'

'You've not been, then?' Luke asked before he could check himself. Of course she hadn't been. She hadn't been anywhere that was further away than this beach. She hadn't even seen the other end of the village. 'Orla – I know we've had a disagreement about this already, but I do think you're missing out on so much here. It seems such a shame to be in this beautiful place and not see any of it.'

'But I do!' she said, motioning to the sea and the beach all around them.

'Yes, I know you come here.'

'And you can see for miles from the castle rooftop. You saw when you went up.'

'Yes, it was amazing, but it isn't the same as going out and seeing new places and meeting new people.'

'Luke – I've told you—'

'I know you have and, at the risk of you throwing me out again, I want to bring it up once more – not because I want to upset you, but because I really believe that it would do you good to get out. It would build your confidence too.'

'I don't need to build my confidence. I'm happy as I am. Besides, you must understand now how I feel about going out.'

Luke suddenly realised how insensitive he was being in trying to encourage her to venture outside.

'Yes, of course,' he said. 'I'm sorry, Orla. I didn't mean to upset you.'

She gave him a tight smile. 'Besides, it's not good for me to go outside. My mother told me that.'

Luke frowned, shocked by her words. 'She said that?'

'It's not good for me to be out in public. She said that, even if people aren't dangerous, they'll always be staring at me and that isn't good for me. She said . . .'

'What did she say?' Luke encouraged after Orla had stopped.

'She said that I would be putting myself at risk every time I left my home.'

Luke swore under his breath. 'She really told you that?'

'Yes. And she was right too. She knows me better than anyone and she was there with me every day in the hospital, and she knew that I'd be happier on my own.'

Luke shook his head. 'Well, I don't believe that.'

Orla glared at him. 'Why not? *Why* do you find it so hard to believe that I'm happy?'

'Because people need people. We're not made to isolate ourselves. Even after what happened to you. Think about it – think of your presence on Galleria and how much you enjoy that connection with other people.'

'I enjoy that because it's on my terms. It's safe.'

'I don't know about that,' Luke said. 'A lot of crazy things go on online.'

'I know and, if they do, I simply delete it or block the crazy people.'

'But don't you think it's time to venture out again? I mean, how long have you locked yourself away like this for, Orla? It's been a couple of years, hasn't it? And don't forget that Helen didn't want you to isolate yourself like this either.'

Orla shifted her feet in the sand. 'Luke—'

'I know – I shouldn't interfere.'

'No,' she said, her tone managing to be both calm and frustrated all at once, 'you really shouldn't.'

She whistled for One Ear and he trotted over to her, his big paws foamy with the surf he'd been paddling in.

'He's a great dog,' Luke said, thinking it best to change the subject before she decided it might be better to throw him out again.

'He's the dog version of me, isn't he, with just the one ear?'

Luke gave a nervous sort of laugh at Orla's humour.

'We had that connection, you see. We're the perfect pair – quite literally – him with no right ear and me with no left. We balance one another out.' She stood up, brushing the sand from her legs. 'He's all I need.' She gave Luke a resolute look before replacing her sunglasses and he read her message loud and clear.

Later that evening, as the blue summer sky was slowly fading into a soft pink, Orla ventured out into the garden. She liked this quiet time at dusk, as the birds found their way to bed and the first stars of the night made their presence known in the endless sky above the castle.

As One Ear poked around the flower beds, Orla walked around the garden. She hadn't seen Luke since their meeting on the beach that morning. She thought he was probably keeping a diplomatic distance between them. She'd heard the occasional bang of his workman's tools and had given him some privacy at lunchtime, grabbing a quick sandwich for herself and moving through to the china room. He hadn't tried to find her and she was glad of that because she'd needed some space and time to think about what he'd said. What he *kept* saying to her.

Sitting down on a wooden bench, she looked up at the great stone walls of the castle. They were fading into shadow now, having been lit up in the most glorious pink light a few minutes before. Wasn't it every little girl's dream to live in a castle? And a pink castle at that! Orla smiled at the thought, and then she remembered Luke's words to her: *'People need people. We're not made to isolate ourselves.'* Orla knew that, and she knew that Helen had also wanted to reach out and help her, but she still thought it very unfair of Luke to keep bringing it up after what had happened to her. It wasn't as if she'd always been this way. In London, she'd had lots of friends and she'd gone out to dinners, to the theatre and to parties. She'd loved her life, but everything had changed with the attack. Not only had it taken away the face she'd known, but it had taken away her inner peace – that sense of self – and she'd felt herself withdrawing from the world, shutting out her friends and removing herself from her old routine.

Orla had done her best not to think about the life she'd lost. Instead, she'd focused on the new life she'd created for herself within the safe walls of the castle – a simple life of collecting beautiful broken things and photographing them. It might sound odd to some people, but it had given her a focus. A *safe* focus. And it made her happy, it really did. It might not seem fulfilling, but it was to Orla, so why should Luke think that it wasn't enough? Why was it so important to him that she leave the castle? It was as if he'd become obsessed with the idea, and a part of her couldn't help thinking that he was burying his own grief for Helen by focusing so fully on her.

She whistled for One Ear and he came trotting towards her.

'What do you think I should do? Throw him out again?' One Ear whined as if in understanding. 'No, I won't do that. You like him, don't you? I like him too. So, what *should* I do? Listen to him? Is that what you think I should do?'

Orla rested her head on top of One Ear's and let him lick her hand as her mind spun. Something in her was changing. Perhaps it was having Luke staying in the castle. He was the only guest, other than her mother, who'd ever stayed there, and it had taught her that she genuinely missed conversation – exchanging everyday pleasantries and thoughts and ideas. Luke was a link to the outside world. He'd come into her life because of something so sad and awful, but he'd brought such joy and positivity and Orla found herself drawn to that, even if it went against everything she'd been building for the last few years. But to leave the castle – to venture into the outside world, even if that was just her own village – seemed truly terrifying. She couldn't do it, could she?

One thing was for sure, if she didn't do it now, with Luke's help and encouragement, she knew she never would.

Luke had been working on a large section of wall in the great chamber. He'd taken out the old lime mortar and had applied a scratch coat. It was satisfying work, but he would now have to leave it for up to ten days before applying a second coat. That gave him time to start another job and, although he had an idea of what he'd like to tackle next, he found himself drifting around the castle. There was so much he could do with the place, but he quickly reminded himself that Orla had set a tight budget and that his time with her wasn't unlimited either. He couldn't stay for ever. Indeed, he'd been wondering just how long her hospitality would hold out for. Probably not long if he kept badgering her about leaving the castle. He'd noticed that she'd kept her distance from him since the morning and he couldn't blame her for that, but her response had been a little less explosive than the last time he'd dared to broach the subject and there was a part of him that believed he just needed to chip away at the tough wall she'd built around herself a little bit more and she would relent. Yes, indeed – he believed that the wall Orla had built around her heart was as deep and strong as those of the castle she'd chosen to live in.

Luke sighed, acknowledging the fact that, perhaps, he was using the castle in exactly the same way – as a wall around his own grief. What would Helen make of him staying here, he wondered? It was one thing to deliver Helen's gift to Orla, but quite another to live under her roof. Would she understand that he'd needed to get away from home for a while? To escape the onslaught of phone calls and sympathy cards and to find a little space of his own? He hoped she would.

Luke made his way down the spiral staircase, marvelling at the stone construction as he reached the upper first floor and saw the room that would have once been a highly decorated chapel. Orla hadn't done much in this part of the castle yet. Her living quarters were centred on the second and upper second floors. Now, Luke continued his journey down, venturing into the lower hall and, from there, towards the basement. It was certainly a lot colder in this part of the castle. It seemed to Luke as if the temperature dropped a degree with each step down he took and that the decades and centuries melted away to reveal the bare bones of the past. Well, not literally. At least, he hoped not. But what a privilege it was to see the little alcoves, the arrow-slit windows and ancient graffiti carved deep into the stone walls, although his eye caught plenty of things that weren't so wonderful, like the great ugly blobs of cement that had been splattered onto the walls and would do more harm than good. Yes, there was certainly a lifetime's work here for any builder who wanted to take the task on.

Luke descended further, passing the lower hall and reaching the very bowels of the castle: the basement. He'd only been down to this part of the castle once before and he hadn't really taken it all in. It had reputedly been the dungeon. He grinned at the thought. Imagine living in a place with its own dungeon. Its own well, too. Luke got his pocket torch out and shone it through the scratched Perspex cover over the well's opening, marvelling at its depth. He was glad to see that an iron grid had been placed over it to prevent accidents.

Swinging his torch, he looked around the rest of the basement. There was a section of wall down here that was boarded up and he approached it now. It was modern plasterboard that had definitely seen better days and was probably masking a ton of trouble. It would have to be removed, he decided. No doubt it was harbouring damp; the wall needed to be allowed to breathe. He gave it an experimental tap, wondering what was behind it, and shone his torch at the place where it joined the wall, but couldn't make anything out.

'Luke?' Orla's voice broke into his thoughts, echoing down the spiral staircase. 'Where are you?'

'I'm in the dungeon!' he yelled back, and he heard her footsteps hastening towards him.

'What are you doing down here?' she asked a moment later, looking around as if he might have been up to something without her permission.

'Just scouting for jobs to do while I'm waiting for some plaster to dry in the great chamber, and I came across this. Did you put this up?'

'No, it was here when I bought the castle.'

'I thought it might have been. Do you know what's behind it?'

'No. Is it something I should be anxious about?'

Luke rubbed his chin. 'No, not anxious. But curious maybe. I can't see any reason why this section of wall would be boarded like this. This column too,' he said, noticing that one of the stone columns supporting a window arch was concealed. 'It's Caen stone, isn't it? I was reading about it. It's a hard limestone from Normandy. Beautiful for carving.'

Orla didn't seem to be interested.

'Everything okay?' Luke asked her.

'Yes,' she told him. 'No.'

'Can you narrow that down a bit?'

'I don't know.'

'Anything I can help with?'

Orla chewed her lip, looking anxious. 'I've been thinking about what you've been saying. I mean, thinking *a lot*.'

'Okay,' Luke said, wondering exactly what it was she was referring to.

'And I think it might not be a bad idea. To go out, I mean.'

'You want to go out?'

'Yes!' she said with a nod. 'No!' She shook her head. 'I don't know.'

Luke smiled, thrilled by her declaration. 'So, where do you want to go?'

'Somewhere not too far away. Somewhere there isn't going to be people.'

'Okay.'

'In your van. I'm not walking anywhere.'

'Right. No problem.'

'And I don't want you putting any more pressure on me. If I don't want to get out of the van, I won't, okay?'

'All right.'

'I don't want you saying that I should or that it'll do me good.'

'Orla – this can be whatever you want it to be. I'm just happy that you're even thinking about it.'

'One Ear comes with us,' she stipulated.

'Of course.'

'Okay, then.'

'Okay.'

She gave a little nod. 'I'll leave you to . . . whatever you were doing.'

Luke watched as she disappeared up the spiral staircase, listening to her footsteps on the cold stone, and a huge warm smile spread across his face.

Chapter 12

Orla looked around her bedroom in desperation. What did she need to take with her? She hadn't been anywhere but the beach for the last two years and felt a little lost at the prospect of driving beyond the castle gates and actually leaving the village. What did women take when they went out? Orla tried to think back to her days as a normal woman. What had she had in her handbag? She'd emptied it out long ago and tucked it in the back of her wardrobe but now she brought it out and looked into its cavernous depths with a feeling of approaching doom. She remembered she used to always carry a couple of lipsticks, but she'd dispensed with such things since the attack. What was the point in trying to look pretty? There really wasn't any, so Orla simply used a clear lip balm for moisture.

There would have been a hairbrush and a compact with a mirror, but that had been thrown away long ago. The only mirror Orla had in the castle was a tiny one which she kept wrapped in a scarf. It was for fly-in-the-eye-type emergencies only. It wasn't as if Orla didn't care about her appearance any more – she kept her long hair tangle-free and washed and moisturised her face – but she refused to venture back to that place where physical beauty dominated. She'd lived in that world mercifully briefly during her time as a model, and it had brought her nothing but pain.

She popped a lip balm into the bag, and a paperback from her bedside table because you never knew when you might be in need of something to read.

'Purse!' she cried. She'd almost forgotten the need to carry money with her, seeing as all her transactions were done online these days, including paying Bill, the gardener. Orla had no need for cash and she probably wouldn't on this particular outing. Not that she was planning to go shopping or anything that adventurous, but it was always wise to be prepared.

Moving through to the great hall, she caught sight of One Ear and added a handful of dog biscuits to her bag. Her coat pockets were usually full of them, but a few more wouldn't go amiss. She also added a bottle of water for her and One Ear to share. She always took one with her when walking along the beach and would pour a fountain for her boy after he'd had a good run.

'Keys!'

Again, Orla tended to keep the keys to her home in her pockets, and it would feel funny putting them into a bag. She then grabbed a couple of tissues and her favourite hand cream.

Just when she thought she was all set to go, her mobile rang from the table and she realised that she'd nearly left the castle without it. She picked it up, seeing her mother's name on the screen.

'Darling?'

'Mum! How are you?'

'I was going to ask you the same thing. I haven't heard from you *all* week.'

'I'm sorry. I've been busy.'

'Busy?' Her mother sounded incredulous. 'Doing what?'

Orla bit her lip, knowing that she couldn't divulge the fact that she had a man staying with her. Her mother would worry herself silly over that.

'Work. My work,' she said instead.

'I wasn't aware you were working.'

'My photography.'

'That's work now, is it? It's paying the bills?'

'Not exactly.'

'You can't not work, you know, darling. That cumbersome castle of yours won't pay for itself.'

'I know. I've still got some money left over from the modelling.'

'Yes, well, that won't last for ever. Not with that big place of yours to restore and run.'

'I know. I will find work at some point.'

'I really don't know *why* you lumbered yourself with that old pile.'

'Don't let's go through all that again, Mum.'

'But really – it's such an extravagance! Why couldn't you just buy a nice little penthouse near me?'

'You know I couldn't stay in London.'

She heard her mother sighing. 'Yes. I know, darling. But it is a pain for me having to hike all the way out to Suffolk to see my daughter.'

'You really don't need to any more.'

'What do you mean?'

'I mean, you've got to let me try and take care of myself, Mum. I'm making progress, I really am. This place has been good for me.'

'Well, that's wonderful to hear, of course, but I think I should see the evidence for myself. You were . . .'

'What?'

'Very fragile when I visited last time.'

Orla closed her eyes and sighed inwardly. Her mother probably didn't realise it, but Orla couldn't help feeling more fragile when her mother was around than when she wasn't. Bernadette could be a formidable presence and Orla always felt herself slinking away inside herself, becoming the dependent daughter instead of the strong, independent woman she longed to be.

'I'm feeling fine.'

'Are you sure? You don't sound fine.'

'I'm sure. You don't need to keep worrying.'

'Well, that's easier said than done, isn't it?' her mother snapped.

Orla glanced around the room, looking desperately for an excuse to end the call.

'I've got to go,' she said. Again, she wasn't able to say she was going out because that would raise too many questions and would probably have Bernadette on the first train out of London. 'I'll call you later.'

'Make sure you do!'

Orla quickly switched her phone off in case her mother tried to ring back and breathed a sigh of relief at the silence which greeted her. Bernadette Kendrick meant well, Orla was quite sure of it, but her intentions and the actual effect they had on Orla were two very different things indeed.

'Orla?' Luke called, entering the great hall a moment later. 'You ready?'

Orla nodded, glad of the distraction from her mother's call, although she had huge misgivings about the whole idea of going out. Why had she let herself be persuaded to do this? She took a deep breath. Maybe she was ready. Maybe the time had come at last to put her fears and doubts behind her and step into the wider world, and Luke was the catalyst to help her do that.

She opened the front door and walked outside. No, she thought, she definitely wasn't ready.

'It's okay, Orla,' he told her, obviously sensing her fear. 'I'm right here with you. One Ear too.'

She swallowed hard, closing her front door and locking it and then placing a tentative foot on the first step down to ground level. One step at a time. She could do this, she told herself.

'You're doing great!' Luke said in encouragement.

She glanced at him. He looked so calm and happy to be venturing out. Was that what normal looked like, she wondered? She'd forgotten. She'd closed normal out of her life that day in the park when she'd sunk deep inside herself, trying to find a space where nobody and nothing – not even acid – could touch her.

With shaky legs, Orla descended the steps from her front door. Normally, she left the castle by the back door, sneaking out into the garden and along the secluded footpath which led to the beach. She rarely, if ever, saw anyone by that route. Now, leaving the castle by the front entrance, she felt horribly exposed. It wasn't just the village of Lorford that lay beyond the gates, but the whole world – the world that had wounded her so deeply that she hadn't wanted to have anything more to do with it.

Suddenly, Orla felt her vision blurring and an icy coldness washed over her skin.

'No!'

Luke turned around at her cry.

'I can't.' Orla was frozen in panic and she felt as if she was going to hyperventilate as her breath became fast and furious.

Luke was by her side in an instant. 'It's all right.'

'I'm sorry. I'm sorry.'

'Don't apologise.'

One Ear, who'd run up to the van in happy anticipation, was now by his mistress's side, and the three of them returned to the castle. Orla's hands were shaking too much to be able to use the key so Luke gently took it from her and let them in.

'Lock the door!'

'Of course,' he said, locking them inside once more as Orla retreated to her bedroom. Once the door was closed, she leaned her head against it, the dizzying sensation she'd felt outside slowly lifting now she was safely back inside. What must Luke think of her, she wondered? Turning around, she walked across the room to her bed as hot tears slid down her cheeks. She'd tried, she told herself. She'd dredged up every bit of courage she had and she'd walked out of her front door with the intention of going out into the world. It hadn't worked, but she had at least tried.

Luke had done his best not to show his disappointment as they returned to the castle. Getting Orla to even agree to *leave* the castle was progress so they were definitely moving in the right direction.

He gave Orla all the time and space she needed and, as he expected, she hid herself away in the china room for the most part, photographing cups and bowls for Galleria. He understood why; he too found solace in his work and he had felt a kind of peace settling upon him recently.

For a moment, he thought back to the Luke he had been at home – the one who had counted down the hours of each day until he'd felt it was a reasonable hour to pour himself a drink. He had only had one single glass of wine since he'd been at the castle and that had been on the night Orla had told him about her attack. She'd been drinking too, and he was glad that he hadn't seen her drinking since. That, he knew, wasn't the answer to anything.

He was hoping that he and Orla being under the same roof was of some benefit to both of them. He certainly felt calmer living at the castle, and being able to help Orla by listening to her and encouraging her was, in some small way, helping him with his own pain, and that could only be a good thing, couldn't it? Helen would approve of that, wouldn't she?

He'd been thinking about how Helen would have reacted to Orla's story. Helen had known that Orla had been hiding away from the world and had wanted to reach out to her, but could she ever have guessed what had happened to her? There was a huge part of Luke that felt that he was very much carrying the spirit of Helen with him in helping Orla, and that made him feel good.

Luke continued with his work. He was just about to return to the basement to inspect the boarded-up section of wall when he noticed that a window frame in one of the passages was in imminent danger of disintegrating if not attended to, so he began making arrangements to repair that first.

The next day, Orla surprised Luke by saying that she'd try again. Like before, she made it down the steps of the castle and began walking across the driveway to Luke's van. This time, however, she managed to get inside. Luke had made room in the back for One Ear, who hopped in without any great concern, instantly at home.

'Right – ready?' he asked Orla. 'Belt on?'

Orla nodded. She'd lost the power of speech, it seemed.

Luke had already opened the gates and he slowly put the van into gear and drove through them. But, before he'd managed to turn onto the road into the village, Orla screamed.

'Stop!'

'You don't want to go?'

She shook her head.

'Okay, no problem.'

'I'm sorry. I'm sorry!' The tears were coming thick and fast now.

'It's all right, Orla. Don't get upset about it. It's okay.'

As soon as the van was parked, Orla stumbled out, almost falling up the steps to the front door. As before, her shaking hands wouldn't allow her to use the key so Luke unlocked the door and, like before, gave her plenty of space to recover.

It was two days later before Orla approached Luke again with the idea of going out. By the look on his face, he was surprised that she'd suggested it, but he quickly cleared away his materials and they were, once again, leaving the castle.

'How are you feeling?' he asked as the three of them walked down the steps for the third time.

'Determined,' she said.

'Good.'

Orla watched as One Ear jumped into the back of the van, as calm as he was the first time. If only she could feel as relaxed as he did, she thought as she climbed up into the passenger seat.

Having opened the gates, Luke started the engine and the van moved down the drive. She could feel Luke's eyes upon her as they reached the road. This is where she'd bottled out last time and she could feel her heart was racing as the van left the grounds of her home. They were out! They'd made it. Luke turned and grinned at her.

'Okay?'

She nodded. 'Okay.'

So, this was her village, she thought as they drove past the red-brick cottages to enter the market square. She really couldn't remember much about it at all. She'd only driven through it a couple of times when viewing the castle and making the necessary arrangements for moving. She'd gazed down onto the streets from the top of the castle, of course, but it was quite a different experience seeing it from street level. It really was very pretty. There were people too. Orla felt a little shocked to see them at first and pushed her sunglasses further up her nose, making sure, quite unnecessarily, that they were on securely. But nobody was paying her the slightest attention. These were people simply getting on with their day-to-day living – shopping, walking the dog, waiting for a bus or venturing to their allotment.

'Bill!' Luke suddenly called, sounding his horn and waving.

Orla nearly leapt out of her seat.

'Sorry!' Luke said quickly as Bill waved back at them.

Orla took a few deep breaths before settling down again.

'That was Bill,' Luke said.

'So I gathered.'

They turned out of the village onto a road that went past the primary school and playing fields. Orla didn't remember any of this at all and she looked at it now as if for the first time. She had managed to shut herself off from the village, but life still very much went on without her.

The van picked up speed as it left Lorford behind, entering the countryside. It was a hauntingly beautiful landscape of massive fields and ebony-dark pine trees, great expanses of heather and, over everything, the deep blue of the sky.

'Wonderful day to be outside, isn't it?' Luke said. 'How about parking somewhere and going for a walk?'

One Ear barked from the back.

'Sounds like he's on board with the idea.'

'Okay.' Orla nodded. A walk sounded safe. She could do a walk. A couple of moments later, Luke pulled into a little car park by one of the heaths. Pushing her glasses up her nose again and making sure her hat was firmly in place, she opened the van door and got out. Luke had the back door open for One Ear and he jumped out with one quick move and trotted to his mistress's side.

The sky was a peerless blue and Orla could hear the spiralling song of a skylark high above. The heath stretched for miles and she imagined that it would be even lovelier when the purple of the heather coloured the landscape later in the summer. Silver birches dotted the heath, their trunks straight and bright. Luke was right, Orla thought. It was a good day to be out amongst it all. She'd done well and Luke had done well to make her do this.

She watched as One Ear poked his nose into the heather, no doubt picking up the scents of rabbits and other rodents. It was good for him to have a new environment to explore. She felt guilty that he didn't get to go anywhere other than the beach. Not that there was anything wrong with the beach. It was their own little paradise and she felt very lucky to have it on her doorstep, but perhaps it was unfair that One Ear only ever had that place as his playground because of Orla's angst.

Orla knew that she could never begin to relax in a public place, but she felt something akin to happiness spreading through her as they continued walking. She'd always found that there was something in the very action of walking that helped to still the mind and quell anxiety. The movement of the body was good for the mind, she believed. She'd walked her way out of so many bad moods and sad moments and she was determined that this walk was going to be a positive one too.

That was before she saw the stranger.

It was just a normal man wearing a T-shirt and a pair of jeans. He was in his late thirties and was walking with a Border collie close by his heels. He didn't even look their way as he approached. He was far too interested in looking at the screen of his mobile phone but, even so, Orla could feel herself starting to panic. Luke, obviously sensing this, was by her side in an instant, making sure he was the one nearest as the man passed them.

'Okay?' he asked, once the man was on his way.

She nodded, thankful that there were no other people in-between them and the horizon.

They walked on in companionable silence, the sun gloriously warm on their backs and the earth sandy and soft beneath their feet. When they came to a natural crossroads, Luke took the right turn, which led into the cool shade of a wood. It seemed strange to leave the wide landscape behind them and to be surrounded by trees. Everything seemed hushed. Orla, who was used to the open expanse of the beach, realised quickly that she didn't like being enclosed like this. Anyone could hide amongst the trees and get close to her.

Suddenly, she started looking around as if there might, in fact, be someone in there.

'Orla?'

'I need to get out.'

'Of the wood?'

'Get me back.'

'Okay, we'll get you back. Take my hand.'

Orla felt Luke's hand close around her own, strong and supportive, as everything else seemed strange and nebulous. She was having one of her dizzy spells, which often came on when she felt threatened. The slightest thing could bring it on – the sighting of someone she didn't recognise, like the man with the Border collie, or a movement caught out of the corner of her eye.

'Nearly there,' Luke said as they reached the van a few minutes later.

Orla felt exhausted, her body drenched with fear, and she sank back into the passenger seat, closing her eyes against the world as if that would make it all go away.

'Shall we just drive around for a while?' Luke suggested.

Orla nodded. It was all she seemed capable of doing. Finally, after a few minutes, she opened her eyes. They were still in the countryside, passing a broad river edged with blond reed beds which danced in the summer breeze. Luke wound his window down a little and the fresh salty air filled the van and One Ear started sniffing in appreciation. They passed fabulous flint churches and thatched cottages huddled around village greens and, turning a corner in an easterly direction, they caught a tantalising glimpse of the sea.

Orla was finally beginning to feel a little more normal and, although she wasn't completely relaxed, she was able to enjoy her surroundings now that she was safe in the van.

As they passed a little garden centre Luke sprang a new challenge on her.

'Fancy going in?'

Orla didn't need to think about it. She hadn't done any shopping in a real shop since before the acid attack. 'Not today,' she told Luke.

'Mind if I pop in quickly?'

'Erm, no,' Orla said as he pulled into a farm track to turn around and go back.

'Anything you want?'

'No, thank you,' she said politely. As fun as it might be to look at the plants and the seeds, Orla left that side of things to Bill.

'Well, I won't be long,' he said a moment later, parking and getting out of the van. Orla watched and One Ear whined, wondering why he wasn't being allowed to follow Luke on this new adventure.

'It's all right,' Orla assured him, when she wasn't altogether sure herself. She looked out of the window, hoping to spot Luke, but she couldn't see him anywhere. She could so easily have opened the door and gone to join him, but it wasn't easy at all, was it? That was the problem. The opening of the door and the walking to meet him were just the mechanics of the thing. But there was a whole psychology side to it which prevented her from doing it. The fear

162

of the unknown – of what might be on the other side of that door. Or *who* might be on the other side of that door and if they might wish her harm.

And so she sat, rigidly staring straight ahead, ever mindful of the people coming and going around her. Where had he got to? He was taking an absolute age in there.

Finally, he returned, a huge smile on his face as he opened the door and got into the van, presenting Orla with a voluptuous pink geranium in a terracotta pot.

'For you.'

'You bought this for me?' Orla was genuinely surprised by the gift.

'I wanted to celebrate. You've done so well today.'

'But I haven't! I've been hopeless!'

'No, you weren't! Not at all. And "hopeless" is the very *last* word I'd use to describe today. For me, it felt *full* of hope.'

'It did?'

'Yes! Look!' He pointed to the milometer. 'We've driven over twenty miles so far. That's twenty whole miles you've explored after having explored precisely none in the last couple of years. Surely *that's* worth celebrating.'

She looked down at the beautiful plant which sat on her lap. 'You're right,' she said at last. 'It is worth celebrating. Thank you. Thank you so much.'

'You're welcome. And I know Helen would be so proud of you.'

'She would?'

'Absolutely,' Luke told her, knowing it to be true. 'Where to now?'

Orla stared out of the window. They'd gone twenty whole miles and had seen places she hadn't known existed before. And here was this kind man willing to take her anywhere she wanted to go.

'Home,' she said at last.

'Yeah?'

Orla nodded. 'Yes.'

'No problem.'

She wrapped her hands protectively around the pot and a little smile began to play around the corners of her mouth. She had left the castle. She had been out into the big, wide world. And now she was going back home.

The slow summer days turned into weeks and June became July. Luke continued his work on the castle, repointing, replastering and repainting, and, each week, he and Orla would venture out in the van, driving a little further and walking a greater distance. Orla's confidence was building and she'd even ventured into the garden centre with Luke one time, glasses and hat firmly in place, and had bought a large heather to plant in her garden and remind her of the heath and of her first walk with Luke.

Luke was delighted with her progress. So much so that he dared to broach the subject he'd been skirting around for some time now. It was one evening, when they were sitting in the great hall, having walked for two hours across the heath, which was now wearing its magenta blooms so prettily. He cleared his throat.

'There's another horticultural club meeting at Bill's on Friday.'

'Oh?'

'Yes. Thought I'd pop along.'

'Right.'

Luke waited, hoping Orla might surprise him and volunteer to go with him. But her eyes remained fixed on the book she was reading.

'I was wondering . . . now that you're going out more . . . now that you're more confident around people . . .'

Orla closed her book and gave him her full attention. 'Luke, I only went into a garden centre.'

'Yes, but you bought that plant and took it to the till and everything. You didn't so much as flinch, let alone start hyperventilating!'

'Are you making fun of me?'

'*God*, no! I'd *never* do that. I'm really proud of you, and I don't mean that to sound condescending or anything. I really admire what you've done, but I can't help wanting to see you do more. You've got so much to give, Orla, and I think the people in the horticultural club would love to meet you.'

'Well, I'm not going.'

Luke watched in exasperation as she opened her book up again. 'But it's just a little get-together at Bill's home, and you know him already, and his wife's great. The rest of the group are really friendly too.'

'I don't need any friends.'

'We all need friends, Orla.'

'You go, if you need friends.'

'I will. I am. But I'd like you to come with me.'

Orla sighed. 'Why?'

'Because I think it will do you good. How long have you been here on your own now? How many people do you know in the village you've chosen to live in? You have to admit that it's not normal.'

Orla sighed, clearly exasperated. 'Not everybody needs to be around people all the time.'

'I know that, and I'm not suggesting that you should be *all the time*. But once in a while might be nice, don't you think?' Luke realised that his voice had raised a little with the passion behind his words and so he made a conscious effort to tone it down a little. 'You can't live in these little boxes you create for Galleria. It just doesn't seem healthy to me. I think you need to reach beyond those boxes and stop talking to people online and start talking to them in real life.'

'But my online friends are very real. It's how I met Helen.'

Luke swallowed. 'I know. But it's a different kind of friendship, isn't it? It's all at a distance. I think you need to meet people – in reality. In the flesh!'

'You're in the flesh.'

'Yes, I am, but I'm only one person and I'm not going to be here for ever, am I?' His question hung in the air between them.

'But I don't feel I need—'

'You didn't want to leave the castle and come out with me in the van a few weeks ago, but look at how much you enjoy that now.'

'That's different – I'm with you.'

'And you'll be with me at this meeting at Bill's. Come on, Orla – come with me. If you don't like it, we don't have to stay long.'

'They'll stare at me.'

'They won't stare at you. I'll make sure of it, okay?'

'They won't know what to say. Either that or they'll start asking questions I don't want to answer.'

'Do you want me to tell them what happened before we go?'

'No!'

'Okay,' Luke said, amazed that she was even considering his suggestion.

'One single question – or one odd *look* – and I'll leave,' Orla vowed.

'Understood.'

Orla glared at him from across the room. 'I don't know how I let you talk me into these things, I really don't.'

'It must have something to do with my innate charm,' Luke said with a grin.

Orla shook her head slowly and sighed out a huge sigh. 'If it all goes horribly wrong, I'm locking you in the dungeon.'

'Fair enough,' Luke said. 'I'm actually growing quite fond of it.'

Chapter 13

Orla didn't quite know how she was feeling as they arrived at Oyster Cottage. She was nervous, of course, and could feel a whole meadow of butterflies fluttering inside her, but it was more than that – she felt like she was on the edge of a panic attack and that she was only just keeping it in check because of the calming presence of Luke by her side.

They'd walked through the village together, which was a feat in itself as Orla had never actually done that before. As always, she'd popped a big hat on her head and wore a pair of oversized sunglasses, looking like a fifties movie star who was trying to hide from the press. The outfit might well have masked her scars but, in a little English village, she soon realised that it only really succeeded in drawing attention to her, which was the very thing she was trying to avoid.

'I rang ahead,' Luke told her. 'Bill's delighted you're coming and he's promised to brief everybody before they arrive, so there won't be any questions or undue attention.'

'How can I be sure of that?' Orla asked.

'He's a man of his word is Bill, isn't he?'

'But the others . . .'

'I'm sure they're all good people. There's nothing to worry about.'

Orla wasn't so sure and was beginning to regret her decision to come along with Luke, however well meaning it all was and no matter how many promises and assurances had been made.

It was Bill who greeted them at the door of Oyster Cottage, with Bosun by his side.

'What a pleasure to see you, Miss Kendrick,' he said.

Orla nodded. 'Hello. Thank you for letting me come.' She might be nervous, but she wasn't going to forget her manners.

'Our pleasure. Come and meet Margy.'

They were shown through to the kitchen, where Margy was hastily getting the tea things together.

'Margy – this is Miss Kendrick.'

Margy put her polka-dot teapot down and her hands flew to her face. 'My dear!' she said, her face quite flushed now. 'It's so lovely to meet you. May I take your hat for you?'

Orla saw Luke visibly blanch and then look surprised as her hands reached up to remove the hat and smooth her dark hair around her face.

'I'll pop it on this hook by the door,' Margy said, taking the hat and glancing only briefly at Orla's face. 'Why don't you go through and meet everyone and make yourself comfortable?'

Orla almost laughed. The last thing she would feel tonight was comfortable.

'Bill?' Margy said as they were about to leave the room. 'Take this up to Beth, will you? I promised her one.' She passed her husband a plate with a large chocolate chip and raisin cookie on it, warm from the oven.

'We have our granddaughter staying with us,' he explained to them, 'and she's being spoilt rotten.'

'Tell her to brush her teeth afterwards and to get straight into bed,' Margy added.

Bill nodded. 'I'll just take these two through first.'

He led Orla and Luke through to the living room, where six other members were already seated. All looked up and smiled as they walked in.

'Everybody, this is Miss Kendrick,' Bill announced.

Orla, who was still wearing her sunglasses, turned to Bill. 'I think you can call me Orla now.'

He nodded and smiled. There was a chorus of hellos from the room and she and Luke sat down on the sofa. Margy came through with tea and cookies for everyone and then sat down, picking up her knitting which, that evening, was sky blue and yellow. Introductions were made. Unsurprisingly, Orla had never seen any of these people before, but they all seemed friendly and polite and, thankfully, nobody stared at her. There was none of the awkwardness or fear in people's eyes that she had been expecting and dreading and, for that, she was truly grateful.

Luke threw her a smile.

'Okay?' he whispered, and she nodded. So far, she was fine.

Once Bill rejoined them, the meeting started. Orla soon learned that it wasn't a themed meeting, as Luke had told her the earlier one had been; it was more of an informal discussion about what people were growing in their gardens – the successes, the failures and what could be done even better. If there was one thing Orla soon picked up on from her neighbours, it was that gardeners were great optimists and, in spite of beasts, bugs and other natural disasters, they always planned ahead, with their hope and joy undiminished. She liked that and, much to her astonishment, she found she was smiling as the talk went on around her.

They talked about whether it was best to grow tomatoes in a greenhouse or outside, their favourite flowers to use when companion planting, the best way to keep pots hydrated when away from home during the summer and whose seed catalogues were the most beautiful *and* the best-value product – the two not often going hand in hand, it seemed – and Orla couldn't help but make a few mental notes and determine to spend even more time in her own garden.

One of the older members of the group, George, sat forward on his chair. 'So then, Luke – what are you growing in your garden?'

Luke wasn't one to blush, but Orla could definitely see his face heating up at the question.

'I'm ashamed to say that I couldn't tell you. You see, that was my wife's department.'

'Plenty of time to learn,' George told him.

Luke nodded. 'I think there's some lavender somewhere.'

There was a pause after he said this because nobody knew whether it was meant to be funny or not, and then Bill gave a chuckle and everybody joined in – including Luke, who was obviously able to see the humour in his ignorance.

'Lavender's a very good place to start,' Margy said, and Luke seemed to relax a little. Orla smiled at him as he turned to look at her, then she did something that took her completely by surprise because she really hadn't planned on doing it at all: she removed her sunglasses. There were a few quick glances, she noted, but more because of her sudden movement than because of what it revealed. Orla looked down into her lap, aware that she was causing a little ripple of sensation.

'Any more tea, anyone?' Margy asked, getting up and taking the attention away from her.

'Oh, do let me help you,' one of the other women said, and the two of them left for the kitchen.

Bill cleared his throat. 'Talking of lavender,' he said, 'I've been thinking of growing Hidcote Pink. Any thoughts?'

A woman in her sixties shook her head and tutted. 'To my mind, lavender is purple. Any other colour is a sacrilege!'

Bill grinned, as did Orla, and a few others scoffed at this declaration.

It was as they were debating purple lavender over pink that a young girl came into the room.

'Beth! What are you doing up?' Bill asked, obviously embarrassed by the interruption of his young granddaughter in a pair of pyjamas covered in red hearts.

'I couldn't sleep,' Beth explained, looking around the room and deciding that things were much more exciting in there than upstairs. Then she saw Orla, and Orla saw the expression on her face change. Her eyes widened and her mouth formed a perfect 'o' shape, and there was an anxious moment when Orla wondered what would happen next.

Orla saw Luke glance at Bill, who looked as if he was about to say something, but Beth beat him to it, cocking her head to one side as she looked directly at Orla.

'What happened to your face?' Beth asked, without an adult's filter to guide her.

Orla felt her throat tighten at the blunt question and her fingers twisted themselves into knots in her lap. But the child's eyes held hers and there was something about that direct look that demanded complete honesty.

'I was attacked,' Orla said calmly. 'Somebody threw something very nasty into my face.'

The girl didn't flinch. 'Did it hurt?'

'Yes.'

'And does it hurt now?'

'No. Not now.'

There was a pause when Beth continued to examine her. 'Will your ear grow back?'

Somebody to Luke's right gasped at this bold question.

'No,' Orla told Beth. 'It won't grow back.'

'Can I touch it?'

'Beth!' Bill cried in horror. 'That's enough now, darling.'

'It's okay,' Orla assured him as Beth came forward, her small child's fingers reaching out to touch Orla's face. She could sense that Luke and the rest of the room were staring at her and Beth now, but that no longer worried her.

'Does it make you sad?' Beth asked at last.

Orla took a moment before answering. 'Yes.'

'But you're still pretty.'

As the little girl smiled at Orla, she could feel tears pricking her eyes.

'You're pretty too,' Orla told the girl as Margy came back into the room with the tea tray.

'Beth!' Margy cried. 'What are you doing in here? You should be in bed!' Margy looked around the room. 'What is it? What did I miss?'

Orla saw Luke exhale a deep breath and Bill shook his head.

'*What?*' Margy asked.

Everyone looked at Orla and she gave Margy a little smile. 'I'll tell you later,' she said.

'You were amazing tonight,' Luke told her as they walked through the darkened streets of Lorford.

'Thank you and . . . *thank* you.'

'I get two thank yous? What for?'

'For making me do that. You were right – they're really good people.'

'They are, aren't they?'

'And I love that little girl.'

'I think you've got a fan there.'

'Well, she's got one too,' Orla assured him.

'I don't think Bill's got over that yet. He was still a bit red in the face when we left.'

'But Margy was so sweet.'

'I think she was very touched when you told her your story.' Luke smiled. They'd waited for the other guests to leave and then Orla had opened up to her hosts, answering their questions just as honestly and confidently as she had Beth's.

'It's wonderful,' Luke went on.

'What is?'

'How you're growing in confidence all the time.'

'Am I?'

'Sure you are! You don't feel it?'

Orla stopped walking and looked up at the star-spangled sky, inky dark and so inviting on that summer evening.

'It's happening so slowly, I'm not sure I'm feeling any confidence at all.'

'But to even leave the castle – let alone go into a stranger's house and not only talk to people, but to share your history with them – you've got to admit that's pretty incredible. Compared to when I first met you and you wouldn't even open the door.'

They began walking again.

'I suppose.'

'There's no supposing about it, Orla. You're opening yourself up to the possibilities of life again,' Luke told her but, seeing her flinch, he asked, 'What is it?'

'It's scary.'

'What scares you?'

'Just . . . everything! That phrase you use – opening yourself up – that scares me because, well, I might be experiencing lovely things like trips out with you into the countryside and evenings with friendly neighbours, but I'm opening myself up to the other things too – the things I've tried to shut out.'

Luke sighed. 'I don't think you can have one without the risk of the other. I haven't yet met anyone who's had a trouble-free life. I'm not sure how you'd go about it, to be honest. What would you do – write a letter to the universe saying you only want to be sent all the good bits of life? I don't think it works that way.'

'No, of course not. And you've had more than your share of the bad stuff.'

Luke didn't say anything. The truth was, he was doing a pretty good job of shutting out the bad stuff while staying at Lorford Castle, which was ironic really because he was quite intent that Orla should get out of the castle and open herself up while he was happily shutting himself away in this little corner of Suffolk.

'Sorry,' Orla suddenly said, interrupting his thoughts. 'That came out wrong.'

'What did?'

'It sounded awful – I didn't mean to dismiss Helen's death as *bad stuff.*'

'But it is.'

'Yes, but those words weren't right.'

'No words are right for it.'

'I know.'

They walked in silence for a few moments, Luke desperately trying to shut out an assault of upsetting thoughts about Helen. She would have loved a night like this, he thought – an indigo sky full of gentle starlight and a cool breeze following the warmth of the summer day. And how she would have loved a place like Lorford, with its pretty homes and quirky residents – like Margy with her ever-present knitting. He just knew she'd be fascinated by it all. Luke smiled and blinked away a rebellious tear, glad the darkness shielded his face from Orla.

When they reached the castle, they were greeted by One Ear, who was thrilled to see them both.

'I'll just give him a quick run in the garden,' Orla said, leaving Luke alone for a few minutes. He needed that time. He needed to collect his thoughts and settle his agitation because he'd come to a realisation and knew that, in helping Orla with her problems, he was successfully shutting out his own.

Bill arrived at his usual time to attend to the garden at the castle the morning after the meeting but, for the first time in the two years he'd been gardening for Miss Kendrick, it felt different. He had now met his employer and oh, how lovely she was. He still couldn't believe the events of the evening before and how she'd not only attended the meeting in the first place, but had sat amongst them all, hat and glasses removed, and had openly answered all of Beth's questions. He'd never forget the initial feeling of horror he'd felt when his little granddaughter had come into the room and clocked Orla. He'd had a moment of pure terror, wondering if the girl was going to scream or make some kind of scene. Well, she'd made a scene of sorts, that was for sure, but everyone had been riveted by it, and Bill had a feeling that those innocent questions had done Orla the power of good to answer. It had certainly broken the tension between everyone; they had all, he felt, been made a little anxious by Orla's presence – not because they didn't like her, but because they were being overly careful not to say the wrong thing or to look at her in the wrong way. Orla had marked herself out as different by hiding away from them all for so long and everybody had been moving around her with care and caution.

He glanced up at the castle now as he began work and wondered what she'd made of them all. He'd liked that she'd stayed behind after everyone had left and had told Margy what she'd missed when she'd been making the tea, and Bill's soul had ached for Orla when he'd heard her story. No wonder she'd closed herself off from the world and feared the whole of mankind. He really couldn't blame her. He might well have done the same thing.

Bending down to pull out a couple of dandelions that really should have known better than to grow where they knew they wouldn't possibly be allowed to stay, Bill thanked his lucky stars that he'd never really known true fear, as Orla must have in her relatively short life. There'd been the time Margy was rushed into hospital with appendicitis. That had been scary, but she'd been young and strong and he'd been surrounded by family. He'd lost his share of friends over recent years, but that was life, wasn't it? No, he didn't have cause to complain. He was a lucky man.

It was as he was trimming the edges of the lawn after mowing it that he saw her, and he did a double take, imagining it was a mirage in the summer heat. But, no, it was definitely Miss Kendrick and she was walking straight towards him. She wasn't wearing her sunglasses today, although she did have a straw hat on to protect her face from the sun, which was already hot and high in the sky. The hat had a pretty sky-blue ribbon tied around it and shaped her face perfectly.

Her face.

Bill looked at it again, his stomach twisting in anger at what had happened to her. If he could get his hands on the people who'd hurt this lovely young woman . . .

He took a deep breath. Violent thoughts weren't the answer, he knew that, but he couldn't help thinking them all the same.

Now, as she crossed the grass to greet him, he tipped his cap in his old-fashioned way.

'Good morning, Miss Kendrick.'

'Bill, you really must call me Orla.'

He scratched his chin. 'That'll take some getting used to.'

She smiled, and it lit up her whole face so beautifully and, once again, he felt sad that she'd hidden away for so long.

'I wanted to thank you for last night,' she began.

'Thank me? It should be me thanking you.'

'Whatever for?'

'For being there.'

'Did I shock everyone?'

He took a moment to consider this. 'I wouldn't say shock so much as surprise.'

'Well, I hope it was a pleasant surprise.'

'Very. I hope we'll see you again.'

'I hope so too.'

He smiled and was just about to turn back to his work when she surprised him yet again.

'Can I talk to you about something?'

'Of course.' Bill gestured to the bench under the rose arch and they both sat down on it together as if they were old friends. 'What's on your mind?'

'I'm worried about Luke,' she said at last. 'He's been so focused on helping me and I can never repay his kindness. He's helped me so much.' She paused, looking down at her hands.

'So, what's the problem?'

'I'm not sure he's mourning properly.'

'How do you mean?'

'He hardly mentions about Helen. He only really talked about the accident when he first arrived and we haven't spoken about it since. It's touched on every now and then, like last night, but . . .'

'What?'

'I don't know. Shouldn't he be talking about her more?'

Bill sighed. 'Who can say? He might be processing everything quietly.'

'He is.'

'Then I wouldn't worry.'

Orla knitted her fingers together. 'But I do. I think he's hiding away here.'

'Like you did?'

'Exactly! It's easy to do.'

'Then you should understand.'

'I do, but he's helped me to see how unhealthy it is.'

'And it's unhealthy for him?'

'I think it might be. You see, he's been sleepwalking.' Orla turned to face Bill now. 'He did it shortly after arriving and a couple of times since. At least, that's when I've known about it. He might do it more often than I catch him. I'm a pretty light sleeper these days. Anyway, I can't help feeling that his locked-in emotions are trying to find a way out.'

'In sleepwalking?'

'I read about it a bit, and sleepwalking can be linked to stress.'

Bill nodded.

'What do you think?' Orla asked.

'What do *I* think?'

'Yes.'

Bill stared out across the garden as he thought about the young man he'd first seen collapsed on the beach. The same young man who'd brought Orla out into the community, but who was obviously fighting his own battle.

'Our neighbour lost his wife a few years ago,' Bill began. 'They were both in their late eighties. Spent their entire lives together. He took it bad. We used to hear him crying through the walls.' Bill shook his head at the memory. 'Margy couldn't bear it. Used to go round and cook for him, listen to him, and hold him as he cried. But time passes, doesn't it? The pain becomes a little easier to bear.'

'You think we should do nothing?'

'I didn't say that. But I think we have to let him process all this the way he needs to. We can be there for him, but we can't do his mourning for him.'

'I know.'

'Just as you had to heal yourself your way,' Bill said. 'The way I see it, there's no right or wrong way. There are as many different ways to go through an experience as there are people in the world, and Luke will do it his way.'

'Yes, you're right.'

They sat in silence together, and it felt so natural. They were becoming friends, he thought, sharing stories and asking for help. That was good. That was as it should be.

'Well, I'd better let you get on,' Orla said at last, standing up and adjusting her hat.

Bill stood up too. 'I'm always here, you know, if you need anything. Always have been.'

She smiled. 'I know. It just took me a while to realise, didn't it?'

Orla returned inside, her sun-warmed limbs cooling in an instant within the ancient walls of the castle. She took off her hat and went in search of a jumper, pulling it on and suddenly realising that she'd gone outside without sunglasses. When she'd removed them in front of everybody at the meeting the night before, it had been one of the most nerve-wracking moments of her life. How she'd found the courage, she'd never know, but part of it came from having Luke beside her. He believed in her and now she wanted to reach out to him in the same way he'd reached out to her.

Only she had to find him first.

Luckily, it didn't take her long. He was working on a section of wall in a small chamber off the upper hall, his sheets and tools laid neatly around him.

'Hey – how are you getting on?' Orla asked as she entered the room with care.

'Good, I think.' Luke stood back from the wall and removed the goggles he'd been wearing. 'Don't touch anything. It's all setting.'

'It looks great.'

'Well, it's better than it was. The lime plastering will allow everything to breathe.'

Orla gave a little laugh. 'Yes, it's good to breathe, isn't it? I think this castle's been holding its breath almost as long as I have.'

Luke smiled. 'But you're both breathing now.'

'Yes.' She watched him as he tinkered around, building up the courage to say what she had come here to say.

She took a deep breath. 'Luke, you know, you've helped me so much.'

He turned back to her. 'You're doing a lot of the work yourself. Don't forget that.'

'I wouldn't have, though, if you hadn't come here.'

Luke smiled and then turned back to his work.

'I'd like to help you, Luke.'

He looked back at her and frowned. 'What do you mean? With the plastering?'

'No, not the plastering. I want to help – if you ever want to talk about anything. About Helen. I'm here and I'm happy to listen.'

He looked at her blankly, as if genuinely confused about what she might mean. It was the strangest sensation to see him like that because he was usually so warm and open, but she could see that her words had closed something up in him and that she wasn't going to get through to him.

181

'I'm fine,' he said in a dreadfully distant monotone.

'Are you?'

He picked up one of his tools. Orla had no idea what it was, but his message was clear – he didn't want to talk to her.

'Luke?'

'I'm *fine*,' he told her again, making her flinch.

'Okay,' she said, feeling deflated and defeated as she left the chamber.

Chapter 14

There was a genuine uneasiness between Luke and Orla over the next few days, with both of them concentrating on their respective work, conveniently at opposite ends of the castle. Orla was quite sure Luke had arranged things that way, working in parts of the castle where he was least likely to run into her.

Orla did her best not to be upset, but it was hard. She bought more damaged crockery that week than she had in a long time. Box after box was delivered to the castle and great mountains of bubble wrap and tissue paper soon accumulated. Orla tried not to think about it, although she felt horribly guilty about the waste. She'd have to find a way to recycle it all at some point. There were stacks of boxes and wrapping from her years of collecting. That was one of the benefits of living in a castle, she thought – there was plenty of room for rubbish.

For now, though, she was focused on her art. It was a while since she'd posted to Galleria and she'd missed the friendly community, but it felt funny going back there now, having been out in the real world. She allowed herself a little time to acclimatise, scrolling through her favourite accounts, liking photos and leaving comments. Then she got down to business, looking through her new acquisitions for the piece to showcase to the world. She'd bought a job lot of blue and white china and she looked through the pieces now. Some of it wasn't very old at all and so wasn't of interest to Orla, but there was a handful of pieces that were very pretty indeed and she placed them on one of the wide windowsills in the great hall, which was a favourite place of hers to photograph things.

The light was honeyed and warm there and gave the plates and cups a glow which was beautiful to photograph. She took some photos from above so that you could see the whole pattern on the plates, then some from the side so that the cups were shown in their full glory. It was a delightful dance with the camera that she always enjoyed, finding that angle which brought the true beauty of something to the fore. Orla was used to bending down on her knees or clambering up a step ladder in order to find just the right place to be. That was her job – an angle explorer, teaming the objects she'd sourced with the light available on any given day. And light could be a very fickle business partner indeed.

Once she was happy that she'd got a few images that would work, she took the cups and plates back to the china room to store safely. One Ear knew that this was the one place in the castle where he wasn't allowed. It wasn't that Orla didn't trust him, but the mere size of him and the enthusiasm of his tail could easily wreak more havoc than the proverbial bull in a china shop and so he would wait in the hallway outside.

When everything had been safely put away, Orla sat down with her camera and her phone, doing a quick deleting round of the photos she deemed hadn't worked as well as she'd hoped. This left her with a shortlist of two dozen or so and she loaded those onto her laptop so she could view them better before whittling them down further. This process took another half an hour and she chose three photos to use over the coming weeks, uploading one to the Galleria site that day. She was instantly hit with 'likes', and comments quickly followed, filling her with gratitude for her online friends, who had an eye for beauty too, even in the broken things in life.

I love the way the light plays on the chip in that cup, somebody wrote. And the way that hairline crack travels just beneath the pagoda – as if there might have been an earthquake.

Orla had liked that too. She always tried to imagine what might have caused each little chip and crack. A clumsy pair of hands, perhaps, or a dog's waggy tail. Life had a way of finding the beautiful things and leaving its mark.

Then came the usual questions from those who only desired to own things after seeing them beautifully photographed by somebody else.

Where did you get those plates from?

Orla would smile. The joy of vintage finds was that they were hard to replicate. One couldn't just log on and buy the exact same thing, and Orla liked that. It made her collection special.

And, finally, the more personal messages came.

So glad to see you back!

Missed you. Hope you're okay.

Orla read them all, choosing not to reply, but touched that, in venturing out into the real world, she had been missed in the virtual one.

But there was a huge void there now. A void that could never be filled. Never again would Helen's voice chime out loud and beautiful amongst the crowd. There would be no more messages, no more sweet exchanges between them and no more photos posted on her *Trees and Dreams* page.

Tears began to fall as Orla felt the loss again. With having been so focused on herself over the past few weeks and being anxious about Luke's state of mind, she'd forgotten about the loss of her friend and realised that she hadn't mourned properly for her at all. When Luke had arrived and told her about Helen, Orla had wanted to be brave for him, but now she realised that she hadn't really made time to think about her own loss. But the tears were coming now, hot and relentless, and she couldn't help but be glad that Luke wasn't there to see them.

Luke was struggling. He'd tried to distract himself with his job, but it didn't seem to be working and he knew why. The twentieth of July. He'd been dreading it.

He'd worked right through lunch, grabbing a sandwich in the middle of the afternoon and taking the shortest of breaks with a quick walk around the village to get some fresh air. Then it was back to it.

But he couldn't very well work right through the night for fear of disturbing Orla. It wouldn't be fair. He hadn't spoken to her – not properly at least – for days now, and it was cutting him up. He knew he was being an idiot, but he was doing his best to keep his emotions in check and, if she started on at him about opening up, he didn't know where it would lead. No. Luke was determined to keep a lid very firmly on his emotions and if that meant that Orla thought him a little gruff, then so be it.

The twentieth of July.

He'd known it was approaching, and he'd known he'd have to face it. It was one of the reasons he hadn't wanted to be at home. Maybe it was one of the reasons he'd been dreaming about Helen too. The last few nights, her face had been so clear to him. Her voice too. Like the dream he'd had just the night before.

'*Let me read you something,*' she'd said, and he'd been smiling, shaking his head, as he knew what was coming.

'*"With the new moon in your sign this week, change is on its way."*
Isn't that exciting?'

'I don't believe in star signs,' he'd told her.

'*I know. I don't either, but they're fun, aren't they?*'

She'd laughed at his seriousness.

'*Let me read yours, you crotchety old Capricorn!*'

He'd sighed in resignation. 'Go on, then.'

'*"Don't let your ambition stop you having a good time. Remember to relax! Life isn't all about work, you know, so put that toolbox down and spend time with loved ones."*'

'It doesn't really say that, does it?' He'd moved to pull the magazine from her.

'*It jolly well does and you should pay attention to it, too.*'

When he'd woken, he realised he'd been crying in his sleep. It had all felt so real. Helen had *been there*. He'd not just seen and heard her; he'd *felt* her. Waking up had felt like losing her all over again and the echo of the dream had haunted him throughout the day.

Looking at the blank wall of lime plaster in front of him now, he still couldn't shake the mood which hung over him no matter how much he tried to focus on the job in hand, switching his radio on in an attempt to fill his head with inane music and DJ babble.

He wasn't quite sure how he got through the day, but he did and, by the time he got into bed that night, he felt utterly drained. He still hadn't seen or spoken to Orla and he was glad he hadn't because he knew he was dreadful company and it wouldn't be fair to inflict himself on her.

He let out a long sigh, staring up into the darkness of the room, and then he closed his eyes on the day, whispering three words before he fell asleep.

'Happy birthday, Helen.'

It was a couple of days later when Orla decided that something needed to be said. Whatever Luke was doing and whatever mood he was in, she was going to confront him because things simply couldn't go on in the way they had been. Selfishly, she thought that she'd been making such good progress and that the gulf that had come between them was a setback. Luke hadn't offered any days out since the day she'd said she'd listen to him if he ever wanted to talk to her. But it was more than that – she was seriously worried about him. Whereas she'd been making progress, she truly felt that he was getting worse. Part of her wanted to confront him about it and just get it all out in the open, but she'd held back because she remembered how difficult it had been for her to navigate her way through troubled times and the last thing she'd wanted was some mad person shouting at her to buck up. So she'd given him time and space. Only she believed he'd had plenty of that now and it was time to start talking.

It was easy to lose somebody in a castle, particularly if you didn't even know they were actually inside, Orla thought as her search for Luke began. He might have taken himself off, for all she knew. With not speaking properly, she wouldn't blame him if he'd downed tools and gone off for the day. In fact, thinking about it now, she wasn't really sure why he was still here. Perhaps he was a man of integrity and wouldn't just walk out on a job he'd promised to do, she thought. But there was another possibility. Perhaps him remaining at the castle was preferable to going home to an empty house – a house Helen wouldn't ever be returning home to. The thought made Orla intensely sad and all the more determined to find Luke and sort things out.

'Luke?' she called as she went from room to room and floor to floor, One Ear by her side. 'LUKE?'

'I'm in the basement!'

'Oh, thank goodness,' she said under her breath, glad that he was still under her roof.

Reaching the basement a moment later, Orla stood at the bottom of the steps anxiously as One Ear barged in ahead of her.

'Hello, boy!' Luke said, ruffling the dog's head affectionately. He then looked up at Orla. 'Hi.'

'Hi.'

Luke cleared his throat. 'I owe you an apology.'

'And I owe you one too.'

'Are you going to make me go first, then?' he asked, a tiny smile lighting his face.

'Yes.'

'Okay. I'm sorry. I'm sorry for being moody and withdrawn and gruff and—' He paused. 'You can stop me whenever you like.'

'No – you can go on,' she told him.

'Well, I'm sorry. There's no excuse for bad behaviour.'

'Yes, there is.'

'No,' he said.

They looked at one another, the space between them suddenly seeming a little less intimidating now that they'd both apologised.

'I missed you,' Orla said.

Luke smiled at that. 'I missed you too.'

'Liar!'

'I'm not lying!'

'You missed One Ear.'

'Well, of *course* I missed One Ear! That goes without saying.' He bent to make a fuss of the dog again, who was very pleased indeed to have so much attention. 'I missed our walks.'

'You could've come along.'

He shook his head. 'I would've been bad company.'

'What have you been doing?'

'Mostly plastering. A bit of carpentry. Got those shutters sorted for you in the west turret, so that room should be cosier, come winter.'

'Thank you.'

'My pleasure.'

'You working in here now?'

'Not sure. I'm still wondering what's behind this,' he said, tapping the board.

'Why don't you find out?'

'I think I will,' he said. 'Maybe tomorrow. Fresh start in case it turns out to be a big job.'

'Fancy a walk now?'

'Yes! I really do.'

One Ear barked at the mention of the word 'walk' and the three of them left the basement together and headed out into the bright sunshine. As usual, Orla wore a hat, but she didn't bother with the large sunglasses today, and Luke noticed.

'I like your new look.'

'What new look?'

He drew a circle around his own face. 'The confident look.'

'I'm feeling braver.'

'You look it too. It suits you.'

'Does it?'

'It really does. You're looking good, Orla. I mean, you always did, but you're not carrying that – that . . .'

'What?'

'That haunted look about you.'

'Oh.'

'Is it all right to say that?'

'Yes, of course. It just feels funny to hear it. But it's good that I'm changing.'

'It is good.'

Orla led the way and, instead of taking the most direct route to the beach, she showed Luke a footpath which led through the reed beds. A perfect V-shape of geese flew overhead, their wings beating steadily, and they spied an egret in one of the ditches, its white plumage bright against the dark water.

'It's beautiful,' Luke said.

'It's even lovelier in the autumn, when the blackberries and rosehips are out.'

'I'd love to see it then.'

'You should.'

'Yeah? You inviting me to stay that long?'

'Of course. We're friends now, aren't we?'

'Absolutely.'

They walked on, climbing over a rickety stile after One Ear had taken it in an easy bound. The footpath then took them up a small hill before descending into the sand dunes and reaching the beach.

The salty air hit them in a refreshing blast and Orla inhaled deeply as One Ear took off at a gallop. Luke laughed and threw his head back to greet the sky. There was something so wonderfully freeing about being there and Orla couldn't help wishing she'd dragged Luke here days ago. But perhaps he would have resisted. Perhaps he wouldn't have been ready. But he was ready now and she took her chance.

'Luke?'

'Yeah?'

'Can I talk to you about something?'

'Sure.'

They made their way across the pebbly beach to where it turned into deep golden sand, damp and firm under their feet.

'I was wondering what Helen looked like.'

He didn't say anything for a moment, but then reached into his trouser pocket and pulled out his phone, turning it around to show Orla a moment later.

Shielding the screen with her hand, Orla looked down at the sweet face of the friend she'd lost. She had warm, chestnut hair which curled down to her shoulders and a happy rosy face, and her eyes shone with love for the man taking the photo.

'She's lovely,' she told Luke. 'I knew she would be. You can just tell with some people, can't you? And I don't just mean beautiful to look at – although she is, of course – but beautiful on the inside.'

'Yes, she was.'

'Her photos showed that. Each one seemed to hold a smile. Does that make sense?'

'Oh, yes.' He put his phone away and turned his head to look out to sea. Orla gave him a moment. 'I'm sorry. I find it hard to talk about all this.'

'I know you do.'

'It was her birthday,' he said at last.

'When?'

'On the twentieth.'

'Oh, Luke!'

'I knew it was coming and yet it hit me so hard.'

'Well, of course it did. You can't shut these things out. You wouldn't be human if you did.'

He wiped the back of his hand across his eyes and sniffed.

'Oh, God! I seem to do nothing but break down on public beaches!'

'There's nobody around and, even if there was, it wouldn't matter.'

Luke hid his face in his hands. 'I'm sorry.'

Orla's heart felt like it was bleeding as she saw his helplessness. 'It's okay,' she told him.

'I feel so – so ridiculous, crying like this!'

'Luke – it's okay that you're not okay. You do know that, don't you? You shouldn't try to hide from this, and I think maybe that's what you've been trying to do, isn't it? You're living with the expert on hiding, don't forget.'

Luke sniffed and Orla handed him a clean tissue from her pocket.

'Oh, God!' he cried. 'When will this stop?'

'I don't know. I think you might have a way to go yet, though.'

He glanced at her and she gave him a little smile.

'I'm sorry. You didn't want to hear that, did you?'

'No, not really. But thanks for being honest.'

'My pleasure. Well, it's not really. I hate seeing you like this.'

'Sorry!'

'Stop apologising,' she told him. 'Anyway, I mean, I think it's healthy to cry, but I wish I could spare you this pain.'

They walked on for a bit.

'I guess it's early days, isn't it?' he said.

'Yes. You're being too hard on yourself. You've got to give yourself time and space to get through this.'

'I want it all to be over.' He sighed. 'And then I feel guilty feeling like that because it's like I'm saying I don't want to think about Helen any more and that I want to get on with living.'

'But that's only natural.'

'Well, nature is cruel, isn't it?'

'Luke – you're alive. You're young. It's only normal that you want to get on.'

'It's not fair, though. When I think of Helen and all the promise life held for her, I feel sick – actually sick. Why did this happen? Why the *hell* did this happen?'

Orla reached out and touched his shoulder, wishing she had an answer for him, but there wasn't one. Life could be cruel, and that was it.

'I miss her,' she said quietly as they walked on.

'You do?'

'I really do. It might seem strange to say that because I know I never met her, but I really feel the loss of her presence.' Orla paused. 'I'm not upsetting you, saying that, am I?'

Luke shook his head. 'No.'

She could hear the emotion in his voice.

'She was a special person and I miss her in my life, even if that was only connecting through Galleria photos and exchanging the odd message.'

'Isn't that how so many friendships are made these days?' Luke said.

'Yes. I suppose they are.'

They walked on for a bit, listening to the roar of the waves as they neared the shore.

'Did she ever tell you about her twenty-eighth birthday party?' Luke suddenly asked.

'No.'

'Well, it fell on a Saturday and she was behaving all moody in the morning because I was making out that I'd forgotten.'

'Oh, Luke! That's so mean!'

'I know. It was a bit, but I had something planned. I told her to come with me into town because I had to pick up some tools and wood and needed her help carrying it all. Well, she wasn't pleased, but she came along.'

'You seriously made her haul wood around on her birthday?'

Luke grinned, obviously enjoying telling the story. 'Ah, but wait! After we picked everything up, I told her I had to deliver some of it to this pub ahead of starting a job. I was worried that she'd guess what I was up to, but her miserable face proved to me that she didn't have a clue.'

Orla gasped. 'You are a cruel man!'

'I know. I know. But it was all worth it when we went in carrying this massive length of wood, only to be greeted by about twenty friends and family all yelling, "Surprise!" You should have seen her face!'

Orla laughed. 'I wish I had.'

'Of course, she was mad at me for not telling her to wear something nicer, but we'd been—'

'Hauling wood around!' Orla said.

'Exactly!'

'That's a rotten trick, Luke! I would've been mad too.'

'But that moment when she saw everyone in the restaurant. She really thought I'd forgotten her birthday. But everyone was there, and there were balloons and cake and candles. The works!' He laughed at the memory. 'I *think* she forgave me.'

'I'm sure she did.'

They stopped for a moment and gazed out to sea, watching a pair of gulls riding the wind.

'Luke?'

'Yes?'

'I didn't know whether to tell you this or not,' she began hesitantly.

'What?'

'You've been sleepwalking.'

Luke looked at her, his eyes still bright with tears. 'You're kidding?'

'Several times now.'

He looked confused. 'Where – how?'

'I've found you sitting in the dark in the great hall a couple of times and, the other night, you were lighting candles.'

'Candles?'

'Perhaps for Helen's birthday?' Orla suggested, now that she had that piece of information.

'It doesn't seem like me.'

'But you're not quite *you* at the moment, are you?' Orla said gently.

Luke closed his eyes. 'No, I suppose not.'

'You've got to be kind to yourself. Make sure you're sleeping well and eating well. Take lots of long walks. Go out and see things. Take time to find yourself.'

He took a deep breath. 'Everything I do seems sad now because it isn't with Helen.'

'Oh, Luke!'

'I've been trying to focus on my work and – well – that's good and it works sometimes. But she's never very far away and I don't want to block her out.'

'And you shouldn't.' Orla watched as Luke gazed out to sea, his brow furrowed with pain. She had an incredible urge to smooth out the skin with her fingers and thought how very like her own damaged skin it looked and how they'd both been hurt and scarred by life.

'I don't know how to do this,' Luke said in a voice barely audible above the waves.

Orla completely understood because, in her own way, she had been there too, only she'd been mourning the loss of her face.

'One day at a time,' she told him. 'That's how you do it.'

He lowered his head as if taking a moment to process this and then he gazed out to sea again, just as One Ear came splashing in the surf towards them, barking at a pair of gulls who were so tantalisingly close and yet so frustratingly far away.

Luke nodded. 'One day at a time.'

Chapter 15

Bill stuck his garden fork in the newly turned earth and stretched his back.

'I don't think I should ask her,' he told Margy as she handed him a mug of tea.

'Well, I think you *should*,' Margy told him. 'It could be just the thing she needs to integrate into village life.'

'But she's doing that naturally on her own. I don't want to push her.'

'You won't be. You'll be offering her an opportunity. It'll be up to her to take it up or turn it down.'

Bill pursed his lips. He didn't like this. Orla was just beginning to trust him and to find her own way back into society. If he dared to push things too quickly too soon, she could easily revert back to her old ways. That was his fear anyway.

'I'm not happy about this,' he told his wife.

'I know you're not. But you can't expect Mildred to do it, can you? She's got enough on her plate and, anyway, you know Orla and she knows you. It'll be better coming from you.'

Bill took a sip of his tea, silently cursing Mildred Smy. Not that it was her fault really. She was merely carrying out what needed to be done. It was just unfortunate that Bill had been roped into this.

'Bill – you've got to do it! If you don't, who else will? Everyone's still a bit scared of Orla.'

'That's nonsense. She's a lovely woman.'

'Yes, well, we know that now, but others don't, do they? She's still the mysterious woman who locks herself away in the spooky old castle, isn't she?'

Bill hadn't thought about it like that. 'I suppose she might seem odd.'

'Oh, Bill! You *know* that's odd. You never stopped going on about it when she first moved here. You said she must be a very peculiar sort not to even bother to say hello to her own gardener. Those were your exact words. *A very peculiar sort!*'

'Margy, shush! For goodness' sake!' Bill said, terrified that the neighbours were out in their gardens and would hear and that word would get back to Orla.

'You know it's true, and you can't blame people for still having – well – misgivings about her. Lorford is a small community and even people who are never seen get noticed.'

Bill frowned.

'Oh, you know what I mean.'

Unfortunately, Bill did. Word soon got around when a property went up for sale, and eager eyes would watch to see the new arrivals. It wasn't just nosiness, but genuine interest in one's neighbours. After all, why would somebody move to a small place like Lorford unless they were going to be sociable? It was why it had been particularly galling to the community when the castle had been sold to a recluse. It had been the main topic of conversation for months as people had speculated about the new owner. And now word was out that she was making herself known and excitement was at an all-time high, although fear was in the mix too, it seemed.

'Okay, I'll do it,' he said at last.

Margy crossed the space between them and stood on tiptoes to give him a kiss.

'You taste of earth,' she said.

'Sorry.'

'No, I like it!'

He smiled and watched as she went back inside with his empty mug, her mission accomplished. Bill sighed. He still didn't like the idea, but he'd do it, and the sooner he got it over and done with, the better, so he brushed the earth from his trousers, cleaned his fork meticulously before putting it away in the shed and went inside to change clothes.

He left the house half an hour later, hair brushed and shirt collar straightened by Margy.

'Just be you,' she'd told him. 'She likes you.'

She might not after what he had to ask, he thought to himself ruefully.

Approaching the castle, he felt like a schoolboy called up to see the head teacher. There was something about being in the presence of the castle when one wasn't invited that was especially intimidating. Perhaps that was another reason why Orla had chosen to live there. It would be a brave person who would just show up and ring that big old bell, wouldn't it?

Bill had never rung the bell at the front door before, although he had been inside that time he'd helped Orla bring Luke back from the beach. That dreadful day seemed like an age ago now and he couldn't help thinking how much had changed in that time with both of them becoming such a part of his life now.

And I might be about to ruin it all, he thought to himself, taking a deep breath and ringing the bell.

Instantly, he heard One Ear and it wasn't long before he heard Orla's voice on the other side of the door.

'Who is it?'

'Orla? It's me – Bill. Bill Wilson.'

'Bill?' Orla said. 'Quiet, One Ear – it's only Bill.'

He heard the sound of a bolt drawing across and a key being turned.

'Hello,' he said a moment later, nodding to her. 'I'm sorry to disturb you, but I was wondering if I could have a word.'

'Is it about the garden?'

'Erm, no. Village business, you might say.'

'Oh, how mysterious!' Orla said with a sweet smile. 'Do you want to come in?'

Bill peered around her shoulder at the great cavernous space of the room behind her.

'Garden, I think,' he said. 'If that's okay with you?'

'Of course,' Orla said. 'I'll just grab my hat.'

Bill took a few deep breaths as he waited. He would feel more at home in the garden, he thought. It would, at least, be one less thing to be anxious about.

A moment later, and they were sitting on the bench that Bill was fast thinking of as 'their' bench.

'Bill, what is it? You look all tied up in knots.'

He blinked, surprised that his demeanour betrayed his inner turmoil so readily.

After a bit of throat clearing and boot shuffling, he began. 'I have a question to ask you.'

'Okay.'

'A request, rather.'

'All right.'

'Now, before I ask it, I have to let you know that I'm dead against asking you this. I don't think it's fair and you have every right to say no.'

'Bill, you're making me nervous now.'

'Sorry.'

'Just ask me!' she said, her eyes wide and anxious.

Bill took one last deep breath. 'Mildred Smy – you've not met her, I think – well, she runs the village show. Has done for as long as any of us can remember, and she's a great one for getting people involved – for giving people little jobs to do. One of life's natural organisers, you know? Well, she's got it into her head that she wants photos – professional-quality photos – taken of the show this year.'

'When's the show?'

'Next week. And, well, she wanted me to ask if you'd do the honours.' He paused, a sense of dread filling him, but at least he'd done his bit now. He couldn't be asked to do more.

'How did this Mildred know I'm a photographer?' Orla asked.

Bill shifted uneasily. 'It's something Luke mentioned to me at the first horticultural meeting. I guess someone overheard us talking about it, and you know what a village is like – word soon gets around.'

'Oh, I see.'

'I'm sorry to put you on the spot like this,' he said, shuffling his boots again. 'Please say no if it's not your thing.'

Orla didn't say anything for a moment.

'It's not your thing, is it?' Bill asked.

'I didn't say that!'

'But you're thinking it, aren't you? I knew it was wrong to ask you. I'm so sorry, Orla. I didn't want to put this pressure on you.' He stood up, ready to leave.

'Bill – I haven't said no yet.'

He turned and looked at her. 'No?'

'But I haven't said yes either. Can I think about it? How long do I have to decide?'

'Knowing Mildred, not long.'

'Give me tonight, okay? And I promise I'll get back to you by morning.'

201

Bill puffed out his cheeks. 'It's more than I'd hoped for. You're a good woman.'

'Am I?'

'Of course you are,' Bill said, smiling at last. 'But you obviously need a few more people to tell you that. Maybe you'll find them at the village show, eh?' He dared to wink at her, and she laughed.

'Maybe.'

It was late afternoon when Luke went to find Orla.

'Hey,' he said, entering the china room, where she was dusting one of the shelves. 'Fancy a trip out somewhere?'

'In the van?'

'Yep.'

'Can One Ear come?'

'Of course.'

'Let me grab my hat.'

Five minutes later, the three of them were in the van and heading out of Lorford.

'Had a good day?' Luke asked her.

'I saw Bill earlier,' she told him.

'Oh, yes? Is he okay?'

'He had a proposition for me.'

'Sounds interesting.'

'That's what I thought.'

'It wasn't?'

'Oh, it was interesting all right, but I'm not sure it's right for me.'

'Tell me.'

'Bill asked if I'd be interested in photographing the local village show next week.'

'And what did you say?'

'I said I'd think about it.'

'So what do you think?'

'My initial response was to run for the hills.'

'I don't think there are many of those in East Anglia!'

'No,' Orla agreed with a laugh. 'What do you think I should do?'

'Well, do you *want* to do it?'

'Not really.'

'Then say no.'

'But Bill's been so kind to me.'

'Then say yes.'

'But I'm scared. I don't know what to do.'

Luke shook his head. 'If you really want my opinion, I think you should do it.'

'Really?'

'I think it would do you good. You've had that camera of yours pressed to your face for so long that you've forgotten there's a whole world beyond it.'

'But I'd still have it pressed to my face if I did this job.'

'Yes, but there'd be people on the other side of it instead of china cups.'

'Don't remind me!'

'It'll be fun!'

Orla stared out of the window as they passed through a deep green wood which cast its shade across the road.

'I did used to love photographing people,' she confessed.

'Well, this could be your way back to that.'

'But I don't want to go back to my old job.'

'Orla – in case you hadn't noticed – you've been asked to photograph a few villagers at a local show, not do an eight-page spread for some highfalutin magazine.'

'I know. But it seems like a very big deal when I've only been photographing cups and saucers for the last couple of years.'

They drove on in silence for a few moments.

'I've got it!' Luke said at last.

'What?'

'Practise on me.'

'What do you mean?'

'Photograph *me*!'

'Are you serious?'

'I'm not saying I'm the world's greatest model, but I'm sure I can keep still long enough for you to take a few shots.'

Orla turned to face him. 'You'd do that for me?'

'Sure, it'll be fun.' He waited for her response. 'So are we on?'

'I suppose we could give it a go.'

After a brisk walk on the heath, they returned to the castle and Orla went to get her camera. Luke, who was suddenly feeling a little self-conscious, went to brush his hair and change his shirt. Why on earth had he volunteered to do this, he wondered? Well, it was to help a friend and put her at ease. Kind of ironic that it was *him* who now needed to be put at ease.

They met up in the great hall a few minutes later and he saw Orla was wearing her camera around her neck.

'No putting these up online,' he joked.

'I wouldn't!' she said.

'Yeah, I'm not as pretty as your china cups.'

She cast him a sympathetic look. 'Nonsense! But you might look a bit out of place on my Galleria feed amongst all the crockery and flowers.'

'Okay, how do you want me?'

'How about leaning against the wall by the window?'

Luke moved towards the wall. 'Here?'

Orla nodded, her camera in front of her face as she took the first photo. Luke stood perfectly still, scared to do something that might displease her.

'You can move,' she said. 'Just be natural.'

'I can't be natural – I've got a camera pointing in my face.'

Orla shook her head. 'I thought this was your way to encourage me to relax.'

'I know,' he said. 'I'm sorry.' He rolled his head from side to side and tried again. 'How about this?' He fixed a smile on his face. Orla lowered her camera and cocked her head to one side. 'Too much of a rictus grin?'

'*Little* bit! Just try to relax.'

Luke nodded.

'You don't need to smile at all. It's probably best if you don't.'

'Have I got a bad smile?'

'No! I didn't mean that. You've got a lovely smile, but it's easier, more natural, if you relax your face. Look out of the window or find something in the room to look at.'

Luke did what he was told, fixing his gaze on a spot in the garden far below the castle window and, after a little while, he almost forgot that he was being photographed.

'That's it,' Orla told him. 'Just hold that for a little longer. And – yes! I think that might do for a first round.'

'Can I look?'

Orla unhooked the camera strap from her neck and Luke looked at the images on the screen, his eyes narrowing as he took them in.

'Wow! Do I really look like that?'

'Of course you do. What did you think you looked like?'

'I don't know. Not that serious, I guess.'

'Did Helen never photograph you?'

'Not like this. I was usually grinning like an idiot on days out.'

'She never took portraits of you?'

'She was more into her trees and landscapes, you know? And I've never been a fan of the official portrait.'

'How did it feel?' she asked him.

'Shouldn't the question be how did it feel *for you*?'

Orla chewed her bottom lip. 'I think I liked it.'

'You sounded as if you did.'

'Did I?'

'Yes. You sounded happy. Slightly bossy.'

'I was not!'

Luke laughed at her obvious discomfort. 'I mean, you're a good director. You put me at my ease.'

'And you put me at mine.'

'So – mission accomplished?' he dared to ask.

'You mean I should take this assignment at the village show?'

He shrugged, trying not to make too big a deal out of it. 'Up to you.'

Orla looked down at her camera, scrolling through the photos she'd just taken.

'I suppose I *could* give it a go.'

'Yeah?'

She nodded. 'Yes.' Her face lit up and her eyes looked almost mischievous but, as quickly as that look of joy came, it vanished, as a dark cloud of fear and insecurity crossed her face. She looked so totally childlike that it made Luke feel instantly protective of her.

'Orla? What's the matter?'

She looked up at him, her face pale and anxious. 'What if I'm making a terrible mistake?'

Chapter 16

The village hall was packed. It looked as if the whole of Lorford was crammed in there, and how splendid it looked. Long tables had been laid with white tablecloths, where vases burst with floral displays and pretty plates proudly showed home-made biscuits, brownies and other scrumptious delights. Orla took a few photographs, marvelling at a particularly shiny chocolate cake and a sumptuous Victoria sponge which seemed to defy gravity.

The children had their own section, which was full of creative fun, and there were plenty of the makers running around the hall. Orla had done her best to capture them. There was one very sweet girl wearing a pink tutu, but she just wouldn't keep still. Orla smiled, acknowledging the fact that, when photographing, things were always much easier than people. You could never guarantee that a person would do what you wanted them to do, whereas a jug or a bowl or a cup would stay put and wouldn't frown or go off in a strop or ruin your picture by not cooperating.

Other than her practice session with Luke, Orla hadn't photographed a person since before her acid attack and the thought of doing so now terrified her, but she needn't have worried about drawing attention to herself; everybody seemed preoccupied with doing their own thing. Everybody except Mildred Smy, whom Orla had been introduced to by Bill just before the village hall opened its doors to the public. She was heading towards Orla now. A handsome woman in her late sixties, she was wearing a smart dress in a particularly hideous shade of green and her platinum hair was swept up in a severe chignon.

'Ah, Miss Kendrick! Is there anything I can get you? A cup of tea, perhaps? A slice of cake?'

'I'm fine, thank you.'

'Well, you're doing a sterling job. *Sterling!*' She gave a tight, uneasy smile and then bustled off into the room again.

Orla took a deep breath. She could do this, she told herself. These were good people – they weren't a threat to her. They were her neighbours. But then a man walked up the steps onto the stage and called for everyone's attention.

'We're about to announce the prizes!' he called out. 'Please help me in gathering everybody inside.'

Orla turned to see a few people leaving the village hall and realised that the room hadn't been full to capacity, as it had seemed to her. But it was about to get very full indeed as a surge of people filed in from the tables of bric-a-brac and the entertainments outside. The noise level rose steadily and the warm day seemed even warmer now. Orla looked around the room in panic. The door seemed a very long way away, but she knew she had to get through it.

'Orla?'

She heard Luke calling from somewhere behind her as she fled. She didn't stop, pushing her way through the throng until she was out of the village hall, and into the relative peace and space of the road beyond.

'Orla!'

Her heart was thudding and she felt hot and chilled at the same time as her breath left her body in great gasps.

'Are you okay?' Luke was beside her now, his hand on her shoulder. 'Let's get you home.'

'I'm sorry.'

'It's okay.'

'I couldn't do it.'

'It's fine. Nobody will mind.'

'But I made a commitment.'

'Don't worry. You did your best.'

Orla felt her eyes filling with tears of frustration at her failure.

'Orla – really – you did so well. I'm so proud of you!'

Orla let Luke take her back to the castle, and relief flooded her as soon as she was through the door. What had she been thinking? She knew she should never have agreed to such an assignment, and yet there was a part of her that longed to reach out and be a normal, functioning member of society again.

Only perhaps not just yet, a little voice said.

Luke made her a cup of tea and Orla sat in the blissful silence of the great hall, One Ear by her side, as if he knew she needed the physical comfort of his great body.

When Orla's mobile rang, she picked it up and looked at the screen. It was her mother. Quickly, without giving it a moment's thought, Orla switched her phone off. Today had tested her quite enough already.

The next day, Luke returned to his work in the castle, which meant venturing down to the basement and the mysterious section of board which somebody had seen fit to place against the stonework. He wasn't sure what he was going to find behind it. It could be anything really.

Carefully, slowly, he began to prise the board away from the wall, revealing the pale Caen stone which had been hidden for so long. Why would somebody just section a random length of wall, he wondered? It didn't make any sense. At least, it didn't until he pulled the last of the board away.

For a stunned moment, Luke just stared. What he'd revealed left him speechless, and he gazed at it for a long time, not quite knowing what he was looking at. He certainly hadn't ever come across anything like this before in the Home Counties he usually worked in.

There was only one thing he could do.

'*Orla?*' he shouted from the basement. Then, climbing a few steps, he shouted again. 'ORLA!' Honestly, he thought, there really should be some kind of bell or phone system in the castle for such emergencies. Luckily, One Ear heard his bellowing and started to bark, and it wasn't long before he heard Orla's footsteps.

'Luke? You down there?'

'Yes! Come and see what I've found.'

One Ear arrived first, charging down the spiral steps like a hairy cannonball. He was quickly followed by Orla, whose face was flushed from her exertion.

'What is it? What's happened?'

'I think you're going to want to see this.' He motioned towards the wall. 'Remember it was boarded up? Well, this was what was behind it.'

Orla's mouth fell open as she stared in wide-eyed wonder. 'What on earth?'

'Did you know this was here?' Luke asked.

'*No.* I'm not even sure what it is.'

'Some kind of green man?' Luke guessed.

Orla inched forward, bending down to take a closer look. The figure was no more than a foot high, carved from the beautifully pale Caen stone and looking so alive that Luke could well imagine him leaping out from the wall at any moment.

'I'm not sure it is a green man,' Orla said. 'There aren't any leaves around him.'

Luke took a step closer. 'He seems to be made completely of hair.'

Orla shook her head. 'Not just hair – scales too.'

'Really?' Luke examined it again. 'You think that's what they are?' He reached out to touch them. 'Not just some random pattern?'

'I don't think there's anything random in its execution, do you?'

'I suppose not. It's just so strange. I was expecting to find a large damp patch, not a work of art like this.'

He took in the strange human-like face surrounded by a wilderness of long hair which flowed down over the scaly body. It had two thick arms and two chunky legs ending in a pair of feet, but there was something about it – an eerie quality – which gave the impression that it wasn't altogether human.

'I wonder how old it is and what it means,' Orla said. 'Do you think anyone in the village will know?'

'I'd say it's been hidden for a fair few years, but we could ask Bill, couldn't we?'

'Good idea. He's been in Lorford all his life. If anybody will know, it'll be Bill.'

Orla was the one to ring Bill, calling his mobile number for the first time.

'I can pop over right now if you like,' he told her. 'I'm just at the allotment. Give me ten minutes to put my tools away.'

Sure enough, ten minutes later and he was knocking on the door, setting One Ear off and alerting Orla to his arrival. He looked anxious, standing there, his cap in his hand as if he was about to enter a holy place.

'Come on in, Bill.'

'Everything all right? Young Luke okay?'

'Oh, he's fine. He's discovered something in the basement and we'd like you to take a look.'

Bill blinked. 'Nothing wrong, is there?'

Orla looked at Bill's anxious face. 'Don't worry! We haven't discovered any old bones. Although I suppose it is a body of sorts.' She laughed as he blanched. 'Come on – I'll show you.'

She led Bill towards the stairs, venturing down into the coolness below, where Luke was examining the wall around the strange carved figure.

'Hey, Bill,' Luke said, briefly looking up.

'Good Lord!' Bill said as soon as he clapped eyes on it.

'It's quite something, isn't it?' Orla said.

Bill scratched his head and looked at the room and the board which Luke had removed.

'I'm taking it you've just uncovered this thing.'

'Yes. Not what I was expecting to find. What do you make of it? We're hoping we can find out something about it.'

Bill looked at the carving and shook his head. 'Remarkable. I think you've got something a bit special here.'

'Any idea what it is?' Orla asked.

'I'd hazard a guess that what we're looking at is a representation of the Wild Man of Lorford.'

'Wild Man?' Luke said.

'It's part of Lorford legend.'

'Do you know much about it?' Orla asked.

'Only what most folks know, that in medieval times – thirteenth century, I think, but I never was much for remembering dates and the like – a wild man of the sea was hauled up by

212

fishermen. Nobody knew where he came from or if it was human or fish or something of the two.'

'A merman?' Orla suggested.

'Your guess is as good as anyone's,' Bill said.

'What happened to him?' Luke asked.

'Ah, well, that's where my knowledge of him begins and ends.'

'Oh,' Orla said, frustrated.

'Sorry to disappoint you,' Bill told her. 'Is there nothing in the castle's records?'

'Not that I remember,' Orla said. 'Nobody mentioned this was hidden away in the basement.'

'That's a shame. The man who owned the place before you didn't really live here at all. He had a bit of work done on it, but he spent most of his time in Italy. I don't suppose he knew it was here either.'

Bill took a closer look at it, a frown of concentration on his face. 'You know, there is someone who might know a bit more about this.'

'Who, Bill?' Orla asked.

Bill pursed his lips, looking as if he wanted to keep the information locked inside them.

'Cranbrook. Ernest Cranbrook. Local historian. Used to live in The Saltings – the big house by the quay – but moved inland after his wife died.'

'Have you a number for him?' Luke asked.

'No, but I know where he lives. We could take a chance and call round. But I should warn you . . .'

'About what?' Luke asked.

'He's a little . . . What's the polite way of saying it? Eccentric.'

Orla smiled. 'That's okay,' she told him. 'I totally get eccentric!'

'You're okay going, then?' Luke asked her.

Orla nodded. She could feel her heart racing, but knew it was with excitement about finding out more about the castle as it was about nerves in leaving its safety.

It didn't take long for the three of them to leave the castle. A short drive in Luke's van took them to the tiny hamlet of Sidbourne, with its fine flint church and a huddle of houses overlooking a green.

'It's that one there,' Bill said, pointing to a red-brick cottage with a wonky chimney and an overgrown garden.

'Ah,' Luke said.

'Shocking, isn't it?' Bill said, shaking his head in despair. 'Before his wife died, she was a passionate gardener. The Saltings was always immaculate. But it was all left to go over after she passed. Used to drive Mildred Smy nuts. She was always banging on doors, trying to get people to keep their gardens neat and tidy. "For the greater good," she'd say. I think she was relieved when Ernest sold up and moved out here.'

The three of them got out of the van and Bill walked ahead, opening a gate that was only half on its hinges and heading up a path made of brick but which had disappeared under a sea of weeds long ago. Bill tutted.

'Breaks my heart. I should come out here and take it in hand.'

He approached the front door. Luke followed next, with Orla behind him. She had grabbed a favourite hat at the last minute but had decided not to hide behind sunglasses.

Bill rapped on the door, which was sun-bleached and had flaking paint. Orla noticed net curtains at the windows which were decidedly grubby. Or maybe that was the windows. Or possibly both.

Bill knocked again and, when the door opened, a curly-haired man wearing tiny round glasses stared at them. He was probably about the same age as Bill, but that's where the resemblance ended.

Whereas Bill always looked completely present and alert, this man looked a little glazed and vague, but his smile was a welcoming one.

'Yes? Can I help you?'

'Ernest? It's Bill. From Lorford.'

Ernest frowned. 'Bill . . . Wilson!'

'That's right.'

'Always loved that name. A good rhyming sound. Bill *Wil*son!' Orla smiled.

'And these are my friends – Luke and Orla.'

They both came forward and shook hands.

'Good to meet you,' Ernest said.

'Orla owns the castle now,' Bill went on.

'Does she, indeed?' Ernest's small eyes lit up behind his glasses.

'Actually, it's that we've come to talk to you about.'

Ernest nodded, his smile still in place, but didn't make a move to invite them in.

'Can we – er – come in?' Bill tried.

'Oh, yes. Of course. Forgive me. Where are my manners? Come in. Come in!' He opened the door wider and they all entered a dark, narrow hallway lined with books, only there weren't shelves or bookcases – only the books themselves, stacked in teetering, tottering piles. Orla glanced at Luke, whose eyes betrayed his amusement.

As they walked down the hall, Orla noticed a door open into a room on the left which, like the hallway, was full of books. These, though, looked a little more organised, sitting on shelves. There was also a single wooden chair and a telescope. That was all.

'This way,' Ernest said, leading them into what, in a normal home, might be a sitting room but was yet another room full of books. 'There's a sofa in here somewhere,' he told them, obviously aware of what the room must look like to visitors.

Bill came forward and moved a heap of newspapers and note-books. There were so many notebooks, all of differing sizes, and Orla couldn't help noticing that the ones that had been left open were full of neat, tiny writing in blue ink. Luke and Orla helped, carefully taking an armful of the books away, placing them on the floor.

'Ah – *there* it is!' Ernest said with a winning smile once the sofa was revealed. 'I can't remember the last time I saw it. Do please sit. Can I get you anything? What is it young people drink these days? I'm sure I could find a teabag of some description.'

'Oh, no – really,' Luke quickly interceded.

'No need to go to any trouble,' Orla agreed, secretly dreading what Ernest Cranbrook's kitchen looked like and not wishing to consume anything that might come out of it.

'We were just hoping for a bit of information,' Bill began as he sat down on the sagging sofa. 'Orla – would you like to tell him what you've discovered?'

'Yes,' she said, sitting next to Bill as Luke examined a couple of old prints on the mantelpiece. 'We've uncovered a rather unusual carving in the basement of the castle. What used to be the dungeon. It was covered up. Luke's just found it. It's carved at the bottom of an arch and looks pretty old.'

'And what does it depict?' Ernest asked.

'Well, I think it might be the Wild Man,' Bill said.

'I had a feeling you were going to say that,' Ernest told him, nodding to himself as he moved across the room towards a precarious tower of books. 'Now, then – where is it? I know it's here somewhere.'

Orla glanced at Luke again and they exchanged a bemused look. Did this man *really* know where all his books were? It seemed unlikely and yet there was a decided purpose about him and, sure enough, he pulled a book out with a triumphant cry. '*The Wild*

Man of the Sea! A Tale of the Suffolk Coast.' He handed the old hardback with the ripped cover to Bill, who flipped through it before handing it to Orla. It was a grubby-looking tome with pages that were yellowing and mottled, but there were some very good illustrations inside of green men, hairy beasts and something that bore a striking resemblance to her very own Wild Man.

'Could we show you our Wild Man?' Orla asked him.

'At the castle?' Ernest said.

'Yes.'

'We could take you there now,' Luke said, on his feet in an instant. 'That is, if you're not doing anything.'

Ernest smiled. 'My dear man,' he said, taking his round glasses off and polishing them with a hanky pulled from his pocket, 'I haven't been doing anything for the last seven years.'

Chapter 17

While Orla's first experience of taking a trip in Luke's van had been absolutely terrifying, Ernest Cranbrook's was one of great joy.

'Well, I say! This *is* exciting,' he said from the back seat, where he sat next to Bill. 'I haven't been to the castle for years. Not since I was a boy and we'd sneak into the garden at night. Remember, Bill?'

Bill gave a funny little cough.

'What's that, Bill?' Luke asked, glancing in the rear-view mirror.

'Just boy stuff,' Bill said elusively.

'We used to go scrumping, didn't we, Billy?' Ernest said with a chuckle. 'Apples, pears, cherries – you name it!'

'There was an orchard?' Orla asked.

'Long gone,' Bill said.

'What a shame.'

'Indeed,' Bill said.

'Used to fill our bellies in there,' Ernest confessed just as they reached Lorford.

Luke was still chuckling to himself as they drove through the market square, pulling into the castle's driveway a moment later.

One Ear was thrilled to see the new arrival and made sure every pocket of Ernest's waistcoat was sniffed and prodded in case there were hidden biscuits. Then it was down to business. Down to the basement.

'What a treat this is,' Ernest kept saying. 'A real treat!' His pink cheeks glowed with anticipation as they descended the spiral stairs in a slow single file. One Ear, eager not to miss out, followed at a sedate pace.

'Well, here it is,' Luke announced as they reached their destination.

For a few moments, all was quiet as Ernest bent double to examine the carved figure, his small eyes squinting and widening and his mouth muttering something only he could hear.

'What do you think?' Luke asked at last. Orla had been watching him and had seen his nervousness. He was even keener than her to hear about the carving, perhaps feeling a kind of kinship with it for having discovered it.

'Yes, we'd love to know,' Orla said.

Ernest stood back up to full height and gave his curly hair a ruffle as if dislodging his thoughts.

'Interesting. *Very* interesting!'

'Yes, we know that,' Luke said, clearly getting irritated now. 'But what *is* it exactly?'

One Ear gave a bark, as if agreeing that the time had come for a full architectural disclosure.

'I would say that what you have here is twelfth century,' Ernest said quietly, each word calm and measured now, his earlier excitement having abated somewhat.

'The castle's twelfth century, isn't it, Orla?' Luke asked.

'Yes.'

'Exactly so,' Ernest said. 'Is it the only one of its kind?'

'I haven't come across any others,' Orla said, 'and I've had a pretty good look around.'

'Me too,' Luke said. 'This was the only section boarded up so, unless there's any hiding behind plaster, I'd say it's a one-off.'

'I think you're right.' Ernest fell silent again, stepping forward and reaching a tentative hand towards the carving and gently touching the flowing hair upon the strange creature's head. Orla noticed that Ernest was still wearing a wedding ring and, remembering that he'd lost his wife some years ago, felt a weight of sadness in her heart that there was so much loss in the world.

'What are you thinking, Mr Cranbrook?' Orla asked gently, not wanting to interrupt his thoughts.

'My first thought was that it was a wodewose.'

'A what?' Bill asked.

'Wodewose. A wild man of the woods,' Ernest said. 'But they were carved in the fifteenth century. They're popular figures on fonts around the county and were thought to be mythical creatures in the same vein as wyverns and the like, although some believe them to be real. Early man in all his innocence. Or depravity – depending on how you look at things. But this is different. It's earlier and the figure isn't holding the club that wodewoses usually hold and, although his body is covered in hair, there are scales too – see.'

Everybody moved forward to look.

'I thought they were scales,' Orla said as she peered closely, observing the rounded shapes which covered the legs and arms of the figure.

'I didn't notice those before,' Bill said. 'You think he's some sort of merman from the sea, then?'

'It would certainly fit in with the legend of the Wild Man of Lorford and, as far as we know, the creature – whatever it was – was brought here to the castle after he was captured in the fishermen's nets.'

'He was *here*?' Orla said, eyes wide.

'Yes, and not treated well, it's said. He was tied up, hung upside down and tortured.'

'Oh, how horrible!'

'They were trying to make him talk, but he had no language,' Ernest went on. 'He was more beast than human, they said. Ate raw fish, squeezing out the blood into his mouth before crunching them, bones and all.'

'Nice!' Luke said.

'No different from One Ear,' Orla pointed out. 'What happened to him?'

Ernest removed his glasses and rubbed his eyes before cleaning his glasses with his handkerchief again.

'It's thought that they soon tired of the Wild Man. Not getting any answers from him, they released him into the river. It's said that he stayed close to the shore for some time, as if not wanting to leave the company of men, but then he disappeared into the depths of the water from whence he'd come.'

'And you truly think this is him and that he was actually here in this very room?' Orla asked.

'I do, and contemporary to the story too, which is particularly exciting.'

Bill scratched his head. 'Aren't there some wild-men-type things on the church font?'

'Wodewoses,' Ernest said. 'It would be worth you paying a visit to compare them to this fine fellow of yours. I'll warrant they don't have his marvellous scales.'

'Could we go there now?' Orla suggested. 'To the church?'

Luke looked surprised by her suggestion to leave the castle twice in one day, but readily said, 'We could stop there before taking you back home, Mr Cranbrook.'

'Wonderful idea,' Ernest said. 'And thank you so much for showing me this jewel. It's the most marvellous thing!'

As they left the castle, Luke sidled up to Orla.

'Two trips in one day?' he said.

'I know. I simply can't help myself!'

He laughed. 'It's great.'

She smiled, feeling the joy that this new-found freedom was giving her.

Orla had never been inside the church before; although she'd photographed the ancient building many times, she'd always done it from the shaded footpath, where she could remain unseen by anyone who might just happen to be around. But she entered the building now with Luke, Bill and Ernest and made her way towards the font, which stood proudly on an octagonal base carved from pale stone.

'Look at these!' Luke cried. 'They're just like our chap at the castle.'

'Well, not exactly,' Ernest said, bending to examine the four wild men depicted on the staves of the white stone font. 'They're three hundred years younger, for a start.'

'And they don't have our Wild Man's scales. They're all hair,' Orla pointed out, noting the wavy lines carved into the stone.

'Exactly so,' Ernest said. 'Quite a different beast altogether. These are the wodewoses or wild men of the woods. Yours is *the* Wild Man of Lorford, I think we can be quite sure of that. It may well have influenced these ones – legends often pass through the generations via architecture, but I have a feeling that these wild men are something else. More akin to the green man stories.'

'You know, I've never really looked at these,' Bill said. 'Or the lions.'

Orla looked at the finely carved lions that flanked the wild men. There were four each around the base of the font, making a wonderful display with their thick manes and regal faces, which were almost smiling at them through the centuries.

'One does tend to take the gems on one's own doorstep for granted,' Ernest said.

The men talked some more, but Orla found herself turning away from the font and walking towards the altar. A shaft of afternoon light lanced through one of the stained-glass windows, throwing pools of colour onto the stone floor. Orla stood in the middle of the rainbowed silence, berating the fact that she had never seen it all before. She would have to come back with her camera and capture some of its beauty. Not for Galleria, of course, because it would give too much away. The pictures would just be for herself – for the joy of capturing a moment of loveliness and for preserving it for ever, much as the sculptors had done with their lions and wild men carved into stone.

'Orla? I'm going to run Mr Cranbrook home now. Coming?'

Orla looked up at the hammer beam ceiling, the intricate carving of the rood screen and a pair of brass figures that she just had to get closer to, and knew she wasn't ready to leave yet.

'I'll walk home,' she told Luke.

'You sure?'

She nodded, and Ernest Cranbrook came forward and took her hands in his.

'Thank you, my dear. It's been so much fun! You will let me know if you uncover any other treasures now, won't you?'

'You'll be the first to know,' she promised him, watching as they all left, Bill throwing her a nod and smile. And then she was left in the silence.

The church was about the same age as the castle, Orla had read. She could feel the kinship of the two buildings, and a sense of pride swelled inside her that she owned one of them. She couldn't help feeling a little guilty, though, that her special home wasn't open to the public so that they could enjoy the delights inside it as they could with the church, but that couldn't be helped, could it? Orla could think of nothing worse than a stream of people coming through her front door.

It was funny that Orla should have such a thought because, a few days later, she noticed a couple of people outside her front gate.

'Do you know them?' Luke asked her as he joined her by the window.

'Of course not.'

'Shall I see what they want?' he asked. 'They're probably just tourists wanting a picture.'

Orla wasn't convinced and shrank back from the window as Luke left the castle. When he came back, he wasn't smiling.

'What is it?'

'They want to see the Wild Man,' Luke told her.

Orla frowned. 'How do they know about that?'

Luke shrugged. 'I don't think Ernest would've said anything, would he? Bill probably mentioned it to Margy, but surely she wouldn't go telling everyone private details about your home to the whole village.'

'But she wouldn't need to, would she?'

'What do you mean?'

'She or Bill or Ernest would only have to tell one other person and then they would tell another and it would be round the whole of Lorford before you knew it.'

'Yes. I see your point.'

Orla sneaked a peak out of the window again. 'Luke – there are even more people now – look!'

He glanced out of the window again and saw that the group had swelled to half a dozen.

'What do you want to do?' he asked.

'What do you mean?'

'Shall we let them in?'

Orla swallowed hard. 'In . . . the castle?'

'They're just neighbours, and they're genuinely curious. They don't mean any harm. Word's obviously got around and I really think they're fascinated by what we've got here.'

Orla looked down from the window at the little crowd of strangers who were expecting to gain entry into her home.

'Look – you don't need to be involved in this if you don't want to,' Luke said, obviously sensing her deep unease. 'I can show them in. They can access the basement without coming through the main rooms and you won't need to see them at all. What do you say?'

She looked at his face – at the bright eyes filled with such life and enthusiasm to share this wonderful thing they'd found with others. The old Orla would have shouted and screamed at Luke for the mere suggestion of such a thing. She'd have probably told him to pack his things and leave, too. But the new Orla – the Orla who was beginning to integrate with her community and reach out to people, who had sat in her gardener's cottage for the space of an entire evening and had told her story, who'd photographed her neighbours at the village show and who'd visited another stranger's house – that new Orla was conflicted. She did have something rather special here, she thought, and did she have the right to hide it away from the village? She might own the castle, but ownership of such a place came with a responsibility and she was beginning to realise that now.

'Orla? What do you think?' Luke prompted.

She took a deep breath. 'Not too many at once.'

Luke's grin stretched from ear to ear. 'You're a star!'

Orla watched as Luke left the castle and ran towards the gate, opening it up, to the delighted surprise of those who'd been waiting there. She wondered whether she should join Luke. It would be polite to welcome these visitors. After all, the castle was a home rather than a tourist attraction. But she felt crippled by insecurity. It was one thing for her to venture out into the world and enter other people's homes, but it was quite a different thing to welcome strangers into her own home. So she stayed where she was and left Luke to it, making sure the main door into the great hall was closed and that One Ear remained with her at all times.

The interest in the Wild Man continued as word spread around the village and a steady trickle of visitors arrived at the castle gate each day, including quite a few members from the village's historical society. They'd heard about the Wild Man and were curious to see it and, judging by their responses, they weren't disappointed. Luke gave them the time and space they wanted to take photographs and ask him questions, which he did his best to answer, and then he led them back up the steps and out into the sunshine.

Luke couldn't help but be mildly amused by it all, but he could tell that Orla was feeling uneasy about the attention. He'd been hoping she'd join them, but she wouldn't, which he thought was a shame because he knew how much she loved her home. She could get so much out of sharing that love with others, but these things took time, he reasoned. She'd made so much progress already and he couldn't expect even more miracles. Not yet, at least.

'I don't like having all these people here,' she told him.

'I know you don't. But it won't last for ever,' he promised. 'It's just something new. Well, old. *Really* old, actually. But interest will wane.'

'I hope you're right,' she told him. 'I don't like living in the spotlight.'

'Don't worry – it'll all blow over.'

Only it didn't. It got worse.

Luke wasn't sure what had made him turn the television on one evening, but he was glad that he had because there was a reporter standing in the middle of the square in Lorford doing a piece to camera. The next shot was of a lone fishing boat down by the quay, and that was when Luke turned the sound up.

'Legend has it that the creature was hauled out and dragged to the castle, where it was locked in the dungeon.'

There was a cut to Lorford Castle.

Luke cursed. Orla would not be happy about her home being all over the local news. Luke watched on as a shaky piece of amateur footage of their Wild Man was shown, probably taken on a phone under his very watch by someone *he'd* let into the castle.

'And here's the carving,' the voiceover said. 'Thought to be a contemporary representation of the legendary Wild Man.'

There were some other shots around the village and then another piece to camera inside the church.

'The castle is now owned by former model, Orla Kendrick, and isn't open to the public.'

Luke cursed again. Why on earth did they need to mention who owned the castle? Orla would be furious if she found out.

The reporter went on, 'But you can see something very similar at the church.' There was a close-up of one of the wodewoses carved into the font.

'Luke?' Orla called through from the kitchen. 'Dinner's ready.'

Luke grabbed the remote control and switched the TV off before Orla had a chance to see it. What she didn't know couldn't harm her, could it?

Chapter 18

The day after the news story aired, Luke realised that he'd been wrong. The interest in the Wild Man of Lorford wasn't going to go away. At least, not immediately. The news story he'd seen had made the situation worse and it was only a matter of time before Orla found out about it.

Sure enough, as he was working on a section of wall in the great chamber, Orla entered the room.

'There are more people by the gate.'

'Really?' Luke tried to sound surprised.

'I don't understand why people are so interested in him,' she said, speaking of the Wild Man as if he were her own personal friend and it was up to her to protect him.

'I guess he's just caught the public imagination,' Luke said. 'I don't know. Maybe it's a slow news week.' He blanched at his reference to the news and hoped she hadn't picked up on it.

'But these aren't all villagers, are they? Surely everyone from the village has seen him by now.'

Luke had his back to her and continued to work, hoping the situation might resolve itself.

'Luke!' she cried. 'I don't want all these people – all these *strangers* – here!'

He turned around and immediately felt guilty when he saw her ashen face.

'I'll go down and tell them to leave. Don't worry about it.'

'What do you mean, *don't worry about it*? Of course I'm worried about it! I chose to live a private life here and that doesn't include half of the world showing up at my gate and demanding to be let inside.'

Luke could hear the distress in her voice and hoped that all this unwanted attention wasn't going to stress her too much. He'd hate to see her upset by it all.

'Okay, okay! Leave it to me,' he told her.

Opening the castle door, Luke saw the flowers. It was a small but beautiful bouquet, tied with a ribbon, just left there on the steps of the castle. He looked around, puzzled, wondering who could have left them there. Leaving them for a moment, he made his way to the gate, where at least a dozen people crowded.

'When's the castle open?' asked a middle-aged man with a large camera swinging around his neck.

'I'm afraid the castle isn't open to the public,' Luke told him.

'But we've come to see the Wild Man,' a woman said.

'The castle's a private home,' Luke explained.

'How can a building like this not be open to the public?' the man with the camera went on. 'It's a disgrace!'

'Something like this is of historic value to the nation,' the woman added.

'The church is worth a visit,' Luke said, doing his best to remain calm. 'There are some fine carvings on the font – very similar to the Wild Man here.'

The man with the camera tutted. 'Not the same. *Not* the same at all.'

There were some disgruntled murmurings of agreement and Luke looked into the small crowd of angry faces, imagining how ugly things could turn if there were even more of them there. It still seemed odd to him that a little carved figure could cause so much interest.

'I'm sorry to disappoint,' he told them and, slowly, they began to move away. Except one man. 'Can I help you?'

The man came forward. He was in his mid-thirties, Luke guessed, and was wearing a baseball cap and a pair of dark sunglasses so that most of his face was obscured. He didn't look like the sort who would spring to mind when thinking of medieval carvings, but Luke supposed you could never tell.

'Is Orla at home?' he asked.

Luke very nearly answered on automatic pilot because of the man's use of her first name, which seemed so familiar, but something stopped him in time.

'Who's asking?' Luke said.

'A friend.'

'And your name?'

The man stared blankly at him. Or, at least, as blankly as only a pair of dark glasses can stare.

'I'll come back,' he said, turning quickly and shuffling off.

Luke remained at the gate, watching the man, who had thrust his hands into the pockets of his jeans and headed into the centre of the village.

I'll come back.

Luke didn't know why, but those words rattled him and he wished he'd responded to them now. They'd almost seemed threatening. For a moment, he thought about going after the man and telling him that he really shouldn't bother wasting his time coming back, but Luke felt awkward and so left it.

Returning indoors with the bouquet of flowers in his hand, he found Orla in the china room, choosing a cup and saucer to photograph.

'Have they gone?'

'Every last one of them,' he told her.

'Good.'

He nodded, wondering whether he should mention the man in the sunglasses to her and deciding against it.

'I found these,' he said, handing the bouquet to her.

'Where?'

'On the steps by the front door.'

Orla turned the flowers over. 'Was there a note with them? A card?'

'No, nothing that I could see.' Luke saw, at once, the fear in Orla's face. 'I'm sure they're meant kindly – whoever left them. Maybe they're for the Wild Man.' He laughed, but Orla obviously didn't find his joke amusing.

'I don't want them.'

'You don't?'

'Take them away, please.'

'Okay. I'll get rid of them.' Luke didn't argue, hearing the anxiety in her voice. 'Orla?'

'Yes?'

'I'll – erm – I'll be in the great chamber if you need me, okay? I'm going to do a spot of work in there.'

She nodded, and he left her.

Luke was uneasy for the rest of the day and spent a fair amount of it pacing back and forth in front of the windows which looked out towards the gate, dreading seeing the man in the sunglasses again. He found it hard to concentrate on his work with the threat of the man's return hanging over him. Then he'd get annoyed with himself because the gates were closed, the doors of the castle were locked and One Ear was most definitely in residence. So why was he feeling so uneasy? It was probably all unfounded and the man in the glasses had been trying his luck to meet the once-famous model, having heard about her on the television. It was a news story which would live only for a few days at most, and then it would be forgotten. He felt completely sure of that. Well, *almost* completely. But, just an hour later, he saw another small crowd outside the gates of the castle and standing there at the back was the man in the cap and glasses. Luke considered what to do. If he went down again, he'd most likely give the crowd false hope. Either that or really annoy them. They would probably lose interest soon enough and give up and go.

But you didn't, a little voice reminded him. *You stayed until she let you in.*

Luke sighed, watching from the window for a while, willing them all to go away. He wondered if Orla had felt the same way when he'd arrived and parked outside her gates. He still felt bad about that, but it had all worked out and he knew he'd done the right thing in trying to see her.

'Back to work,' he told himself. He was probably worrying about nothing. This whole TV thing had knocked him a little, but Orla was still unaware of it, and that was the main thing.

It was when they were having dinner that Luke began to wonder if he should tell her or not.

'I was in the garden earlier and there were still people at the gate,' Orla told him. 'They couldn't see me, but I could see them. I don't like it, Luke. I wish they'd all go away.'

'They will.'

'When?

Luke watched the tortured frown on Orla's face deepen and he could stand it no longer.

'There's something I didn't tell you,' he began hesitantly.

'What?'

'The castle – the Wild Man – it featured on the local news and they mentioned your name as the owner.'

Orla's face drained of all colour. 'How did they find out?'

'I guess it got mentioned somewhere. Social media? Maybe someone tweeted a photo of the Wild Man and it got picked up by the TV station. I'm not sure how all those websites work these days, but it looks like our Wild Man's gone viral.'

Orla's whole body seemed to tighten and, when she spoke, it was slowly and deliberately, each word filled with fear and rage.

'I thought I was safe here.'

'You are,' Luke assured her.

'I don't *feel* very safe!'

'There's nothing to worry about.'

'I don't like being watched, Luke. I don't like being looked at and I don't like random people leaving random bunches of flowers on my doorstep.'

'I know.'

They continued to eat in uneasy silence. Luke wondered whether it would be wise to mention the man in the sunglasses. On the one hand, he might just scare her but, on the other, at least she would know and he wouldn't feel terrible about hiding anything else from her.

'There's been a man hanging around,' he suddenly blurted, taking them both by surprise.

Orla's knife and fork clattered to her plate as she looked up.

'What man?'

'Just a man. He was in his early thirties, I think. Wore a base-ball cap and dark glasses. I didn't think much of it, but he asked for you by name.'

'He *knows* me?'

'I don't know,' Luke said honestly. 'I'm not convinced he did. Your name was mentioned on TV so he might have picked it up from there.'

Orla stared down at her plate, unable to eat any more.

'What if it's Brandon?' she whispered.

Luke swallowed hard. The thought that the man in the dark glasses might be Orla's stalker had crossed his mind too, although he'd done his best to shut the thought out. After all, wasn't he in London? And the story had appeared on the local news, so how would he have seen it? Luke sighed. There were no end of ways he could have seen it, of course. Once information was out in the public domain, it had a way of finding the wrong people.

'It's most likely just some random guy,' Luke said at last.

'But what if it isn't? What if it's *him*? What if he's found me?' She scraped her chair back on the flagstone floor and it screeched alarmingly.

'Orla – you mustn't get all worked up. Whoever he is, he's probably long gone by now.'

But Orla wasn't listening to him. She'd left the room.

Luke followed.

'Orla – talk to me.'

'I'm tired.'

He let her leave, glancing at One Ear as he trotted after his mistress, leaving him alone for the rest of the evening.

Orla couldn't settle that evening and she knew she wouldn't be able to sleep. She felt horribly restless, with the same uncertainty flooding her system as the time after the acid attack. And a part of her couldn't help blaming Luke for what was happening because it was him who'd uncovered the Wild Man and shone a spotlight on her home. But she really shouldn't blame him. It wasn't fair. Besides, she adored the strange stone creature he'd discovered. It was a precious link back to the past and an important part of the castle's story.

She thought about ringing her mother. For all her faults, Bernadette was the one person on the planet who had been there for Orla when she'd been at her most vulnerable. She'd seen the whole horror of what had happened to Orla unfolding and had helped her to pick up the fragile pieces of herself and guide her towards her recovery. A recovery Orla felt still wasn't complete, and she couldn't help feeling it was under threat again with these crowds of strangers at her gate. At her door.

She thought about the flowers again. Luke had got rid of them, but Orla could still feel their malignant presence. If they'd been from a true friend then surely there'd have been a card or note with them. Flowers were something Brandon used to send her. At first, single roses would be posted to her in padded envelopes or left for her where she was working. Then the bouquets started arriving. But he always left notes with them. But maybe he wasn't doing that now because he knew she'd recognise his handwriting. Maybe he was being careful because of the restraining order. If he didn't sign anything, she had no proof they were from him.

Or maybe you're being paranoid, she told herself. Maybe the flowers were some kind of tribute to the Wild Man, or maybe they'd been delivered to the castle by mistake. There were any number of explanations that didn't involve former stalkers, weren't there? It's just that Orla couldn't think of very many of them.

The next day began with a perfect summer morning, and Luke approached Orla after breakfast.

'I thought I'd pop into the local shop and get a few things. Want to come?'

Orla hesitated. She couldn't help it. Staying safely indoors was still her default setting even after all the progress she'd made in recent days, but she found herself nodding and was rewarded when Luke smiled.

'Good,' he said.

They left the castle together, walking through the gate and making their way towards the market square. Orla was thankful that there wasn't anybody hanging around at the gates that morning or she wouldn't have been able to pass through them. Maybe the interest in the Wild Man was waning. She hoped so. Still, she couldn't help feeling anxious as they entered the market square, and she looked around, peering down the little side streets that led off from it. One was full of towering hollyhocks and she could just make out a dark shape in the shadows. She shaded her eyes from the sun, trying to get a better look and then felt a chill run the length of her spine. It was Brandon.

She gasped. 'Luke!' she cried as she saw the man in the shadows turn and walk away.

'What's the matter?' Luke asked.

'I'm not sure. I thought I saw . . .'

'What?'

Orla looked again, but there was nobody there.

'Orla – what is it?'

She swallowed hard. 'Nothing.'

'Are you okay? You seem a bit – twitchy.'

Orla nodded, although she was feeling deeply unsettled, as if a part of her mind had reverted back to a time when she wasn't quite in control of it.

'Do you want to go back to the castle?' he asked her.

She took a moment to think about it, but she wasn't going to let the fear of shadows win over her today.

'No. Let's go shopping,' she said.

The next day, Orla asked Luke to accompany her for her morning walk to the beach. He usually did, so she felt odd asking him, but she wanted to make sure she had somebody by her side – she was still feeling anxious after the incident in the village where she thought she'd seen Brandon. She was wearing her big hat and dark glasses again. They went just a little way towards putting a barrier between her and the world.

'I can take One Ear if you don't want to go out,' Luke told her.

Orla shook her head adamantly. 'I won't be a prisoner to fear. Not any longer.'

'I really don't think you've anything to fear. The crowds have long gone now, haven't they? I haven't seen anyone around for a while now,' Luke said, although she couldn't help noticing the occasional glance he gave over his shoulder as they made their way through the reed beds towards the sea. It didn't exactly put Orla at ease, but she was glad he was there to look out for her.

Reaching the beach, the sea air blew away Orla's cares for a blissful half-hour. One Ear raced and chased, and Luke and Orla crunched across the pebbles and ambled over the acres of wet sand, dipping toes tentatively into the clear waves. It was always good to walk along the beach. No matter what was worrying you, the sound of the sea and the scent of the salty air always made life seem brighter and shinier.

They walked back through the fields, the sun hot upon their backs. Orla had almost forgotten the threat that had been hovering over her since the day before and the fear that had tightened her chest. Almost. Until she saw a figure hovering in the lane at the end of the footpath. It was a man in a baseball cap. He was some distance away, but it looked like the man who'd been hiding in the shadows in the village the day before, and Orla knew it was him.

'Luke!' Her voice was a little pip of despair and Luke's arm was immediately around her shoulders.

'Is that him?'

She nodded.

'What do you want to do? Shall we go back the way we came?'

She saw Luke glance behind them. It would be frustrating to have to double back now when they were so close to home, Orla thought, and yet the fear of getting any closer to this man was almost unbearable.

'No.'

'No? You want to go on?'

'Don't let him near me.'

'I won't. One Ear won't either, will you, boy?'

One Ear looked up from the clump of grass he was investigating and was immediately alert.

'We've got you,' Luke said, and they continued walking.

Orla felt horribly dizzy. The man at the end of the path was clearly waiting for them and he took his dark glasses off as they approached.

'Oh, my God!' he cried. 'It *is* you! I thought it must be.'

Luke's arm tightened around Orla's shoulder as he ushered her past the man, One Ear trotting on her other side.

'I've come all the way from London, Orla! I heard you were here and just had to see you. You disappeared!'

Orla shrank against Luke's shoulder as if trying to make herself invisible.

'Just ignore him,' Luke whispered to her.

'Did you get my flowers? I didn't want to leave a message. I didn't want to scare you.'

'Well, you're scaring her now, buddy – so back off!' Luke shouted.

Orla kept her eyes lowered, her gaze firmly on her feet. Her breath was ragged. It was all she could do just to keep breathing and moving.

'Why did you leave me? What did I ever do to you to deserve that?' The man's tone was changing now, and Luke and Orla picked up speed.

'Don't hide your face from me. I don't mind about the acid attack. You're still beautiful to me!'

'Hey!' Luke shouted, coming to a stop in front of him. 'That's *enough*.'

'Who the hell are you?'

'She doesn't want anything to do with you, so go home before I call the police!'

The man didn't respond to that and Luke guided Orla away from him as quickly as possible.

'*Orla!*' he shouted after her.

'Come on. We're nearly home,' Luke told her.

In truth, Orla didn't know where they were. She felt as if she was in the middle of some nightmare and was only vaguely aware of Luke's voice and his guiding hand.

'We're here now,' he said a moment later, and Orla could see the castle steps. They had never looked more welcoming.

She heard Luke open the door and then shut it behind them, bolting and locking it securely. It felt good to have all that heavy oak and stone between them and that madman, she thought, once again thankful for her decision to buy a castle.

'It's all right now! He's gone,' Luke told her, guiding her into the great hall. 'I'm going to ring the police, okay?'

She nodded.

'There is a restraining order on him, isn't there? He shouldn't be anywhere near you, right?'

At last, Orla found her voice. 'Get rid of him!' she cried, as she fled to her room.

Luke made a call to the police and later spotted a car patrolling outside. He put his tools down and made his way to the front gate, flagging the car down as it doubled back.

'There's no sign of him,' the officer told him.

'Well, he's here somewhere,' Luke told him. 'Please keep looking. He's been hanging around for a couple of days now at least.'

Luke gave the officer his description of Brandon again and watched as the car drove on, silently cursing as he glanced back up to the castle and saw Orla gazing down from one of the windows before edging back into the shadows.

Luke busied himself with his work after that, glad of the distraction. He was so mad at the upset this had all caused Orla and didn't blame her for hiding out in her room, although he was concerned when she didn't surface for lunch.

'Orla?' He knocked gently on her door. 'Come and eat something.'

'I'm not hungry.'

'You should still eat.'

She didn't reply.

Luke worked on through the afternoon, opening one of the windows in the great chamber to let the warm summer air help dry the lime plaster. And that's when he heard it. He didn't really register what it was at first because it was such a slight noise, but it gradually became louder and caught his attention because it simply wasn't going away. He looked out of the window, half expecting to see a swarm of angry bees, but it wasn't bees; it wasn't anything belonging to the natural world. It was a drone.

Luke had never seen one in real life before, but there was no mistaking what it was. It looked like something out of a science-fiction film as it hovered around the castle windows, its evil buzz announcing its presence.

Luke cursed. He was cursing a lot that day. Now, as he looked out of the window to the castle grounds, he felt full of rage. It didn't take him long to spot the guy. He was half hiding in the bushes, but he was definitely holding the control to the drone, which, Luke guessed, would be recording footage.

'Luke?'

Luke turned around as Orla entered the great chamber.

'Orla – go back to your room.'

'What's that noise?'

He pursed his lips, hating that he had to tell her. 'It's a drone.'

'*What?*'

'I'm calling the police again.'

'Is it him?'

'I think it must be.'

Orla cried and her hand flew to her mouth.

'It's all right – I'll let the police know. We just have to remain calm, okay? Orla? You okay?'

She gave a nod and left the room.

Luke wasted no time. He was on the phone straight away to the police. He spoke to somebody who assured them that an officer would be sent out to them immediately and that he wasn't to do anything to alert Brandon. That way, he wouldn't get spooked and they'd have a better chance of catching him this time.

Luke hung up the phone. The sound of the drone could still be heard as it flew around the castle like an angry hornet, and a part of Luke wanted to go outside right there and then and deal with Brandon himself, but he knew that would be foolish and mis-guided. Instead, he closed the window and took a deep breath as he waited for the police to arrive.

It took a full half an hour for the car to pull up outside the gates of the castle. Luke watched from the window of the great chamber. Ever since the night of the train crash, the sight of a police car made him feel uneasy, but this wasn't bringing bad news. With any luck, it was delivering good news for Orla.

The only trouble was, the sound of the drone had stopped about ten minutes before the police car had arrived and Luke hadn't seen any evidence of Brandon since then. Had he known he'd pushed his luck and left before he knew they could alert anybody? Luke waited, watching the policeman as he searched the grounds and glad that Orla was out of the way from the rather distressing scene.

A few minutes later, the bell rang at the front door.

'I'll get it, Orla,' Luke called through, even though it was obvi-ous she had no intention of answering it.

'Mr Hansard?' the young officer said.

'Yes.'

'You're the one who made the call?'

'I am.'

'I'm afraid there's no sign of anybody in the grounds.'

'I thought you were going to say that. Have you checked the lane? And the footpath? He can't have gone far.'

'I'll certainly take a look before I leave, but I'm afraid there isn't much more I can do unless he's actually in the grounds.'

Luke sighed in frustration. 'He's causing a lot of stress.'

'Yes, I'm sorry to hear that.'

'Is there nothing else you can do?'

'Not unless we can apprehend him here.'

Luke grimaced.

'Let us know if he comes back,' the officer said, nodding his head before leaving.

Luke closed the door, angry that he had to break this news to Orla.

He found her in the china room, where she was sitting on a little wooden chair, staring at the floor.

'I'm afraid the police couldn't find him,' he said without preamble.

'Couldn't *find* him?'

'But he's gone. He's not out there now.'

'He won't have gone,' Orla whispered, still looking down at the floor.

'But we know what to do if we see him anywhere near the castle again, okay? Anyway, I don't think he'll come back.'

She raised her eyes to his and he could see the deep fear within them. 'What makes you think that?'

'He'll know he's pushed his luck, and surely he'll have seen the police car if he's still hanging around.' Luke flinched inwardly. He shouldn't have made any reference to the possibility that Brandon was still hanging around. 'I'm sure he's gone. He's violated his restraining order and he's invaded your privacy with that drone. Now, I don't know much about law, but I'm guessing the police won't look too favourably on that, and he's sure to know that.'

'I thought I was safe here.'

'You are!'

She shook her head. 'He still found me. I thought this place would protect me.'

'But it *did*! He didn't get in, did he?'

Orla didn't look at all comforted by this.

'Listen – it's been a trying day and you're tired. Let me make you something to eat, okay? Just try and relax and have an early night.' He moved forward an inch and reached out a hand to squeeze her shoulder and was relieved when she nodded.

Chapter 19

Something felt wrong that night. Orla could just sense it. She couldn't shake the feeling that she was somehow being watched, which was crazy, really, because she was sleeping – or trying to sleep – behind walls that were at least eight feet thick. She couldn't hear any drones, either, so she put it down to paranoia again. But the fact that Brandon had been there – both in the village and in the castle grounds – shook her. Luke was probably right and Brandon had most likely left Lorford hours ago, but what if he hadn't? What if he was still out there now?

Orla turned over in bed and looked at the alarm clock. It was five thirty and already beginning to get light. Orla welcomed it. The darkness always made her anxiety worse.

She got out of bed, knowing that she wouldn't be able to sleep any more and hating the idea of lying there worrying. If she got up, she could do something useful, even if that was only photographing teacups. It would occupy her overactive imagination and she might even create something beautiful, thus turning a negative into a positive. Yes, she thought, as she quickly dressed in a skirt and T-shirt, she'd do that.

It was easy for time to pass when she was photographing and, although Orla didn't completely forget about the fear she'd felt in the night, her pretty china collection at least helped to alleviate those fears.

A couple of hours slipped by and Orla went through to the kitchen to make a cup of tea. One Ear looked up from his basket.

'You want outside?' she asked him, and he got up, stretching his long front legs and yawning. 'Come on, then.'

Orla took him down to the back door and unlocked it. The morning air was cooler than she'd thought and her limbs felt suddenly chilled. If she remembered rightly, she'd left a jumper in the great chamber. She looked at where One Ear was sniffing and, not wanting to rush him, she returned inside for her jumper. It always amazed her how cold a summer morning could be, only for the mists to lift and the sun to rise and the day to be a scorcher later on. It was one of the magical things about summer, she was thinking, as she found her jumper and pulled it on.

And that's when she became aware that something wasn't quite right. There was a strange sort of tension in the air and the faintest scent of something she didn't recognise. It smelled like – what was it? Something fresh and spicy. Orla inhaled, looking around the room as if she might spot something alien there. Perhaps Luke had picked some flowers from the garden she didn't recognise the scent of. She couldn't see any.

Something told her it wasn't flowers. Her skin had broken out in gooseflesh.

She wasn't alone, was she?

Some kind of primitive instinct told her that he was there – right with her – in the castle. She'd only left the door open for the briefest time and One Ear was patrolling the gardens. But that hadn't made any difference. He'd found his way inside, hadn't he?

Knowing he was there before turning around to face the door once more, Orla could feel her heart begin to race.

'I had to see you,' he said.

Her mouth went dry.

'Orla? Look at me! Please look at me! I've missed you so much.'

Slowly, very slowly, she turned around to face him.

'Why do you hide away like this when you're still so beautiful?' he asked, moving forward an inch.

Orla backed away, noticing that his hair looked unwashed and his clothes looked dirty, as if he'd been roughing it. Roughing it in her garden, she thought. She'd been right to be paranoid; there really had been someone watching her home all night, hadn't there? And when she'd left the door open for One Ear, he'd taken his chance to invade her privacy, leaving One Ear out in the garden and her trapped inside with him.

'I didn't know what to do, Orla. There were rumours of you leaving London and I tried to find you.'

His thin face was pale and his eyes had a brightness to them which Orla found disturbing. Perhaps because they were fixed on her so resolutely. She thought of screaming to Luke for help, but she couldn't utter a single sound at that moment. Instead, she watched as he moved towards her in some dreadful kind of slow-motion effect.

'How are you? You look well. I mean, considering what happened to you. That was horrible, Orla.'

She flinched at the way he used her name so familiarly – as if they were friends and he had a right to be there in the middle of her home.

'Don't!' she said at last, finding her voice, even though it was more of a squeak.

'What?' Brandon asked, holding his hands up. 'Don't be scared. I don't mean to scare you. I never meant to scare you. I don't know why you thought I might. Or was it the people around you telling lies about me?' He shook his head, suddenly looking angry. 'I only ever wanted to be with you. I'd never hurt you. Not like the person who did *that* to you.' He motioned to her face and Orla felt tears of rage surging. She couldn't bear to be in the same room as this man. This man who kept coming towards her, and kept using her name in that silky, slimy way.

'I'd have killed that person, Orla. I'd have *killed* them for you.'

Orla looked behind her in desperation and saw something on one of the deep windowsills – something heavy and close by that she could use. She grabbed it. It was a large Victorian wash jug in a pink lustre. She loved it, but she didn't mind using it as a weapon if it kept Brandon away from her.

'Stand back!' she cried at him now.

'What? Or you'll throw that jug at me?' He laughed. 'Let's not fight any more. I just want to talk. To be with you.'

She frowned in horror at his intimacy.

'I want you to leave.'

'No, you don't – not really. You just need to give us a chance, that's all. You need to get to know me. I'm a good person and I'll protect you from anyone who really wants to hurt you. I'll be good for you.'

Orla stared at him in disbelief. How could he not see that he was scaring her and that she perceived him to be one of the very people who did hurt her?

'Get out!' she shouted, finding a mote of inner strength at last. 'Or I'll call the police.'

He shook his head. 'You called the police last time, didn't you? I thought you might. That's why I didn't hang around. But I'll always come back. I'll always be there for you, Orla.'

It was more than she could take and, screaming as loudly as she could, she launched the large china jug at him, hitting him squarely in the chest. He fell back, crashing onto the floor, and looked up, stunned. At the same time, Luke came running through and One Ear was heard barking at the back door.

'What the hell?' Luke cried, sizing up the situation before seizing hold of Brandon.

'Get off me!' Brandon shouted, but Luke was a lot bigger and stronger than him and looked as if he had no intention of letting go.

'Ring the police, Orla,' he said calmly. 'We've got him this time.'

Things got a little chaotic after that and Orla moved as if in some kind of terrible nightmare. She let One Ear back inside and, with some pretty menacing growls, he kept a watch over Brandon, alongside Luke. Mercifully, the police didn't take long in getting there and Brandon was led away.

'That was some wake-up call,' Luke said once they'd driven away from the castle. 'You okay? Cup of tea?'

'I should leave,' Orla told him.

She saw Luke frown. 'Leave the castle?'

'People can find me too easily here.'

'But this is your home now, and it's a good home. A *safe* home.'

'How can you say that after what's just happened?'

'Orla – he's gone. He's in police custody and what happened here won't ever happen again.'

'How can you say that? Can you personally guarantee that?'

'You know I can't, but I wish I could.'

'Have you any idea how hard it is for me to trust anyone? To walk past a stranger in the street? Do you have any idea of what's going on inside my head when I see someone I don't know walking towards me? It was bad enough meeting him out in the lane, but he was right here! Here in my home – in front of me!'

'Please – Orla – you're getting hysterical.'

'I don't feel safe here. I'll never feel safe ever again!'

'But you can't keep running away. That's what I'm trying to say so badly here. This place – this home – it's good. You have people in this village who care about you, and I know how much you love it here. You're a part of the castle's history now. Don't leave it, Orla. If you do, you'll just end up somewhere else where you don't feel safe.'

She stared at him, and she couldn't help feeling utterly helpless, and that, no matter what he said to her, it wouldn't make any difference to how she was feeling.

At last, she spoke. 'What do I do?' she said in a tiny voice. 'I don't know what to do!'

He took a step forward and wrapped his arms around her.

'Just stay.'

She was crying now, and he stroked her dark hair, feeling her sobs and wishing he could somehow help her.

'Come on, let's get you to bed.'

'But it's the middle of the day!'

'Tell me you're not exhausted and that you don't want to go to bed,' he said after the tears had stopped.

She wiped her eyes. 'I won't be able to sleep.'

'You might surprise yourself. Come on – give it a go, at least, okay? I think it'll do you good.'

Orla let herself be led to her bedroom, where she'd left her curtains drawn against the world that had tried to invade her privacy. Luke turned the bedside lamp on, the comforting golden glow filling the little room.

'Luke?'

'Yes?'

'If I do fall asleep, will you leave my light on, please,' she whispered.

'Of course.' He smiled at her and was mightily relieved when she gave a little smile back. 'I won't be far away – if you need me. Me and One Ear both.' He made to leave the room.

'Luke?'

'Yes?'

'Thank you.'

He frowned. 'For what?'

'For being here. I'm sorry if I lashed out. It's just . . .' She stopped.

'Hey! You don't need to apologise.'

'Yes, I do. You've been nothing but kind to me and I've been so horrible.'

He came back towards the bed. 'No, you haven't! How can you say that?'

'I'm sorry.'

'Orla – you don't need to apologise – really.' He moved closer. 'Now, get some sleep, okay?'

She nodded, her sore eyes already closing.

Luke closed her door and went to get washed and dressed properly. When he'd been woken up by Orla's cries, he'd only had time to pull on a pair of tracksuit bottoms. Luckily, he'd been sleeping in a T-shirt, but he wanted a good wash now, feeling slightly dirty, having been in close proximity to Brandon all that time.

He then swept up the broken china jug, had a quick breakfast and took One Ear into the garden for a run.

Despite his best intentions, he found that he couldn't concentrate on his work at all, making little progress between the time he started and lunchtime, so he took One Ear out into the garden again and paced around for a bit before deciding that he really needed to talk to someone. Reaching for his mobile, he made a call.

'Bill?' he said a moment later. 'Can you come over?'

It would have been easy for Luke to walk to Oyster Cottage. He felt as if he could turn up any time, but he didn't want to leave Orla and he'd told her he wouldn't be far away, and there was no way he was going to risk leaving her on her own, even if the police had her stalker in handcuffs.

It didn't take long for Bill to arrive and they sat out in the garden together as Luke filled him in on what had been happening.

'I feel as if I've aged ten years. *Another* ten years!' Luke confessed.

Bill shook his head in dismay and reached into his pocket, bringing out a small white paper bag.

'Have a mint imperial,' he said. 'Margy hates me eating these things, but I think she'll forgive us indulging on this occasion.'

Luke took one and was pleasantly surprised by the soothing quality of the sweet.

'How's she doing now?' Bill asked as he popped a second sweet into his mouth.

'She's sleeping, and I wouldn't be surprised if she slept right through till tomorrow. She looked completely done in.'

'But he didn't hurt her?'

'No, no. I don't think he tried to touch her or anything. But to be in her home! I think that's really shaken her. She was already shaken by the encounter in the lane the other day. But I don't think he's physically a danger to her. I think it's more that he reminds her of that whole period of her life when the attack happened. He wasn't involved in that, but he was a part of the horror of the whole modelling business and I think it just opened up all those painful memories for her. Plus, he's a complete fruitcake, and that's never good to have around, is it?'

'The man who did attack her – he's behind bars, isn't he?'

'He got sixteen years,' Luke told him.

Bill nodded. 'Good.'

'And the model who hired him got a life sentence.'

'Well, that's what Orla's living under, isn't it?' Bill said. 'Her fear and her disfigurement will last a lifetime.'

'Exactly. At least, if she doesn't have more surgery, and I don't think she's planning on having more. She hates hospitals.'

'Are the police going to let you know what happens next?'

'I'm not sure. I'll probably give them a call and make sure he's not likely to show himself round here again.'

Bill leaned forward on the bench and shook his head. 'Poor girl,' he said. 'Let's hope that's an end to the whole business.'

Orla still hadn't surfaced by ten o'clock the next morning, which was very unlike her, and Luke was beginning to get worried. He left a breakfast tray outside her door and knocked quietly.

'Orla? There's some food for you here. I'm going to take One Ear to the beach, okay?'

When she hadn't roused by lunchtime, he became more concerned.

'You want any lunch?' he asked, gazing down at the breakfast tray, which had remained outside her bedroom door, untouched. 'Orla? Speak to me! I need to know you're okay.'

Luke let a couple more hours slip slowly by before he knocked again.

'Is there anything I can do to help, Orla? Is there anyone you want me to call for you?'

He waited a moment, hoping for an answer, and then he heard a noise and looked down to see a slip of paper that had been pushed under the door. He picked it up and read it. It was a phone number.

Luke took the piece of paper into the great hall. He recognised it as a London number and wondered if it was a friend or a relative of Orla's, or maybe even some kind of doctor whom she trusted. There was only one way to find out, so he rang the number.

A moment later, a woman's voice answered.

'Hello?'

Luke cleared his throat, feeling awkward and anxious.

'Hi. My name's Luke. I'm a friend of Orla's and I've been staying with her for a little while.'

'In the castle?' The woman's voice sounded incredulous.

'Yes.'

'Is she all right?'

'Well, that's why I'm ringing. She's locked herself in her bedroom and won't talk to me.'

'What have you done?'

'Nothing!' Luke cried, appalled by her tone. 'I'm trying to help her.'

'I'm on my way,' the voice told him.

'Who are you?' Luke managed to ask before she hung up.

'I'm her mother.'

Chapter 20

Bernadette Kendrick had not come across on the phone as a friendly and understanding human being and, when Luke opened the door to her four hours later, she didn't look like one either. She was a small, slightly built woman, with the same thick dark hair as Orla, but her face had none of the tenderness Luke had seen in Orla's. But Luke guessed he should think kindly of her after her long journey and the stress she must be under worrying about her daughter.

'I'm Luke. Please come in.'

She'd already pushed him out of her way, ignored One Ear, who was barking at her, and dumped her small suitcase in the hallway.

'Can I get you a cup of tea or some—'

'Where is she?' she barked.

'In her bedroom.'

Bernadette was off. Luke made to follow, but she flung a hand out behind her to stop him.

'Leave us!'

Luke stopped dead, turning to One Ear, who looked as nonplussed as he was feeling.

'Well, what do you make of her?' he whispered.

One Ear slunk back to his bed and Luke went to put the kettle on. He'd make that very rude woman a cup of tea whether she wanted one or not.

After Luke had called Orla's mother earlier that day, he'd gone straight back to Orla's bedroom to let her know that she was on her way. Another slip of paper had come out from under the door.

Her name is Bernadette. Do not call her Bernie!

So far, Luke hadn't had a chance to call her anything.

He made three cups of tea and took two through to Orla's room on a tray with a jug of milk and a bowl of sugar and a plate of biscuits. The bedroom door was firmly closed and he knocked on it gently.

'I've made some tea for you both,' he said.

'Please leave us!' Bernadette called, sounding exasperated that he should do such a foolish thing.

'I'll put the tray outside, then,' Luke said with a sigh, hovering for a moment, trying to hear them talking together, but he couldn't really make anything out through the thick wooden door other than low murmurings.

He went back to the kitchen and drank his tea. He knew he wouldn't be able to concentrate on his work now and so called through to One Ear. A trip to the beach was what was needed to calm his anxiety. A big blow of ozone should go some way, at least, to making him feel a little better.

It seemed strange to be at the beach without Orla, he thought, as he strode across the sand. One Ear didn't seem concerned. He wasn't about to reject a walk when it was offered, no matter who was taking him. Luke watched the great dog lolloping in the waves, and his mind flickered back to a walk he'd had along Camber Sands on the Sussex coast with Helen. The weather had been atrocious.

They'd wondered if it was wise to even get out of the car, but they'd set aside a rare afternoon to spend together and they were jolly well going to have their walk on the beach.

The wind had almost taken their breath away as they'd walked. Helen had snuggled into him, her arms wrapped around his. He could almost feel them now, hugging him close.

They hadn't been the only fools out that day. There were a handful of dog walkers braving the elements, including a couple with a yellow Labrador. Helen's favourite dog. She'd laughed when she'd seen it sploshing into the sea, barking up at the sky in utter delight.

'Just imagine if we had a dog like that!' she'd said. 'Welcoming you home after a hard day's work—'

'Making you go out in all weathers,' Luke had countered.

He cursed himself for saying that now because he could totally see the joy of having a dog. Okay, so he hadn't had to walk One Ear in the pouring rain yet, but he sincerely thought that he wouldn't mind now. Coming to Lorford had taught him so many things, but learning to appreciate simple things like walking and breathing in fresh air was pretty high up on the list.

As he walked now, he looked up at the big blue sky and wondered if somehow, somewhere, Helen could see him and if he could share this moment with her – if One Ear could somehow be their dog for a moment. He hoped so.

By the time he got back to the castle, Bernadette was in the kitchen washing the tea things.

'How is she?' Luke asked.

'Scared.'

Luke watched as she angrily sloshed washing-up suds around, waiting for her to elaborate, but she didn't.

'Has she eaten?'

Bernadette didn't answer.

Luke sighed in exasperation. 'Can I see her?'

At last, Bernadette turned around to face him. 'No.'

Luke swallowed hard. It was taking every ounce of his being to remain polite to this woman.

He left the room, taking refuge in the basement, where he was pretty sure Bernadette wouldn't follow him. He was still deciding how best to treat the wall he'd exposed behind the board. Looking at the carving of the Wild Man, he shook his head.

'What on earth did you start, my man?' he said, half wishing that he'd never found the thing.

Bernadette was sitting on the Knole sofa in the great hall, flicking through a magazine she'd brought with her, when Luke dared to surface sometime around seven o'clock.

'Mrs Kendrick?' Luke said as he entered the room. 'I've been thinking about the sleeping arrangements. I've been in the spare room. I think there is only the one made up in the castle, isn't there? Well, I changed the bedding over for you this morning. I'll take the sofa while you're here.'

She looked up from her magazine, not bothering to disguise her disdain.

'That is *my* room you've been sleeping in with sheets that *I* bought,' she informed him, her eyes fixing on him as if he'd done her a great disservice.

'It wasn't being used,' Luke said in his defence. 'Orla allowed me to use it.'

Bernadette put her magazine down and stood up and, although she wasn't tall, Luke couldn't help feeling that he was being looked down upon.

'Who *exactly* are you to my daughter?'

Luke really didn't appreciate this woman's tone of voice. Everything she said sounded like an accusation.

'I'm her friend.'

'Well, I've *never* heard of you.'

'Oh, well, I obviously don't exist, then, if you've never heard of me.' He couldn't help his sarcasm. This woman had been winding him up ever since he'd rung her.

'Are you married?'

Luke was stumped by the sudden question. 'Well, I'm . . .'

'Single?'

'Not . . . exactly . . .'

'What does that mean? Just exactly *why* are you here?'

He put his hands on his hips. 'That's not really any of your business, is it?'

'I'd say it *is* my business when my daughter's locked herself in her bedroom!'

'Did she tell you what's happened?' Luke asked. 'Did she tell you about Brandon and the drone and how he somehow managed to get inside the castle? And how we had to call the police and have him taken away?'

Bernadette didn't seem interested.

'I don't think you're good for her. I think it's best if you leave. I'll take things from here.'

Luke felt as if he'd been flattened. He'd expected a few uncomfortable days while Orla's mother was here. He'd envisaged them carefully moving around each other. But he hadn't expected this.

'Is that what Orla wants?' Luke asked.

'Yes.'

'She *said* that?'

'*I'm* saying that.'

Luke stood his ground for a moment, trying to weigh up his options, but they seemed very limited. This woman was not going to make his stay a pleasant experience and, as much as he didn't want to leave Orla, he didn't want to add to her stress either.

'Orla has my number,' Luke told Bernadette. 'Tell her to call me if she needs anything.'

'She doesn't need you.'

He stared at her in disbelief. Did she really know what was best for her daughter? He hadn't heard Orla mention her mother before, but hers was the number Orla had given him, and who was he to question that now?

So he backed down.

'Right. I'll go. If that's what Orla wants.'

Bernadette didn't say anything, and he was glad of that. She'd said more than enough in the brief time she'd been there. The Kendrick women seemed very good at throwing men out, he couldn't help thinking. Helen had never done such a thing. She'd thrown a fair few of his old bachelor rock-band T-shirts out, but she'd never thrown him out.

Luke packed his things away, loading them all into his van, and then came into the great hall, where Bernadette was sitting on the Knole sofa, her arms crossed against her chest, waiting for him to leave. As if he knew what was happening, One Ear crossed the room and shoved his wet nose into Luke's hand.

'It's okay, boy.'

The dog whined, telling him that it wasn't okay at all.

'We've had some good walks, haven't we?'

One Ear looked up at him, cocking his head to one side as if trying to understand the strange situation.

Luke turned to face Bernadette. 'Right. Well, I'll be off.' He hesitated for a moment. 'Bernie.'

Bernadette's whole body seemed to bristle at his impudence. It was a cheap jibe, but he hadn't been able to resist.

Luke didn't leave Lorford straight away. Instead, he drove down to the quay and sat on a bench for a few minutes, watching as the sun began to set over the estuary and smiling at the comic antics of a little bird on the shore that he had no hope of ever identifying. The truth was, for all the beauty before him, he couldn't help feeling miserable. He felt like he had failed Orla and, in failing her, he'd also failed Helen. He hadn't helped at all, had he? He'd done nothing but cause pain and confusion, and the result was that Orla was locked away in isolation even greater than when he'd first arrived at the castle.

He'd also lost a friend. Because they had been friends, hadn't they? They'd slowly learned to trust each other and there had been some fun times together, but he wouldn't allow himself to take comfort in those now because it had all ended so badly. It was always the end that counted.

Getting up from the bench, he walked the short distance to Oyster Cottage, although he doubted that even seeing Bill and Margy could make him feel any better. If anything, it was bound to make him feel worse because he knew he was going to have to say goodbye to them in the worst of circumstances.

It was Margy who answered the door.

'Hello, Luke. This is a nice surprise. Come in.'

'How are you?'

'Can't complain. Just finishing off this cardigan.' She held up her latest knitting project for his inspection.

'That's lovely,' Luke said, taking in the soft blue and silvery cream creation, which reminded him of the sea. 'Is Bill around?'

'In the garden with Bosun, enjoying the sunshine.' Margy led him through. 'Bill – you've got a visitor.'

Luke walked outside to where Bill was cutting a big bunch of sweet peas. He was half dreading seeing his friend, but he knew that he couldn't leave Lorford without saying goodbye. He watched for a moment as Bill inhaled the sweet peas he'd cut.

'Keeps 'em coming if you cut them regularly,' he told Luke.

Luke inhaled their heady fragrance before Bill handed them to Margy.

'Lovely! I'll pop them in a vase,' she said, leaving them to it.

'Everything okay at the castle?' Bill asked as he bent to pat Bosun's sleepy, sun-warmed head.

'Well, in a manner of speaking,' Luke said, then shrugged. 'I've come to say goodbye.'

'You what?' Bill looked shocked.

'Orla's mother's just thrown me out.'

'Orla's mother's here?'

Luke filled Bill in on what had been going on since Orla had shut herself in her room.

'But she can't throw you out. You've been a good friend to Orla.'

'Not according to her mother. I think she's holding me responsible for Orla locking herself away like that and – well – she's probably right.'

'But that's nonsense!'

'It's okay, Bill,' Luke assured him. 'That castle isn't big enough for the two of us. The only thing that pains me is that I didn't get to say goodbye to Orla. Will you do that for me? And tell her I'm sorry?'

Bill looked confused. 'You don't need to say you're sorry, do you?'

'I feel I should,' Luke said. 'You will tell her, won't you?'

'If it's what you want, then of course I will, son,' Bill promised him, with a gentle clap on his shoulder. 'But maybe I'll wait until her mother's left first.'

Luke gave a tiny smile and then sighed. 'I'm going to miss this place.'

'This place is going to miss you.'

'Yeah?'

'Absolutely.'

'It's funny. When I came here I didn't have any plans to stay, but now it's hard to imagine going home. This feels . . .' He paused, wondering what he'd been going to say. Was it crazy to think of Lorford as home when he'd only been there for such a short time? 'This is a good place,' he finished.

'Oh, yes,' Bill agreed.

Luke looked around the garden in the late evening light, marvelling at the little paradise Bill had made there.

'Can I visit?'

Bill looked stunned by the question. 'You'd better!' he said.

Luke laughed in relief. 'Even if I'm not welcome up at the castle, I'd like to come back.'

'Listen,' Bill said. 'Just give Orla this time with her mother. She won't be there for ever, will she? And I'm sure Orla will want to see you again.'

'I'm not so sure,' Luke admitted. 'I seem to have caused nothing but trouble since I arrived.'

'Are you kidding? You've been the *making* of her! You've brought that poor girl out of her shell and helped her find a way into the community.'

Luke dared to smile. 'Really? You think so?'

'You *know* so,' Bill told him.

'But it's right I should go home,' he said. 'It's time.'

Bill nodded. 'Well, you take care of yourself, son.'

'And you. I won't forget your kindness.'

After a heartfelt goodbye, Luke drove out of Lorford, passing through the square, glancing at the village shop and taking one last look at the towering castle. He followed the road inland, through the great woods and heathland where he had walked with Orla and One Ear. His new friends. How he was going to miss them. They'd so quickly become an important part of his life and he knew he was going to struggle without them for a while.

As Luke settled in for the three-hour journey, he tried not to think about what lay ahead – of the empty house that would greet him, and his new life as a widower. God, what a hateful word that was. He hadn't been able to say it to Bernadette or to admit to his new status. He still felt married somehow.

Sitting alone in his van felt strange too. He was so used to Orla and One Ear accompanying him now. He smiled as he thought of their many days out and how, after Orla's initial terror, they'd fallen into a happy routine, taking little jaunts and exploring the countryside together. He was going to miss that. The beach too. He'd have to make sure he made time to visit the coast more often in his home county. If he'd learned anything over the past few months, it was making the very most of time.

As he neared his village, Luke began to feel anxious. Whoever would have thought that coming home would be such a dreadful experience? Luke never had. But, pulling into the driveway alongside Helen's little red car, he felt an emptiness opening up inside him that had been filled with the people of Lorford for the last couple of months.

He sat in the van for a few minutes, listening to the engine cooling down after the long journey, but he knew he couldn't sit in there for ever. He opened his door and hopped out with what seemed like a Herculean effort, reaching for his keys and unlocking the front door. As he pushed it open, there was some resistance. He peered round the door, switched on the light and sank inwardly at the pile of post that greeted him. There were the usual bills and junk mail, but he could see a fair few handwritten envelopes in there too. He shook his head. Still, the sickly sympathy cards were arriving. Would it never end? He picked up a pile of them and threw them unopened onto the dining-room table. He couldn't face them now. Maybe he never would.

He brought his things in from his van and dropped them down in the hallway, then went through to the sitting room, where everything was just as he'd left it before his trip to Suffolk – the cushions were unplumped, the table undusted and the newspapers unsorted. Helen would not have been impressed and Luke swallowed now as the thought registered.

'Sorry,' he said, imagining her spirit hovering near. He promised to tackle it all tomorrow. Tomorrow, he thought, when he had to go on living.

Chapter 21

Orla's bedroom curtains were thick, but they weren't thick enough to completely stop the sun's fierce progress that morning and she stirred in bed, blinking her eyes open and watching as her room turned a gentle amber colour. How long had she been asleep? It felt like days. She'd certainly been in her room for days, she was sure of that. But today, she felt different. It was as if the weight of fear was slowly lifting from her. Perhaps it had something to do with her mother being there. Bernadette had been with her throughout those awful dark days after the acid attack. Orla knew she wouldn't have been able to cope without her. She would have gone under completely, sinking down deep into herself.

She shook her thoughts away. She didn't want to go back there, especially after the last few days she'd had. The arrival of Brandon in Lorford had dragged her back to that dark place within herself which would never wholly heal and she'd been reminded of just how fragile the human mind was. But she was feeling a little stronger today and, after getting washed and dressed, went in search of her mother and Luke.

One Ear was the first to greet her and she immediately felt guilty at having abandoned her dear companion for so long.

'Oh, my special boy!' she cried as he did a series of little jumps around her. When she'd first brought him home from the rescue centre, he'd jumped up at her and had promptly knocked her onto her back, so she'd had to train him to control his enthusiasm just a little.

The noise they were making brought Bernadette out from the kitchen.

'You're up!' she said, a smile on her face. 'How are you feeling? Can I get you some breakfast?'

'I'd love some, thank you. I'm absolutely starving.'

'Let me get that for you. Why don't you sit down?'

'I'd rather stand,' Orla said. 'I feel it's been a while since I've been upright!' She followed her mother through to the kitchen and One Ear followed her.

'Has One Ear had his walk yet?'

'He's been out in the garden,' Bernadette told her.

'Has Luke been walking him?'

'No.'

'No?' Orla looked around, expecting to see Luke appear at any moment. 'Where is he? He's been working quietly, hasn't he? I hope I haven't made things tricky for him.'

Her mother took a moment before answering.

'Luke's gone, darling.'

'Gone? Where?'

'Home.'

Orla frowned. 'Why?'

'Because I thought that was for the best.' Bernadette filled the kettle with fresh water.

'Wait – you *told* him to go?'

Bernadette sighed. 'Don't make a scene out of it, Orla.'

'What did you do?'

'I simply told him he wasn't needed.'

'How could you do that?'

'How could I *not*? Orla, darling! I arrive to find a strange man in your home and you locked away in your bedroom!'

'But that had nothing to do with Luke!'

'Didn't it?'

'No!' Orla cried. 'Luke was my friend.'

'Well, he wasn't mine, and I didn't like the way he was just hanging around here.'

'But he wasn't just hanging around. He's been working on the castle. He's been doing vital jobs. He's the one who uncovered the Wild Man!'

'*Exactly* my point! If it hadn't been for him, this whole episode with your stalker would never have happened.'

'But that wasn't Luke's fault. Oh, God! I'd better call him and sort all this out. Goodness only knows what he thinks of me.'

Orla left the kitchen and searched the great hall for her phone. She couldn't remember where she'd last used it.

'Leave it, darling. Please!' Bernadette called after her, coming into the room a moment later.

'I can't. He's been good to me, Mum. I can't not call him and explain. What did you do, anyway? Just throw him out?'

'It wasn't like that.'

'No? Are you sure?'

Orla spotted her phone on the windowsill and picked it up.

'Don't!' Bernadette was beside her now, her hand flying out to take the phone from her.

'Mum!'

'Please, darling! Let me have a little time with my daughter. Alone.'

They stared at one another. Orla could feel her heart hammering at the intensity of the moment. Part of her was furious with her mother for what she'd done to Luke, but the expression on her face was more than she could bear.

'Let me text him at least,' Orla said.

Her mother shook her head and, with one slow, purposeful move, she took the phone from Orla's hand.

'Not yet.'

Orla was instantly transported back to when she was in recovery, when she was at her weakest, her most helpless, and when her mother had done everything for her. She'd trusted her. She'd *had* to trust her. And she did so again now, letting her take her phone from her.

'Okay,' she said in a small voice.

'Good,' her mother said. 'Now, I'm going to make you breakfast.'

August trumpeted its arrival with a heatwave. Emerald lawns crisped to brown, field fires broke out and the ice cream aisles in the supermarkets were wiped out. Slowly, Orla was getting back to her old routine. Or rather her *new* old routine – the one she'd happily fallen into since Luke had encouraged her to get out more. Not only did she walk to the beach these days, but she walked across fields and little pockets of woods that surrounded Lorford which she'd never walked to before. She walked right through the market square, passing all the red-brick cottages with their pretty gardens. She sat by the quay, watching the tourist boats coming and going and the play of light across the estuary. She even ventured into the village shop, filling a basket with local produce. Orla Kendrick was now a familiar figure in the village.

Curiously, her mother, who had now been at the castle for a whole two weeks, didn't look happy with this new Orla.

'Where are you going?' Bernadette would ask her every time Orla made for the door.

'Just out.'

'*Where* out?'

'For a walk. To the beach, probably, but maybe across the fields. Would you like to come?'

Her mother never did. 'I'll just tidy up around here.'

'It's a really lovely day,' Orla would say. But her mother never joined her. It was a strange business and Orla was thinking about it as she arrived back from a walk around the village with One Ear. Like her, the dog was making lots of new friends and Orla couldn't imagine not being a part of the village. She knew so many people and had found that the dog-walking community was particularly friendly.

'Ah, there you are,' Bernadette said as Orla entered the kitchen to give One Ear his breakfast. 'I've been worrying about you.'

'I told you where I was going,' Orla said. 'You knew I wouldn't be long.'

'Where did you go?'

'Just down to the quay. You should have come with us. It looked so beautiful today.'

Her mother approached her. 'You're wearing sunscreen, aren't you?'

'Of course.'

'You must look after your skin.'

'I know.'

'Let me look at you.'

'Mum, my skin is fine.'

'Are you still using all the special creams?'

'Yes, of course.'

Her mother sighed. 'I don't like you going out.'

'You could have come with us. I only went through the village. Everyone's so friendly. Luke helped me to realise that.'

Orla saw her mother flinch at the mention of his name.

'You shouldn't take any more risks than you have to.'

'I know, and I don't. Why do you think I didn't go anywhere other than the beach for two years?' Orla sighed. How could her mother not understand that she was doing her very best to recover and lead a normal life, even after the recent upset with Brandon?

'I don't understand why you bought this great fortress of a home if you were going to leave it.'

Orla stared at her mother in disbelief. 'But I'm not leaving it. I'm only walking around the village.'

Bernadette didn't look happy. It was as if she wanted Orla to lock herself away from the world for ever like some fairy-tale princess.

'It's not been easy for me, going out,' Orla confessed. 'It's been the hardest thing I've ever done, especially since . . .' She paused, finding it hard to even speak his name. 'Since *he* came here.'

'Luke!' Her mother spat the name out.

'*No!*' Orla said in horror. 'Brandon! Luke *helped* me! I don't know what you've got against Luke. He's been nothing but kind and good to me.'

'He put you in danger.'

'I'm *always* going to be in danger. We *all* are! Anyone who is around other people is in danger. If there's one lesson I've learned from all this, it's that we can't control anything in this world. But we *can* control our response to it.'

Bernadette was shaking her head again, her lips pursed so tightly they'd almost disappeared completely.

'I don't want you going out again, Orla. I don't want you taking unnecessary risks.'

Orla took a moment to process this, not quite believing what her mother had said.

'What?'

'You heard me. You're not to go out again.'

'Are you being serious?'

'I've never been more serious. And you should start by getting rid of that ridiculous dog. Fancy getting lumbered with a beast like that! Heaven only knows what he costs to feed. If you didn't have him, you wouldn't need to go out at all. And I could come and stay more often. Take care of you, like I did after the attack.'

Orla's mouth dropped open. She was finding it hard to breathe as realisation dawned.

'You actually like me when I'm helpless, don't you?' she said. 'Trapped in a hospital bed or locked away in my room when I'm terrified. You *like* knowing where I am every second of the day.'

'Well, of *course* I do! I nearly lost you, didn't I? Did you know what that was like for me – to see you in that state? My own flesh and blood. Only you were more blood than flesh, Orla! Oh, God! I can hardly bear to remember it.' Her eyes had flooded with tears now and Orla came forward to embrace her.

'But I've got to live, Mum. I feel I've been dead for the last two years, hiding behind these walls and turning my face from the world whenever I dared to go outside.'

'But you've been safe, haven't you?'

'Maybe.'

'Maybe's not good enough.'

Orla took a step back. 'I'm really trying to make progress here.'

'You call putting yourself at risk *progress*?'

'Don't say that – *please* don't say that! I need to do this, Mum – with or without your blessing. It just feels right to me now.'

Bernadette reached out to her, but Orla took a step back, feeling on the verge of tears.

'Orla! My baby!'

'No, Mum. I'm not a baby any more and you've got to stop treating me as if I am. I can't live with you like this. You're suffocating me! I feel like I can't take a single breath without you being there to inhale it. You've got to give me some space.'

Bernadette looked genuinely perplexed. 'What rubbish you talk! You need to rest. Let me help you to your room. You're stressed.'

'Yes! I *am* stressed! And you're causing it.'

'How can you say that? You were helpless when I arrived. Helpless!'

'I know! But I'm trying to get better and . . .' She stopped, wondering how on earth she was going to say it. 'You're not helping.'

'What?'

'At the moment – with where I feel I am – you're really not helping.'

They stood staring at each other as if they were in some terrible stand-off.

'Mum,' Orla said at last, 'I really think it's best if you leave. You do understand, don't you? I need to take care of myself now.'

'But you needed me.'

'I know I did. I *really* did, and I'm so grateful that you came. But I'm all right now. Or, at least, I'm better than I was.'

'You don't want me here?'

Orla swallowed hard. She felt she was being unnecessarily cruel. 'Not at the moment, no.'

Bernadette took a moment to process this, and then a strange, almost strangled sound emerged from her.

'So you call me up and then throw me out when it suits you. Is that it? Is that what you think I'm for?'

'Mum, please—'

'I dropped everything to come here, you know? I have a life in London and yet I make you the centre of my world.'

'I know you do, and I'm so grateful.'

Bernadette's face was flushed with fury now. 'You don't know the *half* of what I've done for you. The sacrifices I made so I could be by your side day and night, month after month, in hospital.'

'Please – don't!' Orla felt like she was losing control again but was quite determined not to this time, so she took a deep breath and spoke slowly and deliberately. 'I appreciate *every*thing you've done for me – really – but I need to be on my own now. That's all.'

There was a tense, silence-filled moment and then Bernadette spoke.

'Very well then.'

Orla watched as her mother turned to leave the room, not wholly convinced that Bernadette would ever forgive her for making her go before she herself was ready.

'Mum!' Orla called after her.

Bernadette stopped by the door and looked back at her daughter.

'Thank you.'

Chapter 22

Once her mother had left, Orla felt like she needed some air so, grabbing a hat, she found herself walking through the village. She hadn't exactly planned her route, but her feet instinctively knew where she needed to go and she soon found herself at Oyster Cottage. She stood for a moment, wondering if she had the nerve just to turn up at somebody's house unannounced. It certainly seemed as if she did, so she knocked on the door, not really expecting anybody to be at home. But, rather surprisingly, Margy answered, a large ball of caramel-coloured wool in her hands.

'Orla!' she cried. 'How lovely to see you. Come in, come in!'

'Oh, no,' Orla said. 'I don't want to disturb you. I was just wondering if Bill was around. I mean, only if he's not busy.' Orla suddenly felt awkward. For two years, she'd ignored her neighbours, and now she was making a nuisance of herself.

'He's at the allotment,' Margy told her. 'You should be able to catch him there.'

Orla smiled in relief. 'I should have thought to check there first.'

'Everything okay?'

'Yes, fine. I just felt like a bit of company.' She laughed. 'I never thought I'd say that.'

'I'm not surprised you have, though,' Margy said. 'And Bill's the best company there is. Now, just you wait a moment.'

Orla watched as Margy disappeared into the cottage. She came back with a brown paper bag which she handed to Orla.

'Flapjacks. Warm from the oven,' she said. 'Enjoy.'

'Thank you,' Orla said, deeply touched.

She made her way back through the village towards the allotments and, with each step, she began to feel slightly lighter in mood. Perhaps it was the blue sky or the warmth of the sun on her back or the delicious scent of the flapjacks she was carrying. Or maybe it was just the fact that her mother had left. As much as she appreciated her being there when she'd needed her, Orla had felt a kind of oppression too, and she'd needed to be free of it. Sighing, she determined to ring her mother later to make sure she'd got home safely and, hopefully, she'd have had time to calm down and would be able to see her daughter's point of view.

But she wasn't going to worry about that now because she'd arrived at the allotments and couldn't help smiling at the view it afforded her of Lorford Castle.

'My home,' she whispered. It was still a strange sensation for her to see it from the perspective of the rest of the village. The views she was used to were from inside looking out, but now she realised just how important this building was within the context of the village. She took a moment to admire the way it perched on its hill, looking down over Lorford and the allotments spread out beneath it. A great stone guardian, she thought, protecting the motley wooden sheds, the polytunnels and the wondrous produce grown by the residents.

Orla surveyed it all now, smiling at the towering sunflowers, the neat rows of chard and salad, the profusion of marigolds and snapdragons, and the towers of sweet peas and beans. It was a feast for the eyes and nose as well as the belly and she couldn't believe it was all on her doorstep and that she'd never spent time here. Well, she'd make up for that now.

It didn't take long to find Bill. He had a central plot with a faded blue shed at the far end. He was pulling some large green leaves from the earth when Orla approached.

'Hello there!' she called, and he straightened up, looking surprised to see her. Surprised, but pleased.

'Hello there,' he echoed. 'What brings you this way?'

'Oh, you know – stretching my legs. Actually, I have a special delivery!' She motioned to the little wooden gate into his plot and, when he nodded, opened it and approached him, showing him the paper bag.

'What's this, then?'

'Flapjacks from Margy.'

'She called at the castle?'

'No. I called round to yours.'

'Everything all right?' Bill asked, opening the bag and sniffing appreciatively.

'Not really. I had a little altercation with my mum.'

'Ah!'

'She's left in a very bad mood.'

'Left?'

'Back to London.'

'I see,' Bill said. 'Might a cup of tea be in order? I have a flask and a couple of enamel cups.'

'Very civilised,' Orla said.

'I won't take offence if you'd rather have a nice cup of tea back at the castle.'

'Where would be the fun in that? I can do that any day,' Orla told him.

'Then come and see the shed.'

Orla grinned. It wasn't every day that you got invited to look at a man's special hideout, and she wasn't disappointed. As with everything to do with Bill, it was meticulous, with its neat shelves on which sat terracotta and plastic pots of all sizes, great fat balls of twine, tins full of seed packets, jars stuffed with plant labels and baskets full of old tools with worn-away wooden handles. And, on a little worktop on the right sat a red flask and two enamel cups. Orla watched as Bill filled the cups and handed one to her. They then went out into the sun again to sit on a bench in the shade of the shed, where Orla opened the paper bag and offered Bill a flapjack.

Orla could feel herself physically decompress from just being there, sitting next to Bill, sipping tea and eating her flapjack while looking out over the allotments and on down to the sea.

'Nice spot,' she said. 'No – not *nice*. Glorious!'

'Can't argue with you there,' he confessed. 'Everyone should have a place like this, even if they don't grow anything – a place to just come and sit. To think or not to think. I do my best no-thinking here.'

Orla laughed and felt herself relaxing even more.

'My mum means well,' she began, not wanting to reopen a painful subject, but feeling the need to talk about it for a moment. 'But she can be a little . . .' She looked out across the allotments as if searching for the right word.

'Domineering?' Bill suggested.

'Oh, yes! But perhaps that's a little harsh.' Orla gazed into the middle distance. It was hard to describe her mother. On the one hand, she'd been there for Orla in some of her darkest hours, and yet she had the capacity to make Orla feel so small and helpless, just when she needed to be built up emotionally. That wasn't healthy, was it? Orla felt instinctively as though it wasn't.

'The strange thing is, she never came with me whenever I went out into the village. How do you explain that?' Orla asked, genuinely perplexed by this. 'One minute, she doesn't want me leaving her sight, and then the next she refuses to come out with me.'

Bill seemed to mull this over for a moment.

'Sounds to me like she didn't want to share you. She wanted you all to herself. Doesn't like seeing you with other people.'

'But that's so weird,' Orla said. 'It's as if she doesn't want me to get well.'

'She probably does – but on her terms.'

Orla shook her head. 'Why are people so complex?'

Bill grinned. 'I like to think I'm real simple.'

'Simple is good.'

They sat sipping their tea in good, simple silence.

'Heard from Luke?' Bill asked at last.

'No. You?'

'Nope. You miss him, don't you?' Bill asked.

'I do. I really do. Isn't that funny? I never knew him before this summer, and he was only here for a few months, but he became such a big part of my life.'

Bill looked out over the allotments. 'He slotted in, didn't he?'

Orla smiled. 'Yes! That's it exactly. He slotted in.'

'Why don't you call him?'

'I'm not sure he wants to talk to me.'

'What makes you think that?'

'The thing with my mother arriving and him leaving. She blamed him for the whole Brandon affair and I locked myself away and couldn't speak to him. It was all such a mess.'

'But it's easier now that your mother's gone, isn't it?'

'I suppose.'

'Then call him.'

Orla finished her tea. Should she call Luke? Would he really want to hear from her? Well, there was only one way to find out, wasn't there?

'Thanks, Bill. It's really helped being able to talk about all this.'

He smiled. 'You should come here more often,' he told her.

Orla took a deep, slow breath of fresh air and gazed out over the allotments towards the coast beyond.

'Yes, I should.'

'Why not meet me here tomorrow? I'll be down after tea to do a spot of watering – once the sting of the day's gone and the air's a little cooler. You could help me, if you like.'

'I'd like that.'

'Good.'

Bill got up and took Orla's cup and Orla made to move.

'Don't be going on my account,' he said. 'I'm just going to do a few chores, but you're welcome to sit a while longer.'

And so she did, watching Bill as he worked, a sense of peace flooding through her. Life was good. Really good. She felt like she was entering a new phase now and that the darkness was behind her at last. Perhaps she'd never feel the total calm that she craved, but who did? What she was feeling right now was close enough – *good* enough. And perhaps some of that had come from her mother having left. She took a deep breath in, inhaling the sweet scent of the allotment, tinged with the salty air coming from the sea.

More than anything, she longed to share that moment with Luke – to reach out to him and share how she was feeling and to apologise and explain what had been going on with her mother and inside her own head. She felt he should know and yet, when she reached for her phone, she hesitated. The truth was, she felt as if she'd lost that special connection with Luke. He'd left and he'd probably written her off as some madwoman, and she really couldn't blame him for that. She'd made his life difficult and decidedly uncomfortable and she wouldn't be surprised if she never heard from him again.

Chapter 23

That first week home was the hardest for Luke. While he'd been staying at Lorford Castle with Orla, he'd forgotten what it was like to live on his own, but there was no escaping it now and the little home he'd shared with Helen suddenly seemed so big without her in it. He tried to love it – he tidied up, he dusted a few shelves, brought some flowers in from the garden and opened windows to inhale the summer air, but nothing could lift his mood and he felt himself slipping into a depression.

'You're living in a twilight time,' one of his neighbours told him when she met him out in the lane. She was a widow, having lost her husband eight years ago. But that was different, Luke couldn't help thinking. She was in her eighties. People were expected to die in their eighties – not their thirties. It wasn't *fair* that Luke was a widower.

'It'll pass, as all things do,' she'd told him. 'The only way to get through this is to get through this.'

Her words sort of made sense, but they didn't bring him any comfort as he crawled into bed alone each night and got up alone each morning. He truly felt as if his sadness would never lift, and it didn't matter how hard he worked or how much he managed to cram into his waking hours because those moments of heartache would still find him.

The only way to get through this is to get through this.

The words of his neighbour seemed nothing more than a taunt.

Evenings were the worst. He could just about fill his days with his work and household chores, but the long, lonely evenings stretched out emptily and he felt unable to reach out to anybody then, because people had their own lives, didn't they, with their own families and things to do. And so he was left to wander around the empty rooms of his home, his mind filled with the dark thoughts of depression.

The only time he didn't think of Helen was when he was thinking of Orla. One evening, after a particularly dusty and dirty day at work, Luke showered, ate a piece of toast because he just couldn't be bothered to make anything else and sat on the sofa with his phone. He was thinking of Orla again, wondering how she was getting on and hoping she was doing okay, or at least doing better than him, which wouldn't be hard.

He visited Galleria, quickly finding her *Beautifully Broken* account and sighing when he saw that she hadn't updated her feed for several days. The last post, in fact, had been a couple of days before Brandon had shown himself. Luke wondered whether to message her via the site. He so desperately wanted to know how she was. Was her mother still there, he wondered? Was Orla still imprisoned in her bedroom by her fears? And, if she was, who was taking care of One Ear? He had to admit to being disappointed that she hadn't reached out to him, but perhaps she really hadn't wanted him there after the trouble with Brandon. It had all stemmed from his uncovering that Wild Man carving, hadn't it? He really couldn't blame her if she'd wanted rid of him.

He looked through the last few photos she'd posted, smiling as he recognised some of the china, remembering when one of the pieces had arrived and he'd helped her unpack it. Now, it was there for the whole world to admire.

While he was on the site, he found himself gravitating towards Helen's account at *Trees and Dreams*. Of course, it was the same as the last time he'd visited it, with that final photo of the oak tree at the top of the feed. That bloody oak tree. He couldn't help but hate that tree now. It had been one of the last things Helen had ever seen. She'd seen hundreds, if not thousands, of things during her last day on Earth and all after her last sight of him. The thought nearly drove him crazy. All those moments she'd had away from him, wasting time on trains and in offices and boardrooms. What had they been thinking of? But that was modern life, wasn't it? One couldn't exist on love alone. One couldn't spend every waking hour with the person you loved. It would be totally unrealistic to think that you could.

He switched his phone off, got up from the sofa and flung his plate in the kitchen sink and went to bed. It was half past nine.

Things got easier after those first few days and Luke got up one morning suddenly feeling lighter and with the need to get out of the house. He knew exactly where he had to go too, and what he had to do.

Getting in his van, he drove a short distance through the Kent countryside, which was looking resplendent in its summer attire. The hills of the Weald were a lemony green against the dark trees of high summer, and the orchards and vineyards were swelling softly with fruit.

Luke turned off a main road into a village he'd never visited before. He thought he had the right address. He hadn't thought to double-check, but he hadn't needed to for, a few minutes later, he'd pulled up outside a seventeenth-century home, recognising the small red van parked outside it.

The front door, a large wooden one which reminded him of the one at Lorford Castle, only on a far more modest scale, was open and the sound of sawing could be heard from inside.

Luke placed his hard hat on his head and walked down a narrow hallway, his boots echoing on the dark stone floor. He entered a room to the right and was greeted by a look of total shock on Chippy's face.

'Luke!'

'Hey, Chippy!'

'I didn't know you were back.'

Luke gave a shrug. He felt a little guilty for having been home so long and not letting his friend know.

'Home for good,' Luke told him.

'Yeah?'

'And ready to work.'

Chippy grinned. 'Well, there's plenty to do.'

Luke looked around the room, which had been stripped back to its original timbers, and smiled. It was a beautiful building and he couldn't wait to get to work on it with Chippy by his side. He'd missed a hard day's work with his friend and the carefree banter they shared. He felt ready for this. For the first time in months, he felt like the old Luke might be ready to make a comeback.

Chapter 24

The summer slipped by in lazy, hazy days on the Suffolk coast. The residents of Lorford kept their curtains drawn against the sun during the day and flung their windows open each evening in an attempt to keep their homes cool. It was a summer they would never forget.

Orla certainly wouldn't forget it. She was spending more time at the allotments with Bill. It was such a special place and she'd found herself becoming a part of the community, chatting to the other people who gardened there. It had been so easy to slip into a new routine and now she couldn't envisage her day without a trip to the allotments fitted into it. Of course, she knew she had Luke to thank for it all. If he hadn't come into her life, she would most likely still be locked away inside the castle, only coming out for her daily walks to the beach.

She missed Luke. But, as the weeks passed without word from him, she guessed that he'd long forgotten about her. At least there was plenty to distract her at the allotments. There was certainly plenty to do during those last hot weeks of summer. Bill's two water butts had been emptied a long time ago and he and Orla were bringing buckets of water with them from home.

'You don't need to carry those!' he chided her each time she did. 'It's easier for me to do that in my car.'

'But I really don't mind,' she told him. 'I've got muscles – look!' She flexed her biceps, which bulged the tiniest amount. 'Well, I'm on the way to *getting* muscles.'

Something else Orla always brought with her was her phone and her camera to photograph the daily changes in the growth of the flowers, fruit and vegetables. It was refreshing to capture something other than china with her camera – something that lived and breathed and evolved over time. She loved the scent of the soil after watering the plants and would often crouch down to inhale the earth and to photograph the jewel-bright stems of the rainbow chard.

August slipped into September, the sun sinking a little earlier in the sky with each passing day and the mornings feeling decidedly cooler. The hedgerows were filled with blackberries and rosehips, and dewy cobwebs threaded their way across the countryside, catching the light and turning everything into a fairy world. Orla helped Bill with his harvest. One of the most rewarding jobs was cutting the squashes. For Orla, who'd lived all of her life in London without a garden, this was a new experience. The only squashes she'd ever harvested before were from a shelf in the supermarket. But how fulfilling it was to lift one of the enormous leaves and to hold one of the swollen fruits in your hands, feeling the full weight of summer inside it, to cut the stalk and place the fruit in your basket and to think of the joy to come in eating it.

Bill was generous, giving Orla armfuls of produce to take away in thanks for all her help over the summer. And she was invited to Oyster Cottage one evening for a celebratory harvest supper where everything they ate had come from the allotment.

When October arrived, it brought the first frosts, and summer suddenly seemed a distant memory. The air chilled and, after months of bare limbs, jumpers were reached for. There was less to do at the allotment now, but Orla still met Bill there. He'd taught her so much over the last few months and she was determined to grow even more fruit, flowers and vegetables of her own at the castle in the spring. He'd promised to guide her through the seasons, and she couldn't wait.

On a crisp October morning after walking One Ear on the beach, she headed to the allotment. Bill had texted her to say he'd be there and that he was going to clear the vegetable beds to make room for some spring greens and to bring a bag to fill for her kitchen. But she couldn't see him when she arrived. She looked around in case he'd wandered into somebody else's allotment. Wasn't that what retired gentlemen did? Stand around with their forks in their hands, putting the world to rights? But the only other person she could see was a woman working quietly alone on her own plot.

Orla turned back to Bill's little corner, and noticed that the door of the shed was open.

'Bill?' she called, walking towards it. He was probably grabbing a tool or perhaps pouring himself a cup of tea, she thought. But he wasn't. As she rounded the door, she almost tripped over his boots. Bill was on the floor, and he didn't look good.

'Bill!' Orla screamed as she fell to the floor beside him. 'What is it?'

Bill's face was screwed up and he was clutching his belly.

'Pain,' he managed.

'I'll get help.'

Quickly, she grabbed her phone, cursing the fact that it was switched off and took an age to turn on. When it did, she left the shed for a better signal and rang 999.

'Ambulance, please. It's my friend. He's in his seventies. He's on the floor in great pain. Abdominal, I think. He can barely speak.'

Orla gave directions to the allotment and was told an ambulance was on its way. She was just about to return to the shed when the woman from the other allotment ran over.

'What's happening? I heard the word "ambulance".'

'It's Bill.' Orla ran back into the shed, followed by the woman. 'Bill? An ambulance is on its way.'

Bill was still writhing in pain, unable to speak.

'What did they say to do?' the other woman asked.

'Not to move him, but to keep him warm.' Orla took her coat off and placed it over Bill. She felt a strange numbing calmness wash over her.

'He'll be all right,' the woman said. 'He's tough as his old boots is Bill.'

Orla nodded. 'He'll be all right.' She reached out to touch his shoulder and then something occurred to her. 'I've got to let Margy know.'

'I'll ring her,' the woman said, getting her phone out.

'I'm sorry, I don't even know your name.'

'It's Pauline.'

'Thanks, Pauline. I'm Orla.'

Pauline left the shed and returned a moment later. 'There's no answer,' she said. 'I'll try again. Should I leave a message?'

'Try again in a few minutes. Where's that ambulance? Bill? We're getting you help. You're going to be all right.'

'I'll walk down to the entrance and wait for the ambulance,' Pauline said, knowing that the entrance was easy to miss from the road.

Luckily, it didn't take long before two paramedics appeared, who asked a bit about Bill before moving him carefully onto a stretcher.

'Is he going to be okay?' Pauline asked. Orla's mouth had gone completely dry by this stage and everything seemed to be passing in a blur. Her eyes moved from Bill to Pauline to the men carrying him and back to Pauline.

'I'll keep trying Margy,' Pauline told her, giving Orla's arm a quick squeeze. 'Quickly – give me your number so we can keep in touch.'

'Are you coming?' a voice finally asked Orla after they'd swapped numbers. She looked up to see that Bill's stretcher was now in the back of the ambulance.

Orla hesitated. Then got in.

Orla lost all sense of time after that. It was a blur of roads as they sped towards Ipswich and then a blur of white corridors as they rushed Bill to hospital There was still no word from Pauline about Margy so Orla texted her to try and find out what was happening.

But there was one person above all others she needed to reach out to: Luke. They hadn't spoken since her mother had thrown him out of the castle and, although she'd wanted to talk to him and explain things, she'd never got up the nerve. She'd been anxious that he might ignore her calls or – worse – that he'd answer and give her a piece of his mind. She'd deserve it too. He'd given her so much and he must think she'd treated him abominably.

But this wasn't about her, was it? It was about Bill, and Bill was Luke's friend. So she made the call.

'Luke?' she said a moment later, relieved that he'd answered. 'It's Orla.'

'Orla?'

'Yes.' She paused, giving him time to say something – anything. 'How are you?' he asked guardedly.

'I'm fine. Well, I'm at Ipswich Hospital.'

'What? Why? What's the matter?'

'It's Bill. He's just been brought in. He's in a lot of pain. I've no idea what's happened yet. I found him collapsed at the allotment.'

'Oh, God!'

'I'm so worried. I don't know what to do.' She could feel tears rising and her throat felt thick with emotion.

'It's okay, Orla. I'm on my way.'

'You're coming?'

'I'll be there as soon as I can,' Luke told her. 'Hold tight, okay?'

Orla hung up and took a deep breath. He hadn't ignored her call and he hadn't shouted at her or refused to come, and for that she was so grateful. She hadn't thought about the implications of asking him to drive all the way from Kent and Luke hadn't seemed to consider it as anything out of the ordinary. She had asked for help and he'd come through for her and she felt all the better for knowing that he'd be there soon.

Luke didn't need to think twice. He dropped what he'd been doing, said something vague about a personal emergency to Chippy and left for Suffolk. He tried to remain calm during the drive, but it was hard not to be worried – worried for Bill, worried for Margy and worried for Orla. How was she coping with being in the hospital? It must be bringing back all sorts of horrific memories for her and he felt terrible for not being by her side right at that very moment. But he would be as soon as he could.

It had been the end of July when he'd left Lorford. Now it was October, another season, but it felt like another lifetime. And yet he hadn't thought about any of the things that might have prevented him from returning. Orla's apparent dismissal of him, her mother's obvious hatred of him, and his own feelings of guilt and shame at having put her in danger. Orla had asked for him and it had been his instinct to say yes.

It was mid-afternoon by the time Luke arrived at the hospital. He found a parking space and quickly made his way to the entrance, finding out where Bill had been taken and making his way there. The walk seemed endless, but he finally saw Orla pacing the corridor ahead of him.

'Orla!' he cried, and she spun around to face him, her complexion pale and her eyes bright with tears.

'Luke!'

They ran towards each other and fell into an embrace, holding one another so tightly that they could hardly breathe.

'How are you? How's Bill?'

'I'm good. He's stable.'

'What happened?'

'They said it was an abdominal aneurysm.'

'What's that? Is it like a burst blood vessel?'

'Something like that. The doctor said all sorts of strange words that I can't remember, but poor Bill's been very lucky, they said.'

'And he's going to be all right?'

'They think so. They had to operate and he's going to be in intensive care for some time.'

'Blimey! And Margy. Is she okay?'

'We couldn't find her for the longest time, but she's here now and she's pretty mad. She doesn't understand what could have caused it. Bill's so fit. She doesn't think it's fair.'

'And you – how are you coping? Really?'

'I'm fine. It was a shock to find him collapsed in his shed.'

'But you're all right? I mean, being here?' Luke stopped. 'In a hospital, I mean.'

'Please don't remind me!' Orla gave a nervous laugh. Then she took a deep breath. 'I'm fine. This is about Bill – not me.'

Luke reached out and took her hand in his, squeezing it tightly.

'Thank you for calling me,' he said.

'Thank you for coming.'

It was then that Margy came out into the corridor, her cheeks flushed pink.

'Luke!'

'Margy, how are you?' He took in her tear-stained face, and the fact that she wasn't holding a pair of knitting needles was a very bad sign.

'I just want to get back home with my Bill.'

'How's he doing?'

'They've sedated him,' Margy said with a little hiccup of fear. 'It's for the best, they tell me. But you can see him if you like.'

'Can we?' Orla asked as Margy led the way.

Luke couldn't help feeling nervous as they approached Bill's bed.

'Hey, Bill,' Luke whispered, feeling a little choked up at seeing his old friend so pale and vulnerable in the hospital bed. Luke was so used to seeing him bare-armed and becapped, a fork in his hand and his face full of sunshine. The contrast between that Bill and this one was startling and scary.

'I haven't thanked you, Orla,' Margy suddenly said, touching Orla's hand gently.

'You don't have to thank me!'

'Oh, but I do! When I think what might have happened . . . if you hadn't been there . . .'

Orla wrapped her arms around her as the tears began to spill.

'It's all right. He's going to be fine.'

Margy sniffed and nodded.

'I think we'd better let him rest,' Luke said.

'Yes, of course,' Orla agreed, and she bent forward to kiss Bill's forehead.

'Bye, Bill,' Luke whispered. 'Rest plenty, now.'

'Let us know if you need anything, Margy,' Orla told her. 'Anything at all.'

She and Luke hugged Margy and then left the ward, standing awkwardly in the corridor for a few moments.

'Can I give you a ride back to Lorford?' Luke asked Orla.

'I don't want you to go to any trouble.'

'It's no trouble. I was kind of hoping my old bed might be available. I mean, if your mother's not still with you. I don't really fancy driving back to Kent tonight.'

'Oh, of course! I'm so sorry, Luke. Yes, please stay.'

'All right, then. Let's get you back. I'm sure One Ear will be pleased to see you.'

'Gosh – One Ear! I have no idea what the time is!'

'He'll be fine, I'm sure. I'll give him a run on the beach if you want to rest.'

They got into the van and Orla immediately closed her eyes. Luke was exhausted after his long drive from Kent, but he guessed that was nothing compared to how Orla must be feeling. She was holding up pretty well, but he guessed that there was more going on with her than she was letting on.

Luke tried to imagine what it must have been like for her to find Bill. Lorford wasn't the easiest place to get to for an ambulance, and the panic at finding somebody collapsed in the middle of nowhere must have been terrifying. He glanced at her now. She looked so pale and he had a feeling she might actually have fallen asleep. Quietly and as quickly as was safe, Luke drove to the castle.

The village should have been a welcome sight to him, but he was so anxious about both Bill and Orla that he didn't have time to luxuriate in being back in the place he'd grown to love.

'Orla?' he said, reaching across the van to touch her shoulder.

She jumped, her eyes opening.

'We're back,' he told her as she looked around, confused.

'Was I asleep?'

'I think so.'

'Sorry.'

'It's okay. Come on – let's get you inside.'

They got out of the van and walked up the steps to the castle door. One Ear was there to greet them and Luke bent to make a fuss of him.

'I'll take you out in a minute, boy,' he promised. 'Can I make you some tea, Orla?'

'Yes,' she said in a vague sort of way, as if she'd only half heard him.

He watched her drift out of the room and wondered if she was going to lie down. He couldn't blame her if she was. So he got on with the task of making tea. Sometimes, something as simple as putting a kettle on and finding mugs was calming. It was a familiar ritual that grounded a person, bringing order to a chaotic day. One might not be able to control the world, but one could at least control a cup of tea.

Luke was just walking through the great hall with two mugs when he heard the noise. He frowned. It sounded like something had smashed.

And again.

One Ear leapt out of his basket and whined as another smash came and Luke hastily put down the mugs and ran out of the room.

'Orla?' he called as he heard another smash. He knew what it was now, and he knew where it was coming from.

He headed to the china room.

Chapter 25

Orla wasn't sure how it began but, all of a sudden, she found herself in the midst of it, the deep fear and anger she'd been carrying inside her erupting in a force she couldn't quite control. The fear of finding Bill collapsed at the allotment, the anger at the way her mother had left the castle, and the horrifying memory of seeing Brandon in the sacred space of her home. It was all too much.

One minute, she'd been hyperventilating in the middle of the china room and then, the next, she'd grabbed hold of her camera tripod and was swinging it through the air like an angry baseball bat, smashing and thrashing all the china around her.

She swung to the left and an enormous jug came crashing to the stone floor, where it broke into a thousand red and gold pieces. She swung to the right, and rainbow shards and splinters flew across the room. The tripod felt lighter in her hands now – she was wielding it more like a sword than a baseball bat, cutting through the cups, bowls, plates and vases that filled the room, and screaming like somebody possessed.

Reds, blues, greens and pinks, silvers and golds, roses and cherries and blue and white willow leaves – all flew through the air before smashing to the floor. Pretty patterns she'd spent hours photographing, gorgeous antique pieces that had featured on her Galleria feed – all were being sacrificed, dying on the grey stone floor of the castle. It was as if all the energy of her body was passing through her arms and into that new weapon – all the anger and the fear that she'd been holding inside her for goodness only knew how long.

The sound was almost deafening and she was only half aware of One Ear barking and Luke shouting something over the noise from the safety of the door. But she couldn't stop now. She just knew that this had to be done.

Her dark hair flew in a frenzy, partially obscuring her vision, but it didn't slow her down as she continued thrashing, her heart racing and her breath ragged.

And then she stopped.

Her whole body was heaving and she was gasping for breath, but the sudden silence that flooded the room was wonderful. It *felt* wonderful.

She sank forward, dropping the tripod and placing her hands on her knees, glad that Luke didn't speak for a moment, but aware that he'd walked into the room, his feet crunching on the china shards.

'Oh, dear!' she whispered, slowly coming back to herself, her eyes focusing on the devastation around her. Just a few items had escaped her wrath and now seemed to tremble in the deep recesses of the castle's windowsills and on the far shelves. 'What have I done?'

Luke came forward. 'I think you needed to do that,' he said, gently putting a hand on her shoulder. 'How are you feeling?'

She looked up at him and blinked, as if settling back into herself at last.

'Strangely calm.'

'Good.'

'*Good?* Look what I've done! All my beautiful things!'

They both looked around the room again. The floor was covered in a china carpet. It was a strange, but rather wonderful, mosaic.

'Well, a lot of it *was* already broken,' Luke pointed out. 'Wasn't it?' Orla saw a smile tickling the corners of his mouth.

'Yes, but only hairline cracks or little chips. None of it was actually *smashed*!'

'Well, it is now!'

'Luke!' she cried as he continued to smile at her, but she was smiling too. 'Oh, my God!'

'This happened for a reason,' he told her.

'You think so?'

'I really do.'

'I'll keep telling myself that then.'

'I think you needed to get whatever was inside you *out*, and quickly. You've been carrying a lot, Orla. And I'm not just talking about today, but for the last few years.'

Orla gazed down at the floor again, knowing that Luke understood.

'I was so worried about Bill,' she said at last.

'I know.'

'He's been such a good friend to me. More than a friend. Like a father, really.'

'He's a very special person.'

Orla nodded. 'I should tidy this up.'

'Not now. It doesn't need to be done now.'

'But it's dangerous. One Ear might . . .'

'We'll make sure the door's closed.' Luke put out a hand, encouraging Orla to leave the room, and that's when he frowned. 'You have a splinter of china in your wrist.'

'Where?' Orla asked. She hadn't felt any injury.

'Right here,' he said, turning her pale arm so she could see it. 'Let me help you.'

He led her gently to the bathroom, holding her arm over the sink and pulling the piece of broken china from her skin.

'Ouch!'

'Best wash it now. Have you got some antiseptic?'

'Yes, in the cabinet. I'll do it.'

'Okay.' He made to leave.

'Luke?'

'Yes?'

'I'm ready for that cup of tea now.'

He grinned. 'Me too.'

Ten minutes later, after letting One Ear out in the garden, they were both sitting in the great hall drinking their tea. Orla looked calm – perhaps the calmest Luke had ever seen her – and he thought it the right time to broach the subject that had been playing on his mind for so long.

'Orla? You know when I left? I feel so awkward about it, and I want to apologise.'

'Oh, Luke! If anyone should apologise, it should be me. I'm afraid I let my mother drive you away and I was too weak to stop her. I wasn't coping.' She paused for a moment. 'I went to a bad place for a while.'

Luke sighed. 'I think I might have put you there.'

'What?' Orla looked confused.

'I brought nothing but trouble with me. That man would never have found you if I hadn't—'

'You can't blame yourself for what happened with Brandon.'

'But if it hadn't been for me being here—'

'If it hadn't been for you being here, I'd still be locked up in a world of my own, only leaving the castle to go to the beach twice a day. I still wouldn't have talked to anybody or gone into the village or made friends, and I wouldn't have known the joy of good friendship with somebody like you.'

Luke was unable to say anything. He felt a hard lump forming in his throat for the second time that day. She didn't blame him for the things that had happened, and she certainly didn't hate him.

'Luke? Are you okay?'

He nodded, still unable to speak.

'I've been worrying about you so much,' Orla went on. 'I wanted to reach out to you, but I didn't think you'd want to hear from me.'

He gazed up at the high ceiling of the great hall, blinking back his tears.

'Luke? How have you been?'

He closed his eyes, trying to find a shred of inner strength.

'I've not been coping very well,' he confessed, and he really wasn't sure why he had. He hadn't meant to say anything. Orla had enough to cope with, without him unloading onto her.

'No?' Orla pressed.

Luke shook his head, not trusting himself to say anything else.

'Come with me,' she told him, putting her tea down and standing up.

'Where are we going?'

Orla didn't reply. Instead, she left the room, and Luke had no choice but to follow if he wanted an answer.

They passed the stairs, which meant that they weren't going down to the basement or up onto the roof. He wasn't sure why he'd thought she'd take him to either of those places, but the last place he'd expected was the one she stopped at. The china room.

She opened the door and gasped as she surveyed the beautiful devastation afresh. But then she walked in and started reaching into all the little alcoves, windowsills and shelves to pick up the pieces that had escaped her lethal swing before. Luke watched, wondering what she was doing as she placed them neatly on the main table in the centre of the room. It was a surprising collection. He hadn't realised how much had got away unscathed, and he was glad for Orla because he knew how much she adored her pieces. But he couldn't have predicted what she'd do next.

She handed him the tripod.

'Go on,' she told him.

'Go on what?'

'Break some.'

His eyes widened. 'You're kidding.'

'I'm not. Go on – it'll do you good, I *promise* you!'

He looked at her as if she was quite mad. 'I can't.'

'Yes, you can! Go on, Luke! Break what's left. Break it all!' Orla bent down to the floor to retrieve some of the larger pieces there and placed them on the table too.

'Be careful – you'll cut yourself!'

'Doesn't matter. It'll be worth it.'

'Orla!'

'Go on! Just do it!'

She was serious, deadly serious, and her strange energy was beginning to infect him too as he looked around the room at the hapless collection of crockery. Suddenly, he didn't see their beauty, only their breakability, and then something fell into his mind, quite unbidden. It was as if it had just been waiting for the right moment. It was a headline in a recent local newspaper about the train crash.

It Should Never Have Happened.

He hadn't told Orla about it, but he thought about it now, and he remembered the anger he'd felt as he'd read it and he used that anger as he took the tripod in both hands and swung it.

He wasn't sure what it was – whether it was the powerful weight of the tripod in his hands, the motion of the swing or the satisfying sound of the china breaking on the floor – but it proved addictive and he found the second swing easier and the third even easier, until he was slicing through the air like a professional swordsman. Orla had moved into the hallway and was cheering him on.

'Go on, Luke! Smash it. Smash it all!'

He swung again. And again. Quickly, he found a rhythm and a release that he hadn't known he'd needed and, when he stopped, he – like Orla before him – was panting. He dropped the tripod to the floor as if it were on fire and tried to take control of his breathing as his heart rate slowly returned to normal.

'You okay?' Orla asked.

He nodded, still trying to corral his thoughts.

'Feel better?'

He turned and smiled. 'I *do* feel better!'

Orla laughed. 'Good! I think you needed to do that just as much as I did!'

'I wish I'd discovered this sooner,' Luke told her. 'Not that I would've come in here and smashed up all your china.'

'We could buy some more.'

'What – just to smash up?' he asked.

'Yes!'

Luke laughed. 'Maybe we should tidy up.'

Orla cocked her head to one side. 'It's kind of artistic in its own way, don't you think?'

Luke bent to pick up one of the larger pieces of broken china.

'You know, I could probably fix some of these. If you wanted them fixed.'

Orla took the piece from him and examined it. 'No. They've had their time. I need to let all this go.'

Luke frowned. 'You mean you won't collect any more?'

'I think I should do something else now. Something that gets me out more. Don't you?' She gave a little smile.

Luke smiled back. 'I think that sounds like a great idea.'

Orla sighed, looking back down at the floor. 'But first, I need to tidy this lot.'

Luke looked at the patterned mess on the floor and watched as Orla lifted her right foot and brought her heel carefully down onto a piece of china.

'What are you doing?'

She bent to pick up the piece she'd stepped on. 'You know what? I've always wanted to make a mosaic. Do you think that could work? To make something beautiful out of all these broken pieces?'

Luke looked at her in admiration, marvelling at the resilience of his friend. 'Absolutely,' he told her. 'You could definitely make that work.'

The Next Summer

Orla took a deep breath before entering the village hall, her camera hanging around her neck like a special kind of talisman. She tried desperately not to think about what had happened to her there the year before, when she'd been asked to photograph the village fete and her fear and panic at being surrounded by so many people had sent her running. That *wasn't* going to happen again. She was quite determined. She was a different person these days, wasn't she?

There had been so many positive changes in her life during the last year and she felt as if she was truly moving forward now. Just five months ago, she'd leased a shop in Woodbridge and had opened a small photography studio. Business was good. More importantly, Orla *felt* good. She genuinely liked being out in the world and meeting people, seeing places and doing her own shopping, especially shopping for books. She'd found a wonderful little shop nearby and loved the experience of holding a book in her hand and flipping through it rather than choosing one from an image online.

She'd bought a small car and was driving into the nearby town four days a week. She'd also been working with the local schools, forming photography clubs and encouraging the youngsters to use real cameras instead of just their phones. She'd seen a few of them today as she entered the village hall, and they'd waved to her, which made her smile.

But there was an even bigger change in Orla. She'd agreed to have more surgery, not because she was concerned about her looks but because her scars were causing her discomfort and she knew she could improve that with a few more simple operations. Luke had encouraged her when she'd told him about it during one of the long weekly phone calls that they'd shared ever since he'd returned to Kent back in the autumn.

'You know, when you were visiting Bill and worrying about him, you totally forgot your fear of hospitals, didn't you?' Luke had said.

That really hadn't occurred to Orla, but she'd had to agree with Luke. Her fear was fast becoming a thing of the past.

Now, in the heart of the village hall, surrounded by her neighbours and so many of her new friends, Orla smiled and got on with her job, moving around the room, taking shot after shot. She photographed the tables with the heaps of wonderful produce and home bakes, she photographed the winners as the prizes were given and then moved outside into the sunshine, where the fun really began, with bric-a-brac stalls, a tombola, and the ever popular attraction: throw-a-wet-sponge-at-your-local-MP, which the vicar seemed to be enjoying a little too much. Orla photographed it all, stretching up on tiptoes and bending down onto knees to get the best angle, capturing all the joy and laughter of the day and feeling so much of it herself too.

When the crowds finally began to drift away, Orla walked across to a shady spot and looked at the back of her camera for a sneak preview of what she'd taken. There was some good stuff there, she thought, pleased with the images she'd caught.

She looked up from her screen, watching as the stallholders began to pack things away and the exhibitors reclaimed their produce or donated it at a collection point which had been set up. These were her neighbours, her community, and they were good, kind, honest people who had welcomed her so wholeheartedly. They hadn't been there to judge her or reprimand her for having shunned them for so long. They hadn't overstepped the mark by staring at her or questioning her, as she had once feared they might. They'd simply acted as if she was one of them, which she was. She was finally beginning to feel that now.

She was just popping the lens cap onto her camera when she saw him across the playing field. He was helping to dismantle a slide which had been set up for the younger children. She walked across the grass towards him and he looked up.

'Luke!' she cried, her pace picking up at the sight of him. 'You made it!'

'Of course I did,' he said with a smile. 'You don't think I'd miss it, did you?'

'I didn't see you in the hall.'

'I came in late, I'm afraid, and I saw you were busy and I didn't want to interrupt. How did it go?'

'Good, I think.'

He grinned. 'As modest as ever. I bet you've got some great shots.'

'Maybe one or two.'

'Fancy an ice cream down by the harbour?' he suggested.

She nodded enthusiastically.

Ten minutes later, ice creams in hand, the two of them walked down to the quay and sat on a bench, staring out at the calm blue of the water.

'How's Bill getting on?' Luke asked.

'Really well. Back to his old self, only Margy fusses around him more since his operation, which drives him mad. She's even been taking her knitting up to the allotment so she can keep an eye on him there.'

Luke laughed. 'I can't imagine him liking that much.'

'Actually, I think he's beginning to get used to it. You should see them. They look so cute together, sharing a flask on the bench outside his shed.'

'Shall we pop in and say hello to them later?'

'Of course,' Orla said. 'I saw Margy buying a rather large Victoria sponge at the fete so we may be in for a treat.'

They sat for a few minutes enjoying their ice creams in silence.

'How have you been?' Orla asked him at last.

'Good,' he said, and then shrugged. 'Well, by good, I mean better.' He paused. 'You know.'

'Yes, I know.' She gave him a gentle smile, remembering some of their long evening phone calls when they'd talked about Helen and how some days just had to be got through. Like Luke's first Christmas Day without Helen – that had been a tough one. They'd spent a good couple of hours on the phone that day. And Valentine's Day, too, which had trooped its colour in hateful splendour, with Luke confiding that he had nobody to leave a card for on their pillow any more. His wedding anniversary had been tricky too, as was his own birthday and Helen's – her second one since she'd died. But Luke was looking well, she thought. There was colour in his cheeks and his eyes were bright with life and light.

'How about you?' he asked. 'You look good. Happy.'

She nodded. 'I am. I had this moment at the fete just as everything was coming to an end and I suddenly realised that I didn't want it to. Isn't that funny? All that time, I shut myself away from the world in the castle, afraid of what was outside my own door, and now I find that a lot of it's rather wonderful.' She popped the last of her ice cream cone into her mouth and crunched. 'Mildred asked me if she could book me for next year's fete.'

'And what did you say?' Luke asked as he finished his own ice cream.

'I said she'd better take a look at this year's photos first.'

'And what did she say?'

'That they were bound to be better than the blurred ones of decapitated prize winners that she's been taking for the last three years.'

They both laughed.

'There's something else I've been meaning to tell you,' she added. 'I've got in touch with some of my old friends in London.'

Luke looked surprised by this. 'Orla, that's great!'

'It is, isn't it?' She gave a little shrug as if it wasn't such a big deal. 'Anyway, I thought it was time. I've missed them all so much.'

Luke smiled and they sat in silence for a few moments.

'You know, I haven't felt this for a long time,' Orla confessed at last with a contented sigh.

'Felt what?' Luke asked.

'This sense of belonging.'

Luke turned to look at her, and then he did something he'd never done before – he reached across the bench and placed his hand on hers. It was such a natural movement that Orla didn't mind at all. Instead, she sat perfectly still and perfectly content, the happy soundtrack of seagulls high above them.

ACKNOWLEDGEMENTS

As ever, thank you to my husband, Roy, for endless trips in pursuit of this novel.

Thank you to Sara Moreton for letting us stay at beautiful Keep Cottage in Orford. To Sue Dixon for advice when needed in an emergency! To Kevin Tatum for advising me about old buildings and planning permissions.

And thank you to Sammia, Katie, Bekah, Laura, Nicole and the rest of the brilliant team at Lake Union. It's so much fun working with you all.

A very special thank you to Dr David O'Reilly, who will be pleased to know that I wrote most of this novel at my new standing desk, and that I am implementing all of his suggested 'lifestyle changes'.

To the lovely people of Instagram who answered my many questions. Do follow their accounts, because they are all gorgeous: Rebecca Lewis @poshyarns, Celia Hart @celiahartartist, Milli Proust @milliproust, Helen Redfern @helenredfernwriter, Becky Cole @beckyocole, Julia Smith @humphreyandgrace, Emma Chessell @mylittlecountrylife and Eva Nemeth @eva_nemeth.

ABOUT THE AUTHOR

Photo © 2016 Roy Connelly

Victoria Connelly studied English Literature at Worcester University, got married in a medieval castle in the Yorkshire Dales and now lives in rural Suffolk with her artist husband, a young springer spaniel and a flock of ex-battery hens. She is the author of two bestselling series, Austen Addicts and The Book Lovers, as well as many other novels and novellas. Her first published novel, *Flights of Angels*, was made into a film in 2008 by Ziegler Films in Germany. *The Runaway Actress* was shortlisted for the Romantic Novelists' Association's Romantic Comedy Novel award.

Ms Connelly loves books, films, walking, historic buildings and animals. If she isn't at her keyboard writing, she can usually be found in her garden either with a trowel in her hand or a hen on her lap.

Her website is www.victoriaconnelly.com and readers can follow her on Twitter @VictoriaDarcy and on Instagram @VictoriaConnellyAuthor.